Instead of You

Anie Michaels

Instead of You

© Copyright Anie Michaels 2016

This publication is protected under the US Copyright Act of 1976 and all other applicable international, federal, state and local laws, and all rights are reserved, including resale rights: you are not allowed to give, copy, scan, distribute or sell this book to anyone else.

In accordance with the U.S. Copyright Act of 1976, the scanning, uploading, and electronic sharing of any part of this book without the permission of the publisher is unlawful piracy and theft of the author's intellectual property. If you would like to use material from the book (other than for review purposes), prior written permission must be obtained by contacting the author at anie.michaels@gmail.com.

This book is licensed for your personal enjoyment only. This book may not be re-sold or given away

Edited by Hot Tree Editing.

~To Myself ~

Is it rude to dedicate a book to yourself?

I don't care.

Chapter One

Cory's Sixteenth Birthday

McKenzie

Like any other day of tenth grade, I spent my lunch break sitting on the brick wall that lined the school property. It was only four feet tall and easy enough to hop onto, and that's where we sat, every day, and ate our lunch. Except today. I was alone. Today was January 10, and Cory was noticeably absent because his brother had taken him to get his driver's license. Well, assuming he passed. If he didn't pass it would be ridiculous as I'd taken the test two days earlier, on *my* sixteenth birthday, and told him all of the questions and answers. I'd also spent the last month studying with him. He had to pass.

Halfway through lunch, Hayes's familiar Mustang pulled into the parking lot. As it drove closer I could make out both Hayes and Cory in the front of the car, Cory in the driver seat. I tried not to get too excited—just because he was driving didn't mean he'd passed. The tinted windows wouldn't give me any more clues, so I waited impatiently for the car to pull all the way up the circular drive, my heart thumping wildly as it came to a stop right in front of me.

When Cory's door flew open and his smiling face popped up over, I knew he'd passed.

"I did it," he said, one fist pumping into the air above his head.

"I knew you could," I said, trying to match his smile.

Cory came around the hood of the Mustang, practically bouncing. It never really got too cold here in the winters, which was why we could eat our lunch outside even in January, but Cory was wearing his signature brown leather jacket that only intensified the blond of his hair. Surely the Florida sun had something to do with his hair color, because he was a stark contrast to his brother.

Hayes stepped out of the Mustang, and I was looking at Cory's antithesis. Where Cory was on the shorter side, Hayes was close to six foot two. Where Cory had light blond, short, manageable hair, Hayes's hair was dark, longer than it needed to be, and quite unruly. Cory was lean and light, running track and swimming the backstroke for the high school swim team, and Hayes was, well, built. Hayes was not wearing a jacket and even though I tried desperately to avoid it, my eyes always seemed to find his biceps.

"Hey, Kenzie," Hayes called as he walked around the front of his car.

"Hi," I replied, smiling. I'd known him my whole life, but I didn't know him nearly as well as I knew Cory. "Did you come home for Cory's birthday?"

"Yeah. Mom would have killed me if I missed my little brother's sweet sixteen." His smile was playful and knowing.

"Only girls have sweet sixteens, Hayes." Cory rolled his eyes, obviously irritated by his older brother.

"Was yours a sweet sixteen, Kenzie?" He'd stopped outside his door, arms folded on the roof of his Mustang, biceps bulging.

"Yeah" was the only thing I could say in response. I was afraid if I said anything else it would be, "Yeah, biceps." Hayes gave me a knowing grin and I felt my cheeks heat, so I looked down at my sandwich.

"Bye, Hayes," Cory said with irritation.

"Later, kids." I watched as the Mustang roared out of the parking lot, and I couldn't help but give a relieved sigh. Recently, Hayes always managed to put me on edge. It was unnerving. Luckily, I only saw him when colleges were on break. He was twenty now and attended Central Florida University two hours away. About the same time he started making me nervous was when he left for college. I remember, sadly, being glad when he finally left for good. Being around him and Cory was confusing for me.

Cory hopped up onto the wall next to me and held out the brand-new shiny plastic license that looked exactly like the one I'd earned two days previously.

"I can't believe we both passed." His words were quiet but full of wistfulness. "We're both sixteen, we both have our license, it's like the one day we've been waiting for since, well, since we were twelve."

Sixteen was a big deal to most teenagers. But sixteen for Cory and me held an unprecedented weight. To say our mothers had built a fantasy around Cory and me dating would have been a massive understatement. It was expected. A forgone conclusion. However, when Cory and I hit a certain age, my father stepped in, forbidding me to date until I was sixteen.

I was so thankful for his rule. Grateful that the decision to date Cory would be put off for a few more years, that I wouldn't have to worry about how I felt until then. But now, it was then. I was sixteen and so was Cory.

"I was wondering," he said, bouncing the heels of his Converse against the brick of the wall, "do you think you'd like to go with me to my party tomorrow?"

I tried to hide my reaction, to keep my breaths even, not let my body show how tense I'd become at his question. He was my absolute, hands down, best friend. But I wasn't sure he was who I wanted to be my boyfriend.

"Cory, of course I'll go with you. I've never missed one of your birthday parties." I made my words light and airy, the exact opposite of how I was feeling that moment.

"No, Kenzie, that's not what I meant. I want you to go as my date."

It was suddenly one hundred degrees hotter than it had been just seconds before and my lungs decided to work overtime. Cory apparently didn't notice my freak-out, as he kept talking.

"I know we've been waiting, but we're both sixteen now. I don't want to wait anymore. I want to be with you." He reached over and took my hand. This wasn't a rare occurrence; we held hands every now and then. He was my very best friend and I loved him. But a lot of the time I wasn't sure if the only reason I loved him was because I'd been trained to do so. But on that afternoon, as we sat on that wall, when his fingers slid between mine and gripped me tightly, I knew he wasn't thinking about our friendship. He wasn't holding Kenzie's hand, the girl who he'd pushed over in the sand box when we were five. No, he was holding Kenzie's hand who he wanted to be romantic with.

God.

Be romantic with.

I couldn't even fathom it, let alone try to put it into words.

How could I tell my best friend in the whole world, on his birthday, that I had no idea what I wanted? That even though we'd basically been primed for this our whole lives, I wasn't sure it was something I wanted? If he was something I wanted?

Easy: I couldn't.

I just smiled at him, gave his hand a squeeze, and let him come to whatever conclusion he would, fully knowing I was taking the coward's way out. When his smile widened and eyes sparkled, I knew I'd started something I wasn't sure I had the power to stop.

Mr. and Mrs. Wallace hadn't spared any expense when it came to Cory's birthday party. They'd rented the ballroom at the local golf club, complete with DJ and dance floor, photo booth, and a wait staff walking around with silver platters of finger food that most of the kids attending couldn't have identified if they'd tried. It was, in a word, fancy.

My birthday party the weekend before had been much more my speed. My parents had let me take five friends to Busch Gardens. We'd ridden roller coasters until we couldn't walk straight. It was awesome. Cory had come, along with my friends Becca, Holly, and Todd. Becca and Holly were my best girlfriends, and Holly practically begged me to invite Todd. I figured it couldn't be bad to have another guy there so Cory didn't feel too out of place. It was a lot of fun, and nothing like the formal affair I was currently observing from my strategically scouted spot where I was doing a fantastic job of holding up the wall.

I watched as my classmates and friends danced in the middle of the room, colorful lights flashing around them. It looked as though they were having fun, but I knew I wouldn't feel comfortable out there like them. My body had always been a mystery to me and I'd never figured out how to properly control it. Sure, I could walk around just fine, but trying to coordinate so many limbs to move at the same time and make it look smooth? I would never be good at that.

Cory was in the middle of the crowd, dancing as if he'd been practicing his whole life for this performance. He'd always been so good at things like that. He was entertaining, confident, and fun to be around. Everyone wanted to be his friend and nearly everyone was. Every person invited to his party coveted their invitations and knew he'd treat them all as if he were genuinely pleased they'd managed to make it. He was a people person, through and through.

I saw my parents in the far corner, only lit by the flashes of light coming from the DJ table, talking with Cory's parents. Our moms were talking to each other while our dads did the same. It was a vision I'd seen my entire life. It was comforting to a point—something I could always count on. But it was also redundant. I wondered if the people I was friends with now—Cory, Holly, and Becca—if that was it for me. I loved them all, but would I ever have more connections with different people? I hated feeling trapped at sixteen, but it was something I was experiencing more and more each day.

I pushed off the wall and started walking toward the doors leading outside, needing a little air. Cory caught my eye and gave me a questioning look, and then signaled that he would come with me. I waved my hand to stop him, then held up all my fingers, mouthing, "five minutes" at him. He nodded, but looked confused. Regardless, he didn't follow me and I couldn't help but feel guilty that I was glad to leave him behind. I just needed a moment.

I walked outside and shut the doors behind me, hearing the music quiet, but not the thumping of the bass. I could still feel the beat vibrating through my feet, still hear it as the windows rattled from it. I continued for about ten steps until I was at the edge of the patio, then took in a deep breath, letting it out slowly.

A few minutes later I was almost to the brink of panic, thinking too obsessively about all that had happened in a matter of days, when a harsh wave of music broke through the quiet. I turned to talk to Cory, who I assumed had come to find me, but practically stumbled when I saw it was Hayes instead.

"Kenzie," he said, obviously surprised to see me. "What are you doing out here all by yourself?" He slowly made his way toward me. He was shrouded in darkness and I couldn't see his face until he was a step or two away.

"I needed a breather." I silently hoped he wouldn't pry.

"I get it" was all he said in response, which made me happy. He came to stand right next to me, but didn't look at me, facing out toward the green just as I had been before he joined me. So I turned and looked in the same direction. There we stood, in relative silence, with only the faint buzzing of the music behind us. I felt the tension start to drift away, the endless loop of stressful thoughts slow in my mind, and the silent hum of the evening cast some sort of soothing magic over me. It was the most relaxed I'd been in days.

Then, as if he'd been waiting for me to be tricked by his silence, he asked, "So when's the wedding?"

Instantly, I was on edge again. I knew exactly what he was referring to, but didn't want him to know that.

"What do you mean?"

"Your and Cory's wedding. When's the date? I need some advance notice so I can tell my professors I'll be out of town."

"Ha ha." That was the best response I could produce considering my heart had started beating a million miles an hour.

"No, seriously, Kenzie. You've both reached that magical age everyone's been waiting for. It's full steam ahead now, right?" The venom in his voice, the disgust that dripped from every word, surprised me. In the sixteen years I'd known Hayes I could remember him being visibly upset so few times, I could count them on one hand. He was aloof, removed, and uninterested in anything having to do with me. His anger toward my would-be relationship with Cory was so shocking, I nearly stumbled.

"I don't know what's going to happen," I whispered, unable to come up with any other answer besides a truthful one.

Hayes turned toward me, coming close enough that I could hear his breath panting out and dragging back in. "Isn't he what you want? What you've always wanted?"

"He's my best friend." Again, the truth fell from my lips.

"Is that all?"

I wasn't sure. I had no idea what I wanted us to become, I only knew what we already were. Best friends. Anything beyond that seemed scary and bigger than I could handle.

Suddenly Hayes was closer, only a breath away instead of a step. I should have taken a step back, should have moved away, but his hand came up to cradle my cheek and all I could do was move my eyes up his chest, over his neck, and meet his gaze.

"Has he kissed you yet?" Hayes's voice was even lower now, somehow rougher, almost as if it hurt him to speak the words.

"No," I croaked out, trying to shake my head, but his big strong hand keeping my face still. Then the other one came to join, starting at my cheek, but slowly moving back into the hair at my nape.

"Good."

Everything went black as his lips pressed against mine. My eyes closed, I could no longer hear the music from the ballroom, and all my senses dulled... except for touch. I felt his lips slowly slide across mine, felt his thumb brush gently over my cheek, even felt the hardness of his chest as my hands mindlessly slid up his front.

Looking back on the kiss I would not remember what prompted me to move closer to him, to angle my head to the right, wanting to give him access to all of my mouth, or even remember how it felt so right to be kissing him, but all of that happened. It was my very first kiss and it should have been awkward and stilted and uncomfortable, but it wasn't.

It was, however, instantly passionate, like every cheesy romance movie where the two lovers kiss and fireworks ignite. There should have been fireworks. When his lips touched mine, nothing short of an explosion took place. We were magnetized to each other, moving closer and closer until there was not one iota of space between us.

I should have felt scandalized when his tongue swept across my lips, but I didn't. I didn't feel anything except ready for whatever came next. Having Hayes's tongue gliding through my mouth, his hand gripping my hair, his body seemingly trying to meld with mine, it was both the best and worst thing to happen to me.

When he finally pulled away, because Lord knows it wasn't going to be me, I stumbled a bit, trying to acclimate myself to being so solitary again. With only minutes of being connected to Hayes, going back to standing on my own was more difficult than it should have been.

He stood just a couple feet away from me, our breaths both panting out, creating the slightest bit of fog.

"I'm a shitty person for taking that first from you and Cory, but I'll be damned if I say I haven't wanted to kiss you for the longest time."

What?

"Hayes," I said, cringing at the wobble in my voice, too aware of the thumping in my heart and other parts of my body that were really unaccustomed to such throbbing. "What was that?" My fingers came to my lips, and even though I knew it made me look like an idiot, I couldn't help but touch the part of my body that had been so intimately connected to his.

He shook his head as a grin came over his mouth. But then he covered it up with his hand and moved his gaze to his shoes. When his eyes met mine again, the smile was gone. "That was just me, taking a risk, and being an asshole."

Before I could even digest the words, he spun around and walked back toward the ballroom. Left standing in the chilly evening all alone with my fingertips still running over the skin left buzzing by his kiss, I was confused as ever.

What in the world?

Hayes had just given me my very first kiss. Stolen it, really. And seemed pleased to do so. And he'd wanted to do it for the longest time? How long? I was sixteen, he was twenty. And his chest was so firm.

I closed my eyes and shook my head at the thoughts running loose in my mind. He'd turned around and walked away, but I was still standing in the cold, my fingers pressed against my lips, somehow trying to hold on to the way it felt to be kissed by him. By Hayes. *Oh, God.*

"Kenzie?" Cory's voice snapped my head back up and my hand away from my lips. "What are you doing out here? Are you all right?"

It scared me how easily the lie slipped from my mouth. "The music was so loud, I was starting to get a headache."

"Do you want me to bring you some water? I could ask my mom if she has any Tylenol."

"No, I think I'll be okay." I stared at him, silently hoping he'd go back into his party where all our friends would be glad to dance with him, to hang out with him, to occupy him while I used what little brainpower I had left to dissect what had happened between Hayes and me. Instead, he stepped closer.

"I was hoping you would dance with me."

"You know I don't dance."

He stopped inches from me, just as his brother had not five minutes before. His hands were in the pockets of his suit pants, and he bent at the knee slightly to look me in the eye. "Come on, Kenzie. It's my birthday," he pleaded, batting his too-long eyelashes at me. "Dance with me." His last words were spoken softly, as if he were embarrassed to be asking me at all. But it was his birthday, and I had technically come to his party with him—I owed him at least a dance.

"Okay," I replied, my voice matching his in softness.

He took another tentative step toward me, his eyes never leaving mine, then pulled his hands from his pockets. One reached out and landed on the curve of my waist, the other he held up, waiting for me to place my palm in his.

Touching wasn't new for us, and dancing wasn't either. But dancing in the dark, alone, with only the distant sound of music in the background was uncharted territory. This was something that, had you asked anyone, was destined to happen. We were both finally sixteen years old: let the relationship commence. I knew it was coming, yet the only feeling I had about it was trepidation.

Could Cory tell I'd just kissed his brother? Could he somehow smell Hayes on me? Were my lips as swollen and sensitive as they felt? Was my waist hot where his hands had been?

I could only hope all the answers were no, pray that Cory had no idea his brother had totally and completely obliterated me with just one kiss.

"Can you believe we finally made it?" Cory asked as we swayed in tiny circles.

"Made it?"

"To sixteen. We finally made it."

"Oh, yeah. Suddenly I feel like the years flew by."

"Really?" he asked, his smile lighting up his boyish face. "The last two years have been torture for me, dragging on and on." His hands slid farther around my waist, effectively pulling me a little closer as his hand came to rest in the small of my back. "But now we're here, and we're both sixteen. All I want, Kenzie, is for us to finally be together."

I saw him duck, watched as his face drew nearer to mine, and tried to hide the horror from my face when I realized Cory was going to kiss me.

His mouth met mine with a little too much force, causing my teeth to painfully press into my lips, but once his mouth was there, it stalled for a moment, leaving me blinking, afraid to move, kissing my best friend. When Cory finally moved, it was to spread his lips, his tongue darting out and forcing my lips apart in the process. Our teeth knocked together as his tongue continued to explore. I pulled away, horrified at how terrible we were at kissing each other, but his mouth followed mine and his hands pulled me closer.

When the kiss was finally over, no less than one million thoughts filtered through my mind. How in the world had I gone sixteen years without one kiss, but managed to get two in less than ten minutes? I tried to focus on the thoughts that told me the quality of the kisses were both based on experience, which would explain why Cory's was the less successful of the two; Hayes obviously had more experience. And while I was busy convincing myself the kiss with Cory was just a matter of practice, I also tried to tamp down the voice in my head that was telling me it was more than that. The small, yet loud, voice that screamed at me that the kiss was about chemistry, and that I had none with Cory. I tried very hard not to listen to my body which, after both kisses, could declare a clear winner.

My poor heart. No one had informed it there'd be a competition. No one had warned me about Hayes.

"Wow," Cory breathed as he pulled away from me, his eyes still sparkling, mouth tipped up into a smile. I tried to match his smile, tried to, in some way, force myself to be just as enamored with that kiss as Cory was. "I know you're nervous, Kenz, I do," he said as his forehead came to rest against mine, both his hands now wrapped firmly around my waist. I let myself lean into him, hoping he could calm the panic rising within me. "But I know we are meant to be together, and I'll spend as long as it takes convincing you of that."

His mouth moved slowly toward mine again, and thankfully, the second kiss was much better than the first. It was soft and sweet, less insistent and less involved. It was the first kiss I imagined us sharing, except it wasn't my first.

"Let me prove it to you." He whispered this against my lips, and I knew I had no other choice except to answer with my own whispered response.

"Okay."

Chapter Two

1:00 a.m., Cory's Seventeenth Birthday

McKenzie

I was startled awake by the unmistakable sound of my window being opened. The sound of wood sliding against wood pulled me from a deep sleep and it took me a moment to realize where I was and what was happening. Once it fully occurred to me that someone was climbing in my window, I shot out of my bed like lightning. I had made it to my feet just in time to see a dark, shadow of a person moving toward me. Before I could scream to save my life, warm and familiar hands rested on my shoulders, and a soothing voice spoke to me.

"Kenz, it's me, don't freak out." Cory's voice was instantly recognizable, and it took me from terrified to irritated in a flash.

"What are you doing?" I whisper-yelled, my eyes starting to make out the features of his face in the darkness. He stepped closer to me, his hands moving down my arms, then landing on my waist and moving upward. It had been exactly one year, to the day, even, since Cory had started touching me less like a best friend and more like a boyfriend. I'd be lying if I said that it didn't take a while to get used to. But I'd also be lying if I said I didn't like it.

I pushed his hands away halfheartedly, grinning when they only started at my waist again and moved up. He was hard to dissuade, I'd found.

"It's our one-year anniversary, Kenzie. I was lying in bed thinking about how much I love you, and I couldn't sleep, so I decided to come over here and tell you to your face." His lips found mine and I could feel his smile against my mouth. His hands traveled north again, stopping very high along my ribcage. "Sweet Jesus, you're not wearing a bra." As if to prove his point, his hands moved all the way to my back, feeling for my bra strap. "Tiny sweet baby Jesus," he whispered as his hands moved toward my front. I rolled my eyes, knowing he couldn't see me. I swatted his hands away just before they covered my breasts. Not because I was particularly against him touching me there, but more so because I knew it would frustrate him and he'd just woken me from a very deep sleep. Karma was a bitch.

"Girls don't normally sleep in bras, Cory." His hands came to my hips again, but this time they moved south. He let out a soft groan when his hands smoothed over the edge of my nightgown, which only fell a few inches below the curve of my rear. Suddenly, his hands moved down even farther, wrapping around the back of my thighs, lifting me. I stifled the yelp I wanted to let out in surprise, and wrapped my arms and legs around him.

He slowly lowered me to my bed, letting his body cover mine, one arm wrapped around my waist, the other pressed against the mattress by my head.

"This is the best anniversary gift ever."

I rolled my eyes playfully, watching a smile spread across his face before he pressed his lips to the sensitive skin of my neck. "I wasn't expecting you, Cory. I didn't put this nightgown on for your enjoyment."

"That's not going to stop me from enjoying it." His mouth moved along my neck and I bit down on my bottom lip to keep quiet.

"My parents are just down the hall," I whispered.

He pulled away and looked me right in the eyes, his nose an inch or two from mine. "Then you're going to have to be really quiet."

Before I could think of a response his lips were kissing mine. As if it came naturally, my knees spread, making room for him, and I felt every movement as his hips settled between them. The rubbing of his denim jeans against the bare skin of my thighs, the zipper of his hoodie snagging on the soft cotton of my nightgown; I felt it all.

This wasn't necessarily an uncommon occurrence for us. We made out often, as any seventeen-year-old couple would. Almost any chance we got alone we spent exploring each other, but I had never let it go very far. Up until that point, our clothes had always remained on, and he'd only ever felt me up on the outside of my shirt. So to feel him hard,

20 | Anie Michaels

pressing against me, well, that was something new to experience.

It had taken me a while to warm up to being Cory's girlfriend. It felt strange and awkward at first, as though it were forced, which made it uncomfortable. But then, one day, I had a moment of realization where I stopped looking at Cory as the boy everyone expected me to spend the rest of my life with, and looked at him as though he were my boyfriend in that very moment. No history, no future aside from our plans the next weekend.

I took the pressure off our relationship and realized it was easier to be with him, easier than constantly thinking about how much everyone expected of us. And even though I wasn't looking into the future with Cory, he definitely was. He'd immediately told me he loved me, which caused an epic panic attack. It was two weeks after his sixteenth birthday. He'd taken me to a fancy restaurant, and from across the table, with a lit candle flickering in between us, told me he loved me. He said he'd always loved me. And while I'd always loved him too, it'd been my best friend I'd loved, not my boyfriend.

When I couldn't say it back, when I wasn't even sure I'd ever be able to say it back, he simply reached across the table, took my hand in his, and told me he'd wait forever—that he knew I'd come around. He'd been waiting almost a year to hear me say those words, and I still wasn't ready.

There were nights I'd lie awake and think about him, think about us, and wonder if I was being fair to him by staying with him, but caring too much about someone seemed like a terrible reason to end a relationship. Because I *did* care about Cory, so much, but I worried it wasn't the same way he cared about me. I also worried that even though he said I'd come around in time, I never would.

All these heavy thoughts seemed to float away like vapor when he kissed me though. When his hands drifted over my body my mind shut down and I didn't think about anything except the way he made my body feel. Tonight was no exception.

My nightgown was a very thin divider between us and offered no buffer to the way his hands were roaming over my breasts, the way he tentatively palmed me through the cotton, gently squeezing. I gasped, my mouth breaking free from his, and my back arched off the bed. I wanted more friction, wanted him to not be so tender with me, but a tiny voice in the back of my mind told me that was slutty, made me feel dirty in some way for wanting those things. It was hard to wrap my mind around, especially when Cory's hands were on me, doing things to me that made me feel good. I just always seemed to want it to be... more... in some way.

His hands left my breasts, sliding down, and he sat up a little when they reached my hips. His fingertips started slowly bunching up the material of my nightgown, pulling it up to my waist. His eyes were locked on mine, silently and respectfully asking permission. I gave him a slight nod, wanting to feel my body on fire again, and my breath hitched as I watched him pull my nightgown all the way up, then over my head, revealing me to him for the first time ever.

I was trapped in a weird moment where I desperately wanted to watch his face, to see his reaction the first time he saw me nearly naked, but I also felt more than a little embarrassed and fought the urge to cover myself. Cory, the boy who'd pulled my pigtails in kindergarten, who'd seen me throw up in the bushes during our families' annual camping trip, was looking at me topless. My best friend was looking at me as though I were the most beautiful thing he'd ever seen, and I had to remind myself that he was my boyfriend, that I should be excited that he wanted to see me naked, not embarrassed.

However, much like all our previous encounters of the physical nature, my thoughts ceased when his hands came to my skin. When the warmth of his skin slid over me, my eyes closed and I was no longer looking at my best friend, I was only feeling. His fingers slid up my skin and I nearly cried out, the tension in my nipple surprising me. They were tight and hard, practically throbbing, and I needed something to take away the ache.

Never in my wildest dreams did I expect to feel Cory's warm tongue circle one of them. We'd never been this intimate with each other and I didn't think he'd be that bold, but I was obviously mistaken. A low moan left me as his mouth closed over my nipple, one of his hands palming my other breast. He sucked me further into his mouth and tingles shot throughout my body while warmth flooded between my legs.

I was moaning and squirming beneath him, trying to deal with all the new and powerful feelings, but also trying to keep somewhat of a level head. We'd never gone this far before, but I knew I didn't want to go any farther. One step at a time. I didn't want my first sexual experience to be in my bedroom while my parents slept down the hall.

"Cory," I whispered. He stopped immediately and slowly removed his mouth from me, only to rest his forehead right between my breasts and let out a groan. "You should go."

He took in a deep breath, but then lifted his head and his eyes found mine in the dark. "I love you," he said. His voice didn't sound loving, it sounded exasperated, and I heard a "but" coming. "Why don't you trust me?" Ah, the "but" came in the form of a question.

"I do trust you. I'm just not ready." I tried to keep my words calm, but I was tired of always having to tell him to stop. I wished he'd stop himself sometimes. "You *know* I'm not ready."

He let out another breath, but this time it was louder and he pushed off me. I pulled a blanket up to cover myself and sat up, readying myself for the argument we'd had a few times already. It always came back to me. He didn't understand my mixed signals. And I would be the first to admit I sent them. There were times, like two minutes ago, when I was totally into it. Times when I wanted to *feel* something, to know what that level of connection felt like. But I also wondered, in the back of my mind, why I didn't feel more connected with Cory to begin with. I didn't long to feel connected to *him*, I just wanted to feel. And it was those doubts that stopped me.

Regardless of all that, I stood firm in my belief that if I wasn't comfortable, for whatever reason, it was my right to be so and to stop him. I didn't like that he sometimes got angry with me for putting the brakes on.

He stared at me for a moment and then flopped on his back, making the mattress shake. He raked his palms down his face and then rested his hands above his head. After a quiet minute he rolled toward me.

"I'm sorry. You're right. I'll try to keep myself under control in the future." Another but was coming. "But, sometimes McKenzie, it really feels like it's not sex you're unsure about."

Panicking a little on the inside, wondering if I were truly that transparent, I had to steel myself on the outside because the last thing I wanted to do was hurt Cory. Swinging my legs around, I lined my body up next to his, propping myself up on one elbow to look down at him. I brought my other hand to his chest, then ran it up over his neck to cup his cheek.

"This is normal, losing-my-virginity jitters. I'll try harder not to get too swept up in the moment. I'm not trying to lead you on or make you angry. I just, quite honestly, don't feel ready. I need you to respect that." My eyes darted back and forth between his, watching as he took in my words.

He closed the small distance between us, bringing his mouth up to mine in a very sweet and chaste kiss. He pulled away after a moment, and we stared at each other. Until he spoke.

"But, if you had to guess a timeframe, when do you think you *will* be ready?"

My mouth opened, jaw dropping, and I scoffed at him. He was smiling, but obviously a little serious. I playfully slapped his arm. "Cory, my God...."

"I'm just kidding. Sort of."

I looked down at my boyfriend, my best friend, and knew he was only being a normal seventeen-year-old boy.

"Tell you what. One year from today, your eighteenth birthday. I'll be ready."

"A whole year?" he practically shouted, a shocked expression on his face.

"Shhhhh," I whisper-yelled, eyes darting to my bedroom door, listening for any sounds of my parents stirring. Hearing nothing from the hallway, I turned back to Cory. "You're ridiculous. You can wait a year. Until then, just assume it's not going to happen. Look at it this way," I said with a smile. "If I change my mind, it'll be a surprise." He let out a loud groan, making me laugh. I took his arm and moved it out so I could put my head in the crook of his neck, and snuggled in. "You know you're my favorite, right?"

He pressed a kiss against my temple. "Yeah."

Chapter Three

Cory's Eighteenth Birthday

McKenzie

"Baby, I'm so sorry."

I turned my head to see Mrs. Wallace shutting the front door behind her. She looked panicked and flustered.

"My late meeting ran over, traffic was atrocious, and I had to stop for gas on the way home." I watched as she came around the couch Cory and I were sitting on, grabbed his face, and planted a big kiss on his cheek. She pulled away, gave him sad mom eyes, and then stood up. "I cannot believe my little baby is eighteen today." She let out a loud sigh, then turned toward the kitchen exclaiming, "Eighteen!" I couldn't see her anymore, but I knew she was throwing her hands up in exasperation.

"Don't worry about it, Mom. Kenz and I were just watching a movie, waiting for everyone to get home."

I felt myself blush and I bit my bottom lip to stop from smiling. Cory was only telling half the truth. Up until twenty minutes ago, we'd been his room fooling around. Cory had yet to let me forget I'd set his eighteenth birthday as *the date*, the one on which I'd give him my virginity. And take his, as well. It was a whole thing. A thing we'd discussed in very thorough detail practically every day since I'd promised him a year ago. One of the things I made clear was that if he wanted us to have sex for the first time, it wasn't going to be in either one of our houses. I wanted something romantic: a hotel room, roses, champagne if he could get his hands on any. I simply was not going to have sex with him for the first time while we were rushed, trying to do the deed before his mom got home from work.

Much to his dismay.

"I promise I'll start dinner right now." She sounded like a little hummingbird flitting around the kitchen.

"Do you need any help?" I called out, hoping she wasn't making anything too difficult that I could possibly ruin. Culinary wizard I was not.

"Oh, Kenzie, sweetie, that's so nice of you to offer, but I have to get my head on straight first."

"All right, let me know." I always tried to be helpful when I was at Cory's house. I knew his parents were almost obligated to like me, since I was the daughter of their best friends and all, but I still wanted them to *actually* like me. It was kind of a complex of mine. I never wanted anyone to be disappointed in me. Cory moved to drape his arm over my shoulders, giving me a squeeze and a half smile; he knew why I always offered, and I think he liked when I helped his mom with tasks around their house. He said it made him feel like I was part of his family. That was important to me as well—I loved the Wallaces. All of them. Even if it was in different ways. Thinking of all the Wallaces made me question, "Is Hayes coming for dinner?"

"Nah, he said he's taking some sort of seminar over his winter break to get a couple extra credits or something, so he doesn't have the time to drive down for one night to have dinner with us on my birthday."

I could hear the vinegar in his voice. He was upset his brother wasn't coming to dinner and I could totally understand that. I, on the other hand, was relieved. Hayes had been so caught up in his schoolwork, I hadn't seen him since the night of Cory's sixteenth birthday.

"I'm sorry, Cory," I said softly. And I was. Selfishly, though, I wasn't sorry I wouldn't see him that night, just sorry Cory was upset about it. I knew I'd have to see him eventually—I couldn't go the rest of my life without Hayes coming around, but as far as I was concerned, the longer the better. Just then the front door opened again as Mr. Wallace entered the house.

"Hey, Dad," Cory called out.

"Hey, birthday man," his dad said with a wide smile.

"Don't call him a man just yet," Mrs. Wallace whined as she came out of the kitchen to greet her husband.

"Okay, okay," Mr. Wallace said, stopping at her side and pressing a kiss to her temple. I looked away, not wanting to intrude on their private moment.

A cell phone rang and I heard Mrs. Wallace ask her husband to answer her phone for her.

"Uh, babe, it's the bakery. They say they're closing in thirty minutes and they wanted to know if you're still coming to get the cake you ordered." Cory and I both turned our heads to look into the kitchen, watching his mother's eyes bulge and hands fist at her sides.

"Shit," Mrs. Wallace cried. "Shit shit shit."

"We'll be there in a few minutes," Mr. Wallace said into the phone. He ended the call then turned to his wife. "It's okay," he said soothingly as he ran his hands up and down her arms, then brought her in close and wrapped his arms around her.

"I was in such a hurry when I finally got out of work, I totally spaced the cake." She sounded close to tears.

"Mom, it's no big deal. Kenzie and I will go pick up the cake."

"You shouldn't have to pick up your own birthday cake, Cory."

"No, this'll be good. We'll go get the cake, then we'll stop at 7-Eleven really quick so I can watch my boy buy his first scratch-off." His dad turned and smiled at us. "We'll get Kenzie some too. There's perks to turning eighteen after all."

I didn't want to burst Mr. Wallace's bubble and tell him I'd driven, at midnight, to the closest gas station and purchased scratch-offs and a pack of cigarettes. Holly and Becca had gone with me, but none of us smoked, so the cigarettes were shoved in my glove box. We didn't win any money on our scratch-offs either.

"No, I need Kenzie here to help me with dinner if you are all leaving." She looked to me, eyes pleading.

"I'd love to help," I said, and stood up.

Mr. Wallace kissed his wife's forehead, then moved to swipe his car keys off the counter. "Let's roll, birthday boy. The bakery closes in thirty minutes."

Cory came up behind me, his hands landing on the curve of my waist, and his lips kissed right where my jaw met my neck. "I'll be back soon, Kenz." His fingers dug into my hips gently as he said, "Love you."

I lifted my shoulder, effectively pushing his face out of my neck, laughing as I said, "Get out of here." I watched as he and his dad left, feeling just the slightest twinge of guilt for not telling him I loved him back. I'd still never been able to say it, but I didn't think saying it simply because it was his birthday was right. So instead, I'd playfully pushed him away.

He wrapped an arm around his mother's shoulders, giving her a side hug and a sweet kiss right on her cheek. "Bye, Mom, we'll be back soon. Hopefully, we'll be millionaires."

"Bye, sweetie. I'm sorry again."

"Don't worry about it," he said as he kissed her again. "Love you, Mom."

I watched as he and his father left the house, trying to imagine in twenty-five years if Cory would look anything like his father from behind. Mr. Wallace still had an inch or two on Cory, but their hair color was identical. Mr. Wallace's shoulders were a little broader, but Cory was definitely the better built of the two, naturally, being an eighteen-year-old athlete. Just before he closed the door, Cory turned his head and caught my eye, winking and grinning, then disappeared.

"I'm making Cory's favorite," Mrs. Wallace said as she tied an apron around her waist, covering the skirt and button-up blouse she had worn to work.

"Lasagna," I said with a smile.

"Lasagna," she replied. "Why couldn't he like pizza the best?"

I laughed. "It's only his favorite because you've never made him help you make it. He doesn't understand the process."

"Something tells me that even if he did," she said, pulling ingredients out of her refrigerator, "he still would want me to make it for him on his birthday."

"Probably," I agreed, laughing again.

Forty-five minutes later the lasagna was in the oven, the table was set, and I had returned to the couch to wait for Cory and his dad to get home. Mrs. Wallace had gone to her bedroom to change.

"Where are those boys?" she asked when she finally emerged ten minutes later.

"Maybe they really won a million dollars." I laughed.

"If they come home with a winning lottery ticket I'm quitting my job tomorrow morning." She walked to the oven, opening the door to check on the lasagna. I got up from the couch and wandered to the kitchen island, leaning my elbows on the butcher-block top. "So," she said, leaning back against the countertop opposite the island, "what did Cory get you for your birthday?"

I immediately blushed, thinking about how he was planning on giving me his virginity, but I managed to keep a straight face. "We decided not to exchange gifts. You know, what with Christmas being, like, two weeks ago."

"Ah," she said, a grin moving across her lips that it looked as though she were trying to hide. She picked up her phone and started thumbing the screen. "I'm going to call them, see what's taking so long."

As she did, I sent a text to Cory.

Are you almost home? And why did your mom give me a weird look when I told her we weren't exchanging gifts?

"He didn't answer," she sighed. "Want to start an episode of *Downton Abbey* while we wait?"

"Sure."

We spent the next hour watching TV. Halfway through the episode, the kitchen timer beeped and Mrs. Wallace got up to remove the lasagna from the oven.

"You don't think Mr. Wallace took Cory to one of those, you know, juice bars, do you?"

"What's a juice bar?" she asked.

I blushed, not wanting to have to explain to my boyfriend's mother what a juice bar was. "Um, it's pretty much a strip club that doesn't serve alcohol, so the age requirement is only eighteen."

"What?" she practically shouted. "That's a real thing? He better not have...." Mrs. Wallace slammed the lasagna down on the stove and picked up her phone again. I watched her as she waited for her husband to pick up his phone, but she must have gotten his voice mail. "I swear on everything holy, if you've taken my baby boy to a strip club, you better not even bother coming home tonight." She paused, took a deep breath, then continued. "But seriously, honey, where are you? Call me."

"They've been gone almost two hours now," Mrs. Wallace said, unable to keep the concern from her voice. It was the same concern that had been creeping into my thoughts for a while.

"Do you think we should go look for them?"

Before she had a chance to answer me, there was a knock at the door.

I didn't know it at the time, but the feeling you get when you've just gotten on a roller coaster and it's climbed that very first peak, and you're waiting to plummet down—that feeling you get in your stomach as you crash forward, that's your body reacting to its instinct. Your body thinks you're about to die, that something really terrible is about to happen, and everything prepares for impact. I got that feeling the moment I heard a knock on the door, and looking back I would tell myself I should have been more prepared. I should have run, should have done anything I could have done to prevent the next few minutes from ever happening.

Mrs. Wallace opened the front door and all I saw was her face go blank and lose all color.

"Are you Mrs. Mark Wallace?" a deep voice asked.

"What's happened?" Her voice was a whisper.

"Ma'am, I'm Officer Davenport with the Florida State Police. Are you the wife of Mark Wallace?"

"Yes, he's my husband. Where is he?"

"The mother of Cory Wallace?"

My heart stopped at the mention of his name.

"What's going on?" she asked, her voice on the verge of breaking.

Another deep voice from outside.

"Do you think we could come in?"

"Sure, is everything all right?" Mrs. Wallace stepped aside and I watched as a policeman entered the house with another man at his side who wasn't in uniform.

The police officer motioned to the couch as the other man closed the door. Cory's mom came to sit next to me, her hands shaking, legs trembling. Without much thought I reached out and took her hand. Something was tragically wrong.

"Mrs. Wallace, it is with great regret that I have to tell you that your husband and your son were both victims in a robbery this evening. And I am sorry to tell you they were both killed in that robbery."

Victims. Robbery. Killed.

"No," she said firmly, shaking her head back and forth. "No, they went to get Cory's birthday cake and then to buy a scratch-off lottery ticket. That was all. I made lasagna."

I could hear her words, could feel the vibrations of her strong argument tingling in my hand, but it was as if I were stuck yards behind her, my feet slowly sinking in quicksand. Or in the ocean as the waves move over your feet and you look down and it feels like you're moving, looks as though the ground is rushing underneath you. But in reality, you are just sinking deeper and deeper into that sand.

"Mrs. Wallace," the other man said, "I know this is difficult to hear."

"There's been some sort of misunderstanding. Let me call him." She stood up, and she took all my balance with her. Her hand was holding me up. My arm fell limply to the couch as I looked at the two men sitting across the room from me.

"They're dead?" I yelled, but the words came out hushed and whispered.

"Are you related?" the officer asked.

"Cory is my best friend," I said automatically. "He's my boyfriend."

"I'm so sorry for your loss." The other man said, confirming my previous question.

"Who are you?" I whispered.

"I'm Father Ryan. I'm the chaplain with the police department."

"Mark, please." Mrs. Wallace's voice was shaking, and I knew she was crying. "The police are here and they're telling me you were in a robbery. *Please*, come home. Bring Cory home, Mark." She started sobbing and I watched the chaplain stand to go to her.

I didn't need to hear any more.

I stood up, walked to the door, ripped it open, and started running.

I heard someone yelling at me, telling me to come back, but I didn't stop. I ran all the way to my house, flung open the front door, and stopped just inside as I saw my parents sitting on the couch in the living room.

"McKenzie?" my mother asked, her voice already tight with fear. She could tell there was something wrong. She stood up immediately and I practically fell into her arms as I stumbled toward her. "McKenzie, tell me what's wrong," she cried, falling to the floor with me.

"Cory," I sobbed, unable in that moment to say the words.

"Sweetie, please, tell me what's wrong." My mother sounded almost as panicked as I felt.

"Cory and Mr. Wallace. They're dead." My arms were around my mother's waist, my face against her lap, my body flat on the floor.

"What?" my father asked, appearing almost immediately at my side. "What do you mean?"

"I don't know. A police officer showed up and just told Mrs. Wallace both Cory and Mr. Wallace were killed in a robbery." I said the words into my mother's thigh, but I knew they'd heard me, knew they were probably just as confused as I was.

"We have to go over there," my mother whispered. "Edward," she continued, her hand rubbing smooth circles over my back, "if this is true, we need to be there for her." I heard my mother's words, her voice crumbling at the end, felt her body shake with silent cries. "Oh, my God, Edward, this can't be happening."

My father picked us both up, and somehow we made it back over to the Wallaces'. There were a few more police cars parked on the street around their house, and some of the neighbors had come out of their houses, standing in their yards, watching, as if it were a spectator sport.

The door was slightly ajar and my mother gently pushed it open, calling out, "Chelsea?"

"Luce?" I heard Mrs. Wallace cry out, then I watched as the two best friends ran for each other, both sobbing. "They're dead," she cried. "My baby boy, he's gone."

I felt my father's arm come around my shoulder, pulling me into his side. I looked up at him, saying, "Daddy, I don't feel so well," and then everything went black.

Chapter Four

McKenzie

When I woke, everything was still dark, but there was faint moonlight filtering in through a window. I blinked, trying to figure out where I was, whose bed I was in, when I heard rustling behind me. I turned my head, rolling fully onto my back, and could see the outline of a man. He turned in my direction, then started moving toward me. I sat up, ready to run, when I heard his voice.

"Kenz, it's okay. It's me, Hayes."

"Hayes?" I was so confused. So many things were running through my mind at the same time that my head started to pound. "Why are you here? Where am I?"

He came all the way to the bed, sitting on the very edge next to my knees. "Did no one tell you?" he asked, voice heavy with sorrow. Suddenly, all the sadness came rushing back. I'd forgotten, but only for one moment, and I knew I'd probably never have that luxury again. There would most likely never be a moment in my life where I wasn't painfully aware that Cory was gone.

"He's gone," I whispered, throat pinched painfully as tears threatened. "This can't be real." Arms wrapped around me in the dark and I was pulled into Hayes, my cheek pressed against his chest where I could feel his breaths stumbling out

41 | Instead of You

and faltering back in. He cried silently, never making a sound. What started as a soft cry, trying to comfort me, slowly melted into Hayes rocking back and forth, silently screaming, mouth gaping, and me being the one holding him.

His hands started as smooth waves across my skin, wrapping around me like a blanket, but soon they were clawing at me, desperately trying to sink into me, as if I were the only thing keeping him from slipping away.

When it seemed like the worst of the waves had passed, he pulled away, his body slowly drifting from mine, the space between us full of grief and sadness.

"I'm sorry," he said, finally speaking after heavy dragging moments of silence.

"You don't have to apologize," I whispered even though I didn't intend to. I wanted to sound strong, as if I meant the words with everything I possessed, because I did.

"Yeah, well," he said, sighing as he stood from the bed, "I didn't mean to come in here and disturb you."

Looking around the dark room, I realized I still didn't know exactly where I was. "Where am I? And how did I get here?"

"You're in my bedroom."

His words registered in my mind and I realized I must be in his bed. It was completely inappropriate the way my body responded to that thought.

I vaguely remembered feeling faint and my father taking me to the back of the house. He had started to head for Cory's room, but I didn't want to be there.

There had been so many lazy afternoons spent napping in Cory's bed, so many late nights when both our parents thought I was at home when I was really lying with him. We'd fall asleep together, setting an alarm to wake us up before dawn so I could sneak back into my own bedroom. I was torn. His bed sounded like the only safe place in the world, but it also felt like it could be the saddest.

Hayes's bed had been comfortable, until I'd realized its owner. Now it felt electric.

"I should probably go see my parents. They're still here?"

"Yes. My mom...." I watched as his shadowed hand came up and ran through his hair. "She's a mess."

I didn't want to go out there. "I should go out there."

"Hey," Hayes said as I started to stand up and regain my bearings. "Are you all right?"

I shrugged even though I didn't know if he could see me. "I don't know. One minute he was here. He was talking and breathing and living, and then someone I've never seen tells me he's gone. It feels like a lie right now, like it can't be possible."

"Well, it's not a lie, Kenz." His voice was tinged with anger, but I didn't think he was angry with me.

"I know. I'm so sorry."

He let out a loud sigh, then said, "Come on, I'll walk back with you." He cracked the door and light slipped into the room, illuminating everything. I walked past him as he opened the door. His hand just barely brushed the small of my back as I passed, gently guiding me through the door. My breath halted as my lungs seized. It had been two years, almost to the hour, since I'd felt Hayes's hands on me, and I'd forgotten their power, forgotten the way they'd lit me on fire. I'd never forgotten how guilty his hands had made me feel, but nothing could have prepared me for the shame of liking his hands on me in the wake of his brother's death.

I hated myself in that moment.

We walked into the living room and I saw my parents and Mrs. Wallace sitting around the table in the dining room attached to the kitchen. They all had coffee mugs sitting in front of them, and used tissues were scattered on the table.

"McKenzie," Mrs. Wallace said, standing and opening her arms to me. I let her hug me, but honestly I was afraid I'd break her. She sounded fragile and I wasn't sure how she managed to seem so put together. "Are you okay, sweetheart?"

"I don't know," I replied honestly.

"You scared us, baby," my mom said, giving me a sad smile.

I took in a deep breath, then let it out, not sure what I was supposed to say next. I took one of the empty seats around the table. "I can't believe this is happening."

"I don't think any of us have really processed this yet," my dad offered. "But it's important that Chelsea and Hayes know we're here for them." He looked at Hayes, who had stopped in the kitchen and was now leaning back against the counter, arms crossed over his chest. "I'm serious, Hayes. You need anything at all, you call us. That goes for you too, Chelsea." Hayes gave a very slight nod of his head, indicating he'd heard my dad, but giving nothing else away, while Mrs. Wallace gave the saddest weakest smile I'd ever seen. She looked terrible, exactly how I'd imagine a woman who'd just been told her husband and son were dead would look.

Her hair, which had been pulled into a tight ponytail, was now just a loose bundle of hair at the nape of her neck with half her hair hanging around her face. Her eyes were red and puffy, her nose a deep shade of pink, and her hands shook slightly as she lifted a tissue to it.

"I'm afraid to go to sleep," she said quietly. "This was the last day they were alive." Her voice dissolved around her words, quaking more and more. "If I go to sleep, I'll wake up, and it will be the first day they're both dead." She dropped her head into her hands, crying in earnest, quiet sobs slipping from her. "I don't want to live in the world I'll wake up in tomorrow."

The tears slipped down my cheeks before I realized I was crying. I hadn't had any time to process what had happened, and suddenly it felt more real than it had before.

Cory was gone.

And he was never coming back.

I had never, not for one single day, gone without a best friend. Cory had always been there. From the beginning. And now I'd have to live the rest of my life without him. It was as though I had been reading a picture book and all the pages were in color, but now the rest of them were just dreary images in black and gray. What had once been a vivid depiction of a beautiful story, a story of a friendship so deep even the word *friends* couldn't contain it, was now a dark charcoal, and each page seemed like it weighed a ton, dripping with wet concrete.

"What happened?" I asked quietly, not even positive I wanted to know the answer, but a large part of me needed to hear the words.

"Honey, we can talk about it later." My mom took my hand, gave it a squeeze, and then shifted her eyes to Mrs. Wallace, raising her eyebrows. It occurred to me she didn't want to talk about it in front of her.

"Lucia, she deserves to know," Mrs. Wallace said through sobs. "I'm okay." She was definitely not okay, but I figured she was as okay as she was going to get that night.

"McKenzie," my father started, his deep voice always soothing, "this is a pretty terrible story, and I don't want you getting upset again. If you need me to stop, let me know."

I nodded, having no other response. There were no appropriate words for this situation.

"Mark and Cory stopped at a convenience store on their way home from the bakery. They were at the counter, trying to buy lottery tickets, when a man entered wearing a hoodie and ski mask."

Just listening to his words made my heart rate speed, thundering through my body, rioting through my veins like stampeding stallions. I closed my eyes, trying to focus on his words and not the way the room felt as though it was getting hotter.

"The man had a gun and demanded the employee behind the counter give him the money from the register. Instead of opening the register and just doing as the man asked, the employee pulled out a shotgun, but before he could shoot him, the robber fired first." My father let out a shaky breath, his voice warbling like I'd never heard in my life. He was a tough guy; only a soft spot for his girls. My mom and I were spoiled by him: loved on, supported, protected. But other than that, he was tough as nails. "The man then turned his gun on Mark, shot him first, then immediately shot Cory after."

Mrs. Wallace broke down, burying her face in her hands. Hayes walked over, knelt next to his mother, and wrapped his arms around her. She melted into him, crying into the space between his shoulder and his neck, her hands grasping at the back of his shirt.

My parents were both crying. My mother cried softly, wiping tears away every few seconds as they rolled down her cheeks. But my father cried silently, holding a tight fist to his mouth. Both were looking at me, watching and waiting for me to crumble.

"So, he just shot them? For nothing?" I asked, confused about every single part of what I'd been told. Confused about why any of this had to happen. Confused about why someone would just randomly shoot a father and son who hadn't done anything to him at all. Confused about why it had to be Cory and his father. And although the confusion was so palpable, so real, it could have had its own seat at the table, it was slowly turning into anger. "Why would someone do that?"

"Sweetheart, we'll probably never really know why," my mother said, reaching for my hand. I let her take it, but I didn't want to be touched. Anger and fear were coursing through me, making my skin feel as if it were electric. I was practically shaking with energy. "Mark and Cory both died, as well as the employee. The robber took the money from the register and ran. The police are looking for him, but odds are, when they find him, he's not going to tell us why he killed them. I'm sorry." She wiped her cheeks again, then took a breath to continue. "He's probably a man down on his luck, and didn't intend to shoot anyone."

"Don't make excuses for a murderer, Lucia." Another first. I'd heard my parents fight before, get into arguments, but I'd never heard my father talk to my mother as though he thought she were stupid. As though he thought her words were careless and insulting.

"I'm not making excuses, Edward," my mother replied, obviously trying to remain calm. "I'm trying to make sense of a senseless act. I'm trying to come to terms with something that has no rhyme or reason. I simply can't believe that someone woke up today and decided to kill three innocent people who have nothing whatsoever to do with him. I can't live in a world like that." The more words she spoke, the harder she cried. My father pushed away from the table and stood, walking into the living room with such purpose it was as if he thought walking away would make the situation less tense.

"If I'd have just picked up the cake from the bakery on the way home, both of them would still be alive."

Her words silenced everyone, made the room stand still like a painting.

"Mom, you can't think that way." Hayes's deep voice finally cut through all of us. He was still kneeling next to his mother, still rubbing his hand on her back, but she was sitting in her chair and looking at nothing in particular.

"It's all I *can* think. Mark and Cory left the house and I know nothing after that. I don't know if Mark knew what was happening until it was too late. I don't know if either one of them died instantly, or if they lay on the floor in pain until they bled to death. I don't know if my baby boy cried out for me. Was he scared? Was he hurting? Did he watch his father die before he slipped away?" She was becoming frantic and yet, she was the only one making any sense. "Did Mark see his son die? Did he try to protect him? Did he die panicking because he couldn't save his son? I'll *never* know the answer to all these questions. But one thing I know for sure is that it never would have happened if I'd just remembered to pick up my son's birthday cake."

The saddest part, the part that I knew would more than likely eat away at Mrs. Wallace for the rest of her life?

She was right.

It wasn't her fault, and no one in their right mind would blame her, but I knew none of that mattered. Mrs. Wallace would blame herself and that was enough punishment—more, in fact.

"I think I'm going to go to bed. I don't want this day to be over, but maybe if I go to sleep, I'll wake up to find it's all been a dream."

Mrs. Wallace stood, didn't say anything to anyone, and walked down the hall. We all watched her go, and when we heard her bedroom door close, we looked to each other again.

"She's going to need a lot of support for the next couple days. Weeks even." Mom wasn't talking to anyone in particular. She might have even been talking to herself; thinking out loud.

"Hayes, is there anything you need from us right now?" Dad's voice had calmed down, and I could tell he was trying to help Hayes in any way he could, trying to do anything to make his loss not seem so huge.

"I don't think there's anything else to do right now." His eyes darted to me for just an instant and the sadness was almost painful to see. He looked back at my father, pulling his shoulders back as if he were trying to appear less broken than I imagined he was. "Nothing to do now until the coroner releases the bodies."

"Right," my father said. There was nothing he could say in response. It was a sentence a twenty-two-year-old man should never have to say about his brother, or his father, and certainly not both of them together. "We'll be back tomorrow, late morning, to see how we can help."

Hayes nodded, but said nothing more.

My mom and I stood to leave. We silently walked toward the door, but I couldn't just leave. I couldn't just walk away from Hayes like that. His mom in the other room, the only person left in his family alive losing her mind. I couldn't just leave him there thinking he was alone. So I turned, walked up to him, lifted onto my toes, and wrapped my arms around his neck. He didn't move at first. I wondered, with my arms slung over his shoulders and my cheek pressed into his chest, if I'd made a mistake and misjudged what he needed from me in that moment. But then, slowly, his arms lifted, closed around my waist, and his cheek came to rest upon the crown of my head.

It was a strange moment. Strange because having his arms around me was comforting, but also confusing because having his arms around me felt like I'd gotten back something I thought I'd lost. I chalked it up to emotions, but let the embrace linger longer than it should have, not caring that my parents were probably watching.

"I don't know how, Hayes," I whispered, "but everything is going to be all right. Eventually." When I pulled away, his eyes found mine, but he looked even sadder than before I'd touched him.

I walked away and left with my parents.

When I made it to my bed, I lay down watching the predawn sky through my window lighten with every minute that passed and I listened to my mother sob and my father soothe her from their bedroom. Only once the house was eerily quiet did my mind finally wander to Cory. I thought about Cory at five, slinging mud at me from across the yard after one particularly heavy summer rain. I thought of Cory at ten, letting me sit on the handlebars of his bike as we rode to the grocery store to buy popsicles to sell to all our friends at the park. I thought of Cory at fifteen, just learning how to drive, his mother practically having a heart attack as he pulled into my driveway, nearly hitting my father's SUV.

There were very few memorable events in my life that didn't involve Cory. He'd been there since day one. And had I known our days were numbered, the last two years would have been very different. I would have made sure of that.

Chapter Five

McKenzie

The next two weeks passed in a blur. My parents didn't make me go back to school immediately; they said I could wait until after the funeral. Because of the nature of their deaths, a very detailed and thorough autopsy was performed on both Cory and his father, which delayed everything.

My mom spent a lot of time with Mrs. Wallace but that wasn't saying much, she was practically catatonic. She rarely got out of bed, and when she did, she resembled a zombie.

I didn't feel like I was faring much better.

The night Cory was killed, I don't think I really comprehended what was happening, or how drastically different my life would become. I woke up the next morning after a horrible night of dreams. Dreams of watching Cory being shot, dreams of his face, dreams of him smiling and winking at me just before he left the house. Each time Dream Cory winked at me, I screamed and yelled at him not to go, to stay with me. That's how I woke up, screaming "Please, don't go!"

After spending a night dreaming about his death, I reached for my cell phone to see if he'd texted me. It didn't occur to me for a few seconds that I'd never get another text from him. I looked at the very last one he'd sent.

I can't wait for tonight.

We were supposed to have sex for the first time the night he died.

But then he died.

He was killed.

So many thoughts were streaming through my mind. *I should have slept with him months ago so he didn't die a virgin.* What a terrible thought. But for whatever reason, I felt like I'd denied him something. I never thought I'd feel guilty for waiting, but suddenly, I did. My reasons for waiting were still valid—I wasn't in love with him. But my need to wait until I was in love didn't seem as important now that he was gone, when weighed against the fact that *he died.* Besides, I'd agreed to have sex with him anyway, regardless of not being in love. We'd set a date, we'd paid for a hotel room. A hotel room we never showed up to. I was going to go through with it because I felt like he'd waited long enough. We'd both waited long enough. I wanted to know, too, what it felt like to be with someone. I was just as curious as any other girl my age, but I was also just as scared. There was also a tiny thought in the back of my mind that perhaps, just maybe, having sex with him would send me over the proverbial edge. I thought maybe if I made love to him, that final switch would flip and I'd finally fall in love with him.

I'd never known anyone who'd been murdered before, but I could officially attest to the fact that the family left behind by someone who died of natural causes had a very different road than Mrs. Wallace and Hayes. Not only were they dealing with the deaths, but they were also dealing with worrying about the man who had killed Cory and Mark.

After he'd shot all three people, the man wearing a mask ran away and the police had no leads on where it was he went or his identity. They knew what kind of gun was used, based on the bullets pulled from all three bodies, but that was basically the only information they had to go on.

This not only caused Mrs. Wallace great stress, understandably, it also caused some degree of paranoia. I'd gone with my mom over to her house a few times and I'd heard her talking about what-ifs. What if the killer had known Mark? What if he killed him on purpose? Targeted him? What if he wasn't finished and came back for her and Hayes?

I didn't see her in hysterics, but I heard her. She'd been in her room with my mom and Hayes and I'd sat on their couch, eyes wide, pulse racing.

It hadn't occurred to me that this might not have been an accident.

Hayes wandered out and I must have looked like a deer in headlights because he diverted from whatever path he was on and came straight to me. "What's wrong, Kenz?"

"Is what she's saying true? Will they come back for you?" I hadn't felt fear in the days since they'd died, but I was feeling it then.

He didn't answer right away, but he looked at me, seeming to just take my face in. "No, Kenz. No one's coming back for us. Mom's just not thinking straight. Her mind's not right."

"But how do you know?" The thought was terrifying.

"Because it doesn't make any sense. That guy was just hard up for money. He probably didn't go in there intending to shoot anyone. He didn't know who my dad was, or even what his name was."

"But he does now! This has been all over the news all week. He's out there and he knows the man he killed has a wife and another son. What's stopping him from finding you and—"

I never finished that sentence because Hayes pulled me into his arms, running a hand down my hair, whispering that everything was okay, that he wasn't going anywhere.

When the day finally came for the funeral, it felt surreal. I had never, not in a million years, thought I'd ever be attending Cory's funeral. Even if we'd grown up and gotten married just like everyone had planned, I'd never thought that far ahead. I thought it would be years before I ever even had to *go* to a funeral. And even though eighteen was too

57 | Instead of You

young, in my opinion, to be going to your best friend's funeral, it was most definitely too young to be dead.

Everything about Cory's funeral felt wrong.

Mrs. Wallace insisted we sit in the front pew, even though I'd wanted to be as far away from the caskets as possible. Hayes sat closest to the aisle, his hand wrapped around his mother's, resting in her lap. I was sure everyone in the church could hear Mrs. Wallace weeping throughout the funeral, and there was no denying it was heartbreaking.

Sometimes, people refer to funerals as celebrations of life. But not that funeral.

No.

No one was there to remember the good times, or think about how much light Cory had brought his parents, or how lucky Mrs. Wallace had been to spend her life with her husband.

No.

Everyone was painfully aware that we were in mourning, that these deaths were a tragedy, and there was no way to lighten the mood. Mrs. Wallace was crying, and she wasn't the only one.

When the pastor of the church neither Cory nor I had ever attended finished talking about life and what a gift it was, and how we can't always understand what was in store for us or our loved ones, he took a step back and I startled as Hayes stood and started walking toward the pulpit. The instant he was absent from his mother's side, Mrs. Wallace slumped toward my mother and I realized she was incapable of even holding herself upright.

Hayes walked past me and our eyes met for just one second and even though I'd never found him to be particularly easy to read, the emotion held in just that one second of contact left me reeling. It was almost as if every emotion he'd been feeling in the last two weeks was stored in his eyes, creating a storm of feelings that was about to erupt right in front of me. I wanted to jump off my seat, take his hand, and just be next to him. I wanted for him to let me help carry some of the weight I could see grasping his shoulders with invisible hands.

But before I could even blink, he pulled his eyes away from mine and continued on his way.

He made it to the little podium, pulled a piece of paper out of his front jacket pocket, and unfolded it, placing it on the wooden platform. He took a deep breath, releasing it audibly as the crowd in the church, which was so full there were people standing in the back, waited with bated breath to hear his broken words.

He finally looked up and the urge to run to him only grew. I didn't want him doing it alone.

"The first thing I'd like to say is that, on behalf of my mother and myself, we'd like to thank everyone for their support. The past two weeks have been trying, to say the least, and things would only be worse if it weren't for the love and support coming to us from our friends and family. You see," he continued, his eyes darting down to his paper, "my mother and I have found ourselves to be in somewhat new territory." His hand came up, running absently through his hair, eyes still downward. "When faced with unimaginable circumstances, there are only a few choices to be made. Among the terrible choices, one has been our mode of operation: cling to those around you. I've been away at college for a few years and even though I think it's normal, I hadn't been talking to my parents as often as I should have, and I definitely wasn't talking to Cory as much as I should have, and that's something I regret.

"My mom called me a few weeks before Cory's birthday and invited me home for his birthday dinner. I wasn't far, just a two-hour drive, but I was too busy. Too involved in my own life. Too cool, maybe? I was a lot of things, but I didn't bother coming home." He let out a loud, swooshing breath, swaying back and forth like he were moving his weight from one foot to another. "I have no idea what would have happened had I come home. There's no way to tell. I like to think I would have gone with them, would have been with them in that convenience store, would have done something to prevent us all from having to be here today, but I'll never know.

"What I *do* know, what I've learned in the last two weeks, is that nothing is guaranteed. Things you think you are owed, you just can't count on. You think you'll never have to bury your brother and your father on the same day? Think again.

You think you'll be old and gray before someone close to you passes away? Nope."

I could see his hands shaking, his body growing restless. I knew he was a ticking time bomb, and knowing that, I felt the same. I was antsy, wanting to run to him, pull him away, tell him he didn't owe anyone any more of his words or thoughts. Enough had been taken from him.

"If Cory were here he'd tell you all, I'm sure, to live as if tomorrow weren't a given, as though you've only got this one chance to take what you want from life. And if you can't take his word for it, take mine."

My breath caught as Hayes's eyes met mine. My chest ached as he spoke directly to me, even though the entire church was full of people holding back cries and wiping their eyes.

"If you let that one moment pass you by where you could have grabbed what you wanted, there will come a day when it's out of your grasp, and regret will haunt you, just like a ghost."

My heart sputtered in my chest, my fingers clenched into a tight fist. I was suppressing every natural instinct I had, forcing myself to stay seated. If I stood, I was either going directly to Hayes, or straight out the door.

"My mother wants everyone to know how much she loved my father." Hayes's voice cracked with his words. The sound pierced my chest and cut my heart right in half. "They had a good life together, and maybe one day she'll be strong enough to tell you all how he earned her love every day. Maybe one day soon she'll be strong enough to tell you how much she loved Cory, how from the day he was born until the day he was taken from us he was her baby. In fact," he said with a sudden short laugh, "he'll always be her baby and I've given up trying to compete with him anymore. The competition is now eternally unfair." He laughed again as a single tear streamed down his cheek, and light laughter came from a few more people in the church.

After a few moments he took another deep breath, then let his gaze sweep the church, seeming to take in the sight before him.

"Again, we're really thankful for everyone's support. We hope the death of Cory and my father isn't in vain, though. If anything, we hope you all will live your life a little fuller, a little more aggressively, and remember that tomorrow is never promised. Nothing is promised to us. The only thing we've really got is the here and the now, and if you let it pass you by, if you sit by and let it go, there's no guarantee you'll get those moments, or those people, back."

He folded his piece of paper up as he walked back down the stairs toward the pews. He came closer and closer to me, and it was almost as if the magnetic force between us grew stronger with each step because the instant he was right in front of me, I stood and opened my arms to him.

I was sure to everyone in the church it looked like one person offering a lifelong friend support during, arguably, the hardest day of his life. I was sure everyone watched us embrace and was happy that Hayes had a friend like me in his life to help him deal with his staggering loss. They all thought my motivations for wrapping my arms around him, for spreading my fingers wide over his back to feel as much of him as I possibly could, was innocent.

I would spend the next few days trying to convince myself of that too.

Chapter Six

Hayes

Funerals were exhausting.

Fuck that.

The last two weeks were exhausting. But yesterday was the most draining day of my existence.

I'd led a pretty low-key life. I wasn't high maintenance by any means. I was focused and driven. I set a goal and I went after it. Well, most of the time. The last four years had been so incredibly concentrated on getting my degree and moving on to my master's program, I'd barely had time to live the normal college life.

It was only now, in the midst of the biggest mind fuck ever, that I've realized I wasn't just focused, or concentrating on life, I was avoiding things.

When Edward Harris had called me late that night, the night my father and brother were killed, he tried not to freak me out. He didn't want me panicking as I made the two-hour drive, so he just told me there was an emergency and that I needed to come home. But I'd known something was wrong. I never could have imagined everything that had happened. But since the moment I walked in that door, I'd been bombarded with every single thing I'd been trying to run away from since I left town.

Oh, and the murder of my dad and brother. That happened.

So even though I'd been exhausted, even though it was all I could do at the end of the night to strip to my underwear and crawl into bed, I never found sleep. Instead, I'd lain in my bed listening to my mother cry through the walls. Or when she'd managed to fall asleep, I'd lain in my bed and thought about Kenzie. But then, like I always had, I'd push thoughts of her away and I'd think about school, wondering how everything was ever going to be okay again. In the midst of all the rambling of my mind, my mom would wake up again, and I'd listen to her crying through the walls.

It was an endless cycle.

When I noticed the sky becoming lighter, I knew I'd been awake all night.

I sat up, reaching for my phone and disabling the alarm that was set to go off in another hour, and headed into the hallway. I stopped outside my mother's door, leaning in, trying to see if I could hear her crying. I could hear her breathing, but there were no cries.

Even if I couldn't sleep, I was glad she could. Although, she'd been put on medication just days after the murder. I made a mental note to e-mail her doctor as obviously she needed a stronger prescription. I didn't want her to cry every night.

She needed rest. Pieces of her mind were slipping away all the time. The sleepless nights, the worrying, the paranoia, simply dealing with something a mother and wife should never have to deal with, each of those things were slowly robbing her of her sanity, and I knew she'd never get better if she didn't get any rest.

I continued down the hall, holding my breath as I passed Cory's room.

I hadn't been able to even open the door since I'd been home. I was terrified of what would happen if I did. So far, aside from kind of losing it at the funeral, I was the only person in my family who wasn't in the midst of a mental breakdown, and I didn't want to take any chances in that department. So Cory's door stayed closed.

I locked myself in the bathroom and prepared myself for another day. Another day where I avoided all the emotions clawing away at my insides, fighting their hardest to break their way free of me.

When I went downstairs thirty minutes later, Lucia was standing at our kitchen sink washing dishes. I'd asked her the day before, sometime during the wake, when forty or fifty people were in our house sharing memories with each other about Dad and Cory, to come and sit with my mother.

She'd given me the same response she had for the last two weeks anytime I asked anything of her.

"Of course, sweetheart. Anything you need."
That was always coupled with a gentle squeeze on
my shoulder and the saddest eyes on anyone I'd
ever seen.

I was so thankful for the Harris family. Lucia and
Edward had done so much for my mom and me
since the murder, but I needed things to start
getting back to normal if I was going to continue to
avoid the feelings I was constantly aware of, just in
the periphery.

That was also why I was glad it was Lucia in my
kitchen, and not McKenzie.

"Good morning, Hayes," she said quietly just
after turning off the faucet.

"Morning."

"Sweetie, you look terrible," she said, that gentle
yet worried tone in her voice.

"I didn't sleep much last night. Mom was crying
a lot."

"I see," she said softly, her eyes moving all along
my face, trying to find the part of me that worried
her the most. Was it the dark bags under my
eyes? My sunken-in cheeks? The red veins in the
whites of my eyes? "Whatever you've got going on
this morning, can it wait? Maybe you should go
upstairs and try to get some sleep. I'll listen for
your mom."

I gave her the best smile I could muster. "Thank
you, but this really can't wait."

Thirty minutes later I found myself in a situation I never could have *ever* seen coming.

"Hayes, it's good to see you. Please, take a seat."

I shook the hand of my high school principal and took the seat she offered me across the table from her at the only coffee shop in town.

"Mrs. Anderson, thank you so much for meeting with me on a Sunday. I know it's a hassle, but it's the only time I could make this happen. Life's been, well, a little hectic."

"I am so sorry for your loss, Hayes. Everyone at the school has been reeling from the loss of Cory, and we all extend our deepest sympathies."

"Thank you," I said with a nod, the words practiced and rehearsed to perfection in the last two weeks. I could take a condolence like a champ. "I don't want to take up too much of your Sunday." That was my subtle hint to Mrs. Anderson to move off the topic of my brother's death, and on to the real issue at hand.

"Yes, well, I think I have all the information I need. I've been communicating with your supervisor at your university and it looks like we've ironed out all the details. But, first, why don't you tell me a little bit about what you've accomplished academically in the four years since you've graduated from my high school."

The smile she gave me then was one of pride, which I welcomed. I could talk about school all day long—it had been my focus every day since I left this town. Talking about it now was the most welcome distraction I could have asked for.

"Well, I went into the university knowing exactly what I wanted to do and I didn't waste any time. All my elective courses were either related to my major, or in my area of study. I took courses all summer every year. I took night classes and at least twenty credits a term and I graduated at the end of my third year with a major in History. I applied to the graduate school of education, was accepted, and now I'm working on my master's. At the end of the year I hope to have my degree and my teaching certificate."

Mrs. Anderson looked at me, a smile still wide on her face. "That's a lot of work, Mr. Wallace."

I shrugged. "It's what I wanted."

"And how has the year progressed for you, academically, up until this point?"

"So far, it's been great. The graduate program started over the summer, so for two terms they really pile on the classes. Then in the fall I was assigned to a classroom and a teacher, and I shadowed. This semester I was supposed to take that class over to get my student teacher practicum completed. It's one of the last steps in the licensure program. I can't get my teaching license without it." I took in a deep breath, knowing we were getting to the point in the conversation where I was going to find out whether or not four years of hard work was getting thrown away. "But, obviously, the high school I was assigned to is two hours from here. And I'm not in a position to leave my mother right now."

"No, I can't imagine you are." Again with the sad voice.

"So, I reached out to my advisor and asked her if there was anything I could do, any way I could finish my practicum here. I believe that's when my university contacted you."

Mrs. Anderson was quiet for a moment, a long moment, but then she spoke, her tone no longer sad. She sounded like a principal. Like someone's boss.

"I called a small meeting with all the social science teachers at the high school. I explained your situation and asked if any of them were in a position to host a student teacher. As you know, since we're so far from the university, we've never hosted any, not since I've been here."

"I know it's a lot to ask, and I wouldn't normally, but—"

"But you've got extenuating circumstances, and we all understand that, and we want to help. Mr. White was planning on starting a new unit this Monday with his senior World History class. The other three teachers are in the middle of units and don't feel like it would be fair to ask you to step in. Mr. White is excited to have you, though."

I felt a rush of tension leave my body as my shoulders slumped forward. She was giving me a chance. There was not one tiny molecule in my body that didn't understand how much I was asking of everyone—of the high school, of my university, of my advisors. They were all bending over backward for me, and I knew it was mostly out of sympathy, but I didn't care. I'd worked so hard to get where I was and I had been so close to the end, just to have it all teetering on the edge of disaster. I couldn't leave my mom. And if there was nothing to be done but postpone my work, then I would have done that, but at least now I can still finish my degree and be there for my mom every night. "Thank you, Mrs. Anderson. You have no idea how much this means to me."

"We're glad to have you. We just wish it were under better circumstances." Sad voice again. "There are just a few things we need to go over still. Then I will let you get back to your Sunday."

"Great. I'm all ears." And I was. I couldn't say I was excited, as that level of emotion was numb to me. But finally, for the first time in two weeks, something *good* was happening, something that could take away just a little bit of the heaviness I'd been carrying around since the night I got that phone call.

"I should tell you that Cory was enrolled in this particular class." Her words were like a bucket of ice water thrown over me. Any lightness I had felt just moments before was pushed back down by her words. "Unfortunately, this was the only class we could assign you. Obviously, I completely understand if you'd like to pass."

I thought about her offer, thought about what it would mean to turn her down. It would mean not being able to complete my practicum until the fall of the following school year. It would mean missing out on one entire season of hiring. I would be sitting for months with no real hope of finding a job.

"If I can be completely frank with you, Mrs. Anderson," I said, leaning toward her slightly.

"Of course."

"I have to spend every evening in the house I grew up in with him. I walk past his bedroom door at least ten times a day. I see his picture hanging on the wall. I see his car in the driveway. There's no way to escape his memory, and I wouldn't if I could. I'm already dealing with his loss, so this is just another log on the fire."

"I understand. I wish it were different—"

"But it's not."

"No, it isn't." She was quiet for a moment, but then she continued on. "That all being said, your advisor, Mr. White, and I have all decided that if you begin the term, but find it to be too overwhelming, you can choose to end your practicum with no repercussions. We want you to succeed, but we don't want your circumstances to hold you back should you find yourself in a situation where you need time to heal."

She was giving me a safety net. I didn't like special treatment, but I knew I was basically asking for it. Besides, I knew she was just being a decent human being. This was such a fucked-up situation, I couldn't fault her for trying to help me.

"Thank you. I'm going to try my best to be just like any other student teacher, Mrs. Anderson."

"I don't have any doubt you will. Your university advisor wants me to let you know that you're still required to attend the biweekly meetings with your cohorts."

"I am pretty confident I can find someone to be with my mom one night every other week. The Harrises have been very helpful."

"That leads me to my final discussion point." My brows drew together in confusion. I didn't know how the Harris family fit into this conversation at all. "The staff at the high school was not blind to the relationship between Cory and McKenzie Harris. And some of the staff has made me aware of the closeness of your two families, which I am so thankful you have in this difficult time."

"Okay," I said, drawing the word out to emphasize my confusion.

"McKenzie Harris is a student in the class Mr. White has offered to you for your practicum."

Shit.

"Now, normally, it would be unethical for us to allow you to be her teacher, Mr. Wallace. But we're aware, once again, of the extenuating circumstances you find yourself in, and we are compelled to help. I've made your university advisor aware of the conflict of interest, and she has made it clear that she trusts me to make the final determination as to whether or not this particular, uh, conflict, is dire enough to prevent you from finishing your degree at my high school. After looking at your college transcripts, and talking with you today, I think you're determined enough, and levelheaded enough, to not let your connection with McKenzie Harris cloud your ability to teach her."

"Uh, Mrs. Anderson, it never crossed my mind that she might be in my class." Why would it have? Surely the universe didn't hate me this much, right?

"Will it be an issue?" she asked, not unkindly. It was very obvious she was trying to help me in any way she could. And I needed her help. I needed this opportunity. This practicum was one of the few things I had that was keeping me from losing my mind every day.

"No," I answered, hoping she couldn't see past my blatant lie. "It won't be an issue."

"Then it's all settled. We'll see you tomorrow morning at seven thirty." She stood up and I did the same, reaching my hand out to her.

"Thank you again, I really appreciate it." She smiled at me, shook my hand, then turned and left the coffee shop. I collapsed back into my chair,

74 | Anie Michaels

hands coming instantly to run through my hair, breath leaving me in one long and exhausted exhalation.

"Shit," I whispered harshly, my eyes on my shoes, elbows on knees, head in hands. "Shit."

Somehow I was going to have to make it through the next five months as the teacher of my dead brother's girlfriend.

The girl I'd known her whole life.

The girl I'd been in love with, in one way or another, since I understood the word and what it meant.

Chapter Seven

McKenzie

Cory had driven me to school for the last year and half. Even though it was, in the grand scheme of things, not the worst thing to happen, stepping up onto the school bus was a terrible way to start the day.

Everyone's eyes were on me; their sad eyes with concerned expressions. I was so tired of everyone looking at me like I was going to burst into tears at any given moment. It felt so displaced. *I* hadn't died. I hadn't lost a son, or a brother. But then I remember what everyone *thought* I'd lost: my boyfriend, the love of my young life, my future, my other half.

Do you know how hard it is to mourn when you're not sure what it is exactly you lost?

I felt Cory's loss profoundly. I missed his laugh, his jokes, his kindness, his friendship. But I hated myself because I didn't miss the other parts of him. In fact, part of me, a part I was so scared to acknowledge or give a voice to, was glad the option of being with him forever was taken from me. I never would have turned him down, would have spent my life hoping to love him in some way I wasn't sure I was capable of, but the man with a gun made that decision for me. And I hated myself for being even remotely grateful for such a fantastically horrible thing.

So all those people who looked at me as though they felt sorry for me, well, it made me sick because I didn't deserve any of it. I was a horrible person.

I found an empty seat, sat down, and curled my body toward the window, hoping it would give off the right message: I didn't want to be bothered.

Holly, Becca, and Todd were all waiting for me when I walked off the bus, all wearing identical pitying faces.

"Hey, McKenzie." Holly greeted me first; she was the most outgoing of the group, the one most likely to talk at inappropriate intervals.

"Hey, guys," I said, adjusting my messenger-style bag on my shoulder. Becca stepped forward and wrapped her arms around me. I let myself take the comfort she offered and tried not to shrug out of her embrace too early. I loved my friends dearly, and they'd been really great since Cory died, but I didn't want that day to be about what I'd lost. I wanted to focus on going back to normal, or building a new normal. Something besides focusing on all the sadness. I'd had hours and hours of sadness as I lay in bed at night, unable to sleep more than an hour or two.

"Are you doing okay, Kenz? Is it too hard to be here, you know, because it reminds you of Cory?" Holly's question was met with glares from Becca and Todd. I tried not to let her question get to me; I knew she meant well. Holly just lacked the part of her brain that evaluated the effect her words might have. She was never purposefully inconsiderate, perhaps just too curious and just maybe lacking a little tact.

I think my friends were expecting me to have some sort of nervous breakdown as soon as I stepped foot onto the asphalt. Expected a new wave of devastation to roll through me. As if just existing in the aftermath wasn't devastation enough.

"Holly," I said, trying to mask a little of my irritation, fully aware I wasn't doing a great job. "Every single piece of my life was intertwined with Cory's. I can't enter a room at my house that doesn't have a piece of him in it. My bed, my living room, even the freaking tree house in my backyard – everything is *filled* with Cory. He's everywhere. So, no, being here isn't too hard. *Life* is too hard right now; this is just par for the course."

"She's just worried about you," Todd said, defending his girlfriend. "We all are, Kenzie. Is there anything we can do to make this easier for you?"

I forced a smile. "No. I'm sorry, Holly." And I was. I didn't want to snap at anyone, I just wanted to progress, to move forward. "Let's just get on with it. This is life without Cory, and I can't hide from it forever." I looked down at my fingers gripping the strap of my bag, knuckles turning white. "He wouldn't want that anyway."

"You're right," Becca chimed in, the smile evident in her voice.

It hit me just then that I wasn't the only one without Cory. Everyone was dealing with his loss. I immediately felt shame for being so selfish all morning. "Are you guys all doing all right?"

"It was weird the first couple of days," Todd said, putting his arm around Holly's shoulders. "Everyone was in shock and talking about it a lot. The counselors made sure everyone knew if they needed to talk to them, their doors were open. It was just, I don't know, sad. But slowly it's all gone back to normal." He paused and as a group we all started migrating toward the building. "But I think when everyone sees you again, it might be a little crazy."

"Crazy?" I asked, confused.

"Well, I think you might be somewhat of a spectacle," Becca said, holding open the door for all of us. I gave her a questioning look, still not sure what they were talking about. "It's always been you and Cory. No one has really seen you since he died, so seeing you might make people act weird."

"Nothing too crazy," Holly jumped in, "just people staring, maybe asking you questions. We just want you to be prepared."

"Okay, well, I appreciate it. But I just want everything to level out."

"Just let us know how we can help." This came from Todd, Cory's best guy friend. I looked at him then, really looked at him, and I could see the residual sadness. He looked tired, his hair a little longer than he usually wore it, shaggier, and he was missing something, some lightness that he usually carried around with him. I wasn't the only one who'd lost a friend. They were suffering right along with me. And yet, they were all there offering to help me in any way they could.

I didn't deserve them.

"Thank you, guys, I appreciate all your concern." I turned and headed up the small staircase that would lead me to the senior hallway where all our lockers were located. "Just make sure you save me a seat at the lunch table and I'll be fine," I said, adding a laugh. It was a forced one, sounding totally fake, but it was the best I could do at that moment.

As was usually our routine, Todd kissed Holly good-bye, and he left with Becca. They had the same first period, while Holly and I had our first class together on the other side of the school. As they said their good-byes, I absentmindedly turned the dial on my locker and pulled it open.

I was face-to-face with my favorite picture of Cory and me. It was taken at a prom after-party from the previous spring. One of Cory's friends from the swim team had invited nearly the entire school to his house, claiming his parents were out of town, so everyone would be chaperone-free. We all brought tents and made campfires and had the best time.

I don't remember who took that photo of us, but I remember it being posted on Facebook and making me smile immediately.

Cory and I were sitting on a log next to each other, both of us with a red plastic cup in our hands, both of us in sweatpants and t-shirts, and we were laughing hysterically. It was a moment caught in time in which we were both completely carefree, young, and happy. I also remembered why I liked it so much the first time I saw it; Cory wasn't touching me.

He didn't have his arm around me, we weren't holding hands, he wasn't pulling me to his side and kissing my temple, like he so often had.

We were just sitting next to each other, laughing. And we looked like the best of friends.

I grabbed the book I knew I'd need for my calculus class and slammed the door to my locker shut, the loud bang echoing down the emptying hallway.

"Everything all right?" Holly asked, giving me another concerned look.

"Yeah," I lied, "I'm just not looking forward to catching up in math."

"Don't worry," she said as she looped her arm through my elbow, "Mrs. Williams will go easy on you. All your teachers will. Everyone wants to help you, not make your life harder."

I hoped she was right.

The day went pretty much as my friends predicted. Whispers and long faces met me at every turn. People who used to give me friendly smiles in the hallway were giving me frowns and sympathetic eyes. There were some friends who avoided me altogether. *That* I could understand and appreciate. I hadn't dealt with much death in my life, but when a friend's grandparents had died, I'd always immediately clammed up. What do you say to someone when something so terribly sad and completely irreversible has happened? I'm sorry? I'm thinking of you? There was nothing anyone could say to bring him back, and the unusual facial expressions drove me crazy—like it physically hurt to talk to me. So the people who avoided me? I silently thanked them for saving us both the uncomfortable encounter.

My teachers had all gone above and beyond, like Holly had said they would. I'd been given packets of work I'd missed with very generous deadlines. My English Literature teacher had even pretty much indicated she'd look the other way if I never turned in the work at all.

At lunch I'd done my best to act like everything was normal. I'd sat at our usual lunch table, I'd eaten my usual turkey sandwich and Diet Coke, and then I sat and listened to my friends trying to make conversation. I watched them try to pretend that every day at lunch they hadn't discussed me, which was why they were having a hard time now carrying on a normal conversation.

So I decided to do them all a favor and remove myself from the situation. They tried to protest, asked me to stay, but I was practically at my breaking point.

My next class was gym, so I headed to the locker room, changed into my uniform, and then went outside to run a few laps around the track.

No one else was using the track so the only things I heard were my feet slapping against the asphalt and my breaths pushing out then pulling back in. I didn't have to avoid anyone's eyes, or listen to anyone tell me how sorry they were. Nope. I just had to feel the sun pounding down on me.

The only problem with the running was that I couldn't escape my own thoughts.

When it finally came to the last class of the day, I knew it would be the hardest one. I'd been anticipating it since first period, knowing if any class would be uncomfortable, it would be World History. It was the one class Cory and I'd had together that year. For the first time that day, I was wishing for either Becca's sad eyes or Holly's uncontrollable mouth. I'd put up with either one of them if it meant a buffer from the wall of emotion I knew I'd hit as soon as I walked in the room.

I stopped right outside the door and steeled myself. I pushed my shoulders back and took in a few deep breaths, blowing them out slowly. This was what I wanted: to return to normal, to try and force life to move forward, to *deal*. So that's what I did. I walked into that classroom. Little did I know, nothing would ever be the same.

Chapter Eight

McKenzie

I walked to my desk, eyes cast downward, hair falling around my face creating my own little bubble. The day had been trying and this last hurdle was going to be the highest to jump over, the most difficult, so the more I could keep out, the better.

I could feel people staring at me, their gazes tingling all over my skin, their whispers burning in my ears.

But this was different. There were way more whispers than I had anticipated, and the air felt almost electric. Something more was going on.

I pushed some hair behind my ear and glanced up.

Mr. White was at the front of the room.

With Hayes.

Hayes had his back to me, hands braced on his hips, and he was listening to Mr. White.

It all started to make sense. Well, not all of it. I had no idea what he was doing there, but it explained why the room was absolutely supercharged.

He was wearing a white cotton shirt, like my dad wore to work, but his sleeves were rolled up to his elbows. My eyes travelled down his arms, noticing every bulge in his forearms and the strength in his fingers as they gripped his waist. He wore caramel-colored pants and a dark belt. The fit of the shirt barely contained the breadth of his shoulders, stretching around his biceps.

I hated the fact that my pulse raced from just looking at him.

I didn't know what he was doing there, but I was going to find out.

I walked to the front of the room, the whispers around me silencing instantly.

"Hayes?" I hated the way I said his name. It was hopeful and frail.

He turned when he heard me, and I was not prepared for what I saw. Hayes's hair had always been longer than a typical "man's" hairstyle. It was long enough to tuck behind his ears, but it was usually down, falling around his face until he swept it back with one hand, only to have it fall back down again.

Today it was pulled back into a neat-enough short ponytail. It had been years since that much of his face was on display for me to admire, and he'd changed a lot. His face was fuller, only emphasized by the ticking in his jaw as he clenched it. I noticed his eyes do a quick scan of my body, so I was hoping he didn't notice me take in a sharp breath at the sight of him.

His cheekbones were broad; his jaw wider than I could remember. Perhaps it looked bigger with the

86 | Anie Michaels

stubble covering it. All the dark stubble only made his light pink lips stand out, which explained why my eyes were drawn right to them. Sometime in the last two years, Hayes had gone from being the boy I remembered growing up with to a man I couldn't take my eyes off of.

When our gazes finally met, his eyes looked sad. The difference between his sad eyes and everyone else's was that his eyes weren't sad for me. They looked sad all on their own. And that made my hand itch to reach up to his face, to try to comfort him, do anything to make him look less broken.

"Miss Harris, I'm glad you're here a few minutes early," Mr. White said, pulling my attention from Hayes. "We should have a short discussion."

"What do you mean?"

"Mr. Wallace is going to be taking this class over. He'll be your teacher for the remainder of the school year." My heart, which had previously been racing, stopped suddenly. Halted. "This has all come together very quickly, and although we know this isn't the optimal situation, it's the only solution we found suitable."

"You're my teacher?" I asked Hayes, my voice shaky and weak. It was then I noticed the red tie around his neck. It wasn't tied terribly tight, loose enough that I could still see down the collar of his shirt. I spied his pulse pounding through the skin of his neck.

"Mrs. Anderson and Mr. White were kind enough to find room for me here. I need to finish my degree, but I can't go back to school just yet."

No, he really couldn't. Mrs. Wallace was a mess. I immediately felt terrible that I hadn't asked Hayes about school since he'd been home. I just assumed he was taking some time off, opting to stay in town to care for his mother. The decision to continue his schooling must have been a difficult one and I hated myself for not thinking about all the hurdles he'd been jumping.

The truth was, I'd been avoiding him. My mind was jumbled. I was constantly dealing with the sadness of losing Cory and the shame of feeling like I'd been given some sort of sick and twisted second chance. I hated myself most of the time. And I seriously hated myself whenever I remembered the way it felt to wake up in Hayes's bed, and to feel his arms wrap around me.

Not to mention, for two years I'd been thinking about his lips pressed against mine.

So, I'd been avoiding him. And myself. And everything that didn't help me erase the thoughts that were drowning me.

"I'm sorry I didn't tell you sooner," he said quickly when I didn't reply. "It all happened so fast and I just found out yesterday."

I'm a shitty person.

"Hayes, don't apologize, please. I'm just surprised."

88 | Anie Michaels

Mr. White cleared his throat. "I know there will have to be adjustments, and we're all kind of winging this, but it's still important to establish that Mr. Wallace is a teacher when he's in this building, Miss Harris. So, let's just be careful and make sure you're addressing him as *Mr. Wallace.*"

"Oh," I said quickly. "Yes, of course. I'm sorry, Mr. White. Mr. Wallace." I met his eyes when I said his name and I watched that muscle in his jaw tick again.

After a moment thick with so much tension it felt like a rubber band, stretched so thin it would snap at any moment, stinging and snapping against my skin, I turned and went back to my desk.

As I walked through the room, I was sure everyone could hear my heartbeat pounding, loud like a bass drum, thumping wildly.

"Okay, class," Mr. White said a few seconds after the bell rang. "Quiet down." He waited a few moments for everyone to settle in their desks and for the whispers to die down. Hayes was four years ahead of Cory and me, so the last time we were all in the same school was when I was in first grade. That was not to say that people in my grade didn't know who he was; especially the female demographic. Hayes was practically high school legend. Him and his Mustang. Anyone who had a slightly older brother or sister had a pretty good idea of who Hayes was, and who his little brother was, too. "Class, I'd like to introduce you to Mr. Wallace. Some of you may already be aware of the fact that Mr. Wallace, here, is the brother of our recently deceased student and friend, Cory. And although this is a very sensitive situation, I wanted to head any rumors off." His eyes did a sweep of the room, landing quickly but effectively on every student in the class. "He will be your acting teacher for the rest of the term. He is completing the last requirement for his teaching degree, and due to unforeseen circumstances, it must be completed here, in our classroom."

At his words, a few whispers flitted through the room. Mr. White cleared his throat again, silencing the class once more.

"I will be here to supervise, but all questions, concerns, and communications about the course should go to Mr. Wallace first."

With that, Mr. White stepped aside and swung an arm out to Hayes.

"Thank you, Mr. White," Hayes said first, giving Mr. White a tiny, unenthused smile. "I'm really glad to be here," he said, turning to the class. "As Mr. White mentioned, I am Cory's older brother." A somber silence fell over the room, but Hayes went on. "I recognize a few of you, but I'm glad I'll get the chance to get to know you all a little better. I've been at Central Florida University for the last four years. I've got my bachelor's degree in history, and as Mr. White mentioned, I'm working on the last piece of my master's degree and teaching license. At the end of this semester, I'll be a licensed high school history teacher. So, you'll all be learning along with me." He gave a nervous laugh, and the class responded with their own laughter. I couldn't help the tiny smile that pulled at my lips. Then, suddenly, a new emotion crept through me—pride. Hayes had gone off and seemingly conquered the world.

"So, it looks as though we are going to spend the first part of the semester covering the Second World War," Hayes said, and I could have sworn I saw a glimmer of excitement in his eyes as he said the words, even though a groan erupted from the students.

I spent the next hour watching Hayes in a whole new light. He wasn't the quiet, sullen guy I'd always been around. He was sure of himself, he was smart, and he was eager to teach all of us. It was refreshing and new, and totally distracting from everything that had plagued me all day long. The only thing that wasn't different was the pull I felt to him. If anything, watching him as a capable man only made him that much more attractive. So, it was no hardship to sit in that room for an hour, my eyes glued to his every movement, every gesture, and every single part of him.

The worst part was, however, that even though my eyes were glued to him, his eyes never once returned to me.

When the final bell of the day rang out, I practically ran for the door. I didn't stop to wait for Holly or Becca, I did nothing except make my way to the bus that would take me home, find an empty seat, curl into the window again, and try to figure out how I was going to finish the year having to look at Hayes every single day.

When I made it home, an empty house greeted me and I was relieved. I needed a little time to decompress, to fool myself into thinking I could handle having Hayes as my history teacher for the rest of the year.

The selfish part of me, which I had realized was a much larger part of me than I had known, was hoping Hayes would leave town soon. That he'd disappear into the same oblivion he had four years ago and all the confusing feelings would disappear, allowing me to mourn my boyfriend without the distraction of *him*. I kept telling myself that as soon as Hayes left, all the confusing feelings would disappear and I'd be able to see the truth again, I'd be able to remember how much I liked being with Cory and how content I'd been with him.

But then that nasty and sneaky part of my brain would surface and compel me to believe that even after Hayes left, I'd never stop wondering why I had those needy feelings in the first place. Something told me that even if Cory were alive and Hayes had returned, I'd still want him, and that even if I could convince myself to never act on those feelings, I'd never be able to force myself to love Cory like he loved me.

I went straight to my bedroom, closed the door, shut the curtains, and slipped under the covers of my bed, and surprisingly managed to fall asleep almost instantly.

When I woke, the first thing I noticed was it was much darker. The sun had obviously set. The second thing I noticed was the sound of my phone ringing in my backpack. I got to my phone just in time to see I'd missed a call from my mom. Her phone call meant she wasn't home, so I listened to the quiet house to see if I could hear my dad, but there was nothing. A ping from my phone told me I had a text.

Hey sweetie, I need a favor. I thought I would be home by now, but I'm still stuck at work. There's a casserole in the fridge for Chelsea. Can you take it over, put it in her oven for 20 minutes at 350, then just sit with her until I can get home? How was your first day back at school?

I replied immediately, even though my stomach plummeted at the thought of being at the Wallace household.

Sure, no problem. School sucked. Everyone whispered about me as I walked past them and looked at me like... well... like my boyfriend had died.

I'm sorry. I wish you didn't have to go through any of this.

I'll make it. You'll come over when you're off?

*Yeah. Shouldn't be too long now.**

*Okay, see you there.**

When I arrived at the Wallace house I knocked gently. I'd quit knocking on their door when I was eleven years old and Cory's mom had told me that if I knocked on their door again, she'd tan my hide. She was kidding, of course, but I got the message. From that day forward I walked right into their house. Suddenly, though, it felt wrong to just go in. Not only had my link to that household been taken from me, Mrs. Wallace was in a delicate position, and walking into her house felt a lot like barging into her sadness.

When no one answered my soft knocking, I gently turned the doorknob, not surprised to find it unlocked. I inched the door open and quietly called out, "Mrs. Wallace? Are you awake?" I figured she wouldn't be, and even if she were awake, I doubted she would answer me. I knew she'd just lie in her bed, staring out the window, just as she'd been doing since the day Cory and Mr. Wallace had been killed.

I moved right into the kitchen and turned the oven on, then started peeling the foil off the casserole.

There were quite a few people who had come together to help Mrs. Wallace out in the last three weeks. There was a calendar hanging on the wall and every day had a name on it of a person who had committed to providing dinner for Hayes and his mother. My mom's name was listed two or three times a week, and she still didn't think it was enough. My mom had been over every day, trying to do anything she could to help her best friend. I was proud of her for it, but I knew it took a toll on my mother as well. Not just physically, burning the candle at both ends, but also emotionally. She wanted so badly to help her best friend, but the longer Mrs. Wallace stayed in her bedroom, the more worried my mother became.

The casserole was halfway done when the front door opened and Hayes walked through.

"McKenzie," he said as he closed the door.

"It's my mom's night to provide dinner and she was running late. I just came over to heat up the casserole."

He came toward the kitchen, stopping at the table and placing his brown leather bag atop it. It was a grown-up bag, not something a college student would normally use, I thought. It was a step up from a backpack and a step down from a briefcase. It looked somewhat expensive. I knew the leather would feel buttery and soft if I ran my hand over it.

"You don't need an excuse to be here," he said softly, his eyes asking me for something, I just couldn't figure out what. "I was just surprised to see you." He ran his hand straight through his hair which was, once again, down and loose, framing his face and hiding so much.

"You put your hair back today." The words toppled from my mouth. "At school, I mean."

"Oh, uh, yeah. I thought it looked more professional." He ran his hand through it again, unconsciously, then continued. "I'm thinking of cutting it."

"Don't," I blurted, immediately mortified as a blush heated my face. "I mean, I don't think you have to. You've already got the job, ya know? Why cut it now?"

"I guess you're right," he replied quietly, with almost a sad tone to his voice. "Listen, about the job, I'm sorry I didn't tell you beforehand. I wanted to, but I didn't want to upset you or cause you any more stress, and then there you were...." His voice trailed away and I was left with just his eyes peering at me from the other side of the table. While everyone else that day had looked at me with pity, Hayes had something else in his eyes.

"It's okay, you don't owe me an explanation."

"I know I don't owe you an explanation, but I feel like you deserve one, that I want to give you one." His voice was pleading, his eyes were asking me for something I couldn't quite pinpoint, and my own body was betraying me by shortening my breaths and weakening my knees.

All of that, however, was interrupted by the sound of the shower turning on at the back of the house.

"Will you help me with something?" Hayes asked, his voice suddenly a little rushed.

"Anything." Again, my mouth went and said something before my brain could process it, and once I heard the word, heard the honesty with which I said it, I knew I couldn't deny it any longer. Hayes was more than just Cory's older brother. Was more than just my temporary history teacher. He'd been more than *just Hayes* for quite a while, but I'd hoped and prayed with time his importance would fade, that I could go back to regular life and be happy with the hand I was dealt. But just then, in that moment, something changed, and I wanted something I knew I could never have.

"When she showers is pretty much the only time I can change the sheets. Will you help me?"

"Of course."

He gave me a sad, small smile, and I followed him down the hall. "She lies in bed most of the time, and only showers every three or four days, so the sheets get dirty pretty fast," he said, whispering to me as he grabbed a clean set of sheets from the linen closet. "I change them while she's in the shower, and I'm not even sure she notices."

I was torn between feeling terrible for Mrs. Wallace and the depression she must be living with, and feeling equally terrible for Hayes, having to watch his mother fall apart slowly right in front of him. Obviously the hope was that eventually Mrs. Wallace would pull herself out of the darkness she'd been thrust into, but it was unsettling watching someone as young as Hayes having to care for his mother as if she were suffering from some other illness besides just grief. It made me wonder, if I were put in a similar situation, would I be able to keep it together as much as Hayes seemed to be.

The answer to the silent question was more than likely a resounding no.

We stood on opposite sides of the bed and pulled sheets off, along with pillowcases, then hastily worked together to replace them with clean ones. Just as we finished and I had scooped up the dirty linens, we heard the water shut off, so I scurried out of the room. I had just closed the lid on the washer when I heard the oven timer go off.

I entered the kitchen and stopped mid-step when I saw Hayes pulling the casserole out of the oven. Perhaps it was stupid, but watching him taking something out of the oven, doing something so domestic, made him seem so much older than he had just a week ago. He was a grown man, an adult, *my teacher* for crying out loud. We were worlds apart, with so much more than time and space between us.

"Well, is there anything else you need help with?" I asked. But I immediately followed up with, "If not, I'll just head home." I was halfway to the door, ready to go home and sleep away the rest of that weird day when his voice stopped me.

"Would you like to have dinner with me?"

Chapter Nine

Hayes

I watched her eyes get wide with my invitation, and I should have expected that reaction, should have anticipated her surprise. It didn't make it burn any less.

I'd spent over an hour ignoring her during class, and that felt wrong. It felt like the biggest crime against nature to purposefully ignore her. To not look at her, to not admire her, or watch her expressions change and wonder what was going through her mind. I'd spent the last two weeks doing just that; using all my time with her, any I was lucky enough to happen upon, to take her in. So, having to pretend I didn't see her all the time while in class, well, it made me hungry for the sight of her.

"Sure," she said quietly. "I can stay."

Not, "I'd love to stay," or "I thought you'd never ask." No, she was just able to stay. I berated myself for acting like it mattered. I'd take pieces of her any way I could get them, even if it was a pity casserole.

I brought the big baking dish to the table as she gathered plates and utensils. I tried not to think about how many times she must have stayed to have dinner with Cory, how she knew where everything was. She might have even known the house better than me at that point. I hadn't come home much in the last two years. Not since I kissed her on my brother's birthday and realized how big of an asshole I was for it. No. I'd stayed away after that. I had tried not to think about them together often, but I knew if I saw them together, once they'd crossed the line from friends to more than that, it would probably hurt more than I could imagine.

We dished up our meals in silence, the only sound was the rain hitting the windows from a typical Floridian rainstorm. After a few moments of chewing and taking quiet drinks of our waters, letting moments fall between us like heavy rocks to the bottom of the ocean, I finally had to admit to myself that eating a sympathy casserole with Kenzie wasn't the life-altering, romantic meal I was delusional enough to hope it would be.

"I think it's great you were able to work something out so you could stay with your mom." McKenzie's voice broke through my depressing inner monologue. "I'm sure she's really thankful you stayed."

I swallowed, but it felt as if I were pushing down more than food; I was forcing down so much, there wasn't room for the meal I was eating.

"I'm not sure she really realizes what's happening." I paused and watched as the confusion moved over her face, starting with her eyebrows moving together, then her eyes narrowing at me, followed by the pursing of her lips, which finally made me look away. "It's not like I sat her down and told her I was staying to make sure she was all right." I shrugged, pushing the food around my plate with my fork. "I'm pretty sure if you went and spoke with her right now she couldn't tell you what day it is, or how many days she's been in her bed. She's just not all there."

It was Kenzie's turn to push her food around for a moment, then she whispered, "I can't imagine."

"How are you holding up?" I asked, even though the answer had the potential to maim me. It was a horrible situation to be in. I wanted the girl I loved to be fine, I didn't want her in pain; but I wanted my brother's girlfriend to miss him, to be somewhat lost without him. "Was it difficult to go back to school today?"

She looked slightly panicked at my question, her eyes widening and mouth parting just slightly. She didn't have time to answer though because at that moment my mother made an appearance.

"McKenzie, honey," my mother said softly as she walked toward her, sniffling, wiping her hand beneath her nose. Her hair was damp and she only wore an old tattered robe my father had gotten her for Mother's Day years ago. "I found this yesterday in the bag that came home from the hospital with all of Mark and Cory's belongings in it." My lungs froze, wondering where she'd hidden that bag. I'd hidden it in the laundry room, knowing she wasn't ready to deal with it, but then it had disappeared. I'd spent hours looking for it, knowing the contents had the potential to hurt. She made it all the way to McKenzie and then held her hand out toward her. Sitting in her palm was a little black velvet box. "This was in Cory's pocket when he was killed," she said, a sob fracturing her words.

If McKenzie had looked panicked before, she looked absolutely petrified now. Her eyes were locked on that little black box, wide with what I could only describe as fear. My mom motioned with her hand, encouraging McKenzie to take it.

Kenzie's hand reached out, shaking, and her trembling fingers closed around it.

Something wasn't right here.

"He must have wanted to give it to you on his birthday," Mom said, no longer even trying to rein in her tears. "I think it's some sort of promise ring."

Shit.

McKenzie slowly opened the box.

Then she not-so-slowly stood and ran from the house.

In an instant I was chasing after her. I ran through the front door she hadn't closed in her haste, and yelled her name as I sprinted down the driveway.

"McKenzie, wait!"

The rain hadn't stopped and it was dark outside, but I could still see her thirty feet in front of me, her arms flailing and feet kicking up water behind her. I pushed myself harder knowing that if I didn't catch up with her soon, she'd reach her house and once inside it would be easy for her to ignore me, to run and hide. I managed to make it to her, wrapped my arm around her elbow, and spun her toward me.

I was unprepared for the tears I saw falling from her eyes, mixing in with the raindrops hitting her face. Seeing her cry was like switching something on inside of me and I was instantly pulling her into my arms, uncaring of the rain quickly soaking through my clothes. All that mattered was that she was upset and I was there to comfort her.

"I'm sorry the ring upset you." I had to speak louder than I wanted to be heard over the rain pelting the pavement. I felt the contents of my stomach churn when I realized what I had to say next. "It must be really difficult to think about what you've lost—what life would have been like for you and Cory."

She went still in my arms. The cries stopped. Her breathing halted. She was like a block of ice pressed against me: cold and hard. Suddenly she was pushing away from me like my touch hurt her, like I'd caused her pain, and that caused *me* pain.

"Kenz, wait, what's wrong?" She kept walking away from me, so I lunged forward and grabbed her arm again. That time she didn't need me to spin her around, because she yanked her arm from my grasp and was suddenly just inches from me, looking up at me with agony in her eyes. "What is it?" I asked, my words a plea. "Please, just talk to me."

"I thought—" she started, but an angry sob escaped instead of words. But she continued. "I thought I was going to spend my whole life with Cory."

The cold rain was no longer a match for the hot pain that came from hearing those words.

"And I thought it was going to be difficult, at the very least, less than ideal, to spend a life with someone I didn't love. But now," she said, throwing an angry hand into the air, "Now I know I'll have to live with the guilt of never telling him how I really felt. Every time someone tells me they're sorry, sorry for *me*, I feel like a fake."

"What are you talking about?" I asked, my heart begging me, pleading with me, to make her talk faster, to make her words come quicker.

"He would have given me that ring, Hayes. He would have slipped it on my finger and told me he was promising to marry me one day. And I would have let him."

"And?" I begged.

"And it would have been a lie," she yelled. Rainwater flew off her lips, dripped from her eyelashes. "I lied to him for two years, maybe longer, and I definitely lied to myself." She dropped her face into her hands, crying, shoulders shaking, and I didn't dare try to guess what it was she meant.

"What was a lie?" I asked as I gently rested my hands on her shoulders.

"Everything."

"Kenzie," I said, stepping as close as I could get. My hands moved up her shoulders, across her neck, and came to rest on each side of her face. The last time my hands were on her face was the one and only time I'd kissed her. "What are you saying?"

"I didn't love him, Hayes. I never fell in love with him, even though, sometimes, I wanted to. It would have been so much easier to love him instead of...."

"Instead of what, Kenzie?" I urged.

"Instead of you."

She was looking up at me, but I didn't see sadness in her eyes, I saw fear. Her words sank into me, absorbed into my skin, and flowed through my veins.

"Me?" My thumbs moved just barely over her cheeks as my hands slid to the back of her neck.

"It's always been you." Her words were just whispers, but they sounded hopeful and shameful at the same time. I brought her shivering frame closer to me, my forehead resting against hers. And the most wonderful part of it was that she let me. She came, willingly, into my arms, wrapping her own around my waist. "Hayes," she said, just a breath, before I felt her lips press against mine.

She was kissing me. *She* was kissing *me*. And I only let my brain ponder that magnificent fact for a nanosecond before I started kissing her back. I'd relived our kiss from two years ago daily in my mind, thought about it many times, always with mixed emotions. Some days I was glad I'd taken what I thought was my one and only shot at kissing McKenzie. Other times I was absolutely overflowing with guilt for kissing my brother's girlfriend. Most days though, most days, I was absolutely broken that it would never happen again.

And here she was, putting me back together again with her lips.

She kissed me slowly, tentatively, as if she were afraid I was going to stop her.

My fingers threaded through her hair, now drenched from the rain, and I gripped it, making sure she had nowhere to go but to me. Her lips were soft but cold, moving over mine as if I were fragile. I stepped into her farther, even though we were clinging to each other with no room between us, but pushing her back made her unsteady and forced her to hold on to me tighter.

I passed my tongue over the seam of her lips, hoping she'd give me the permission I sought. When her lips parted and a tiny sigh escaped her, I was done handling her gently.

My tongue swept over hers, licking her, tasting her, and a growl rumbled through my chest with the feeling of finally getting that part of her back. As I kissed her, my lips moving over hers, her lips responding with so much heat and need, I was aware of her body. Aware of the way she slowly softened against me, losing all the stiffness she'd held on to just moments before. Her hands gripped my shirt at my back, and when her fingers twisted in the material, she pressed herself against me even more. She was holding on to me because she had to; I had her at a disadvantage. But she was also clinging to me because she wanted to, I could tell. She told me in the way her lips sought mine out. If I moved left, she went with me, followed me. When I took her bottom lip between my teeth, sucking on it, she let me and her shuddering breaths told me she never wanted me to stop.

When our lips finally separated, it was only because we needed air, both of us panting to pull in as much as we could.

"Kenzie," I said between dragging breaths, "I won't let you go. I can't walk away and pretend this didn't happen. It'll kill me if I do it again."

"I wish you'd never walked away the first time." Her eyes were so clear, her expression, for the first time in weeks, relaxed and sincere.

"What is this?" I asked on a breath, unsure if I wasn't having some sort of hallucination, my hands back at the sides of her face, examining everything about her in that moment because I never wanted to forget what she looked like the instant I felt my life click into place.

"This is us."

Chapter Ten

McKenzie

Hot water cascaded from the top of my head, down my chest, over my stomach, all the way to the shower floor. The warmth was welcomed after standing in the rain. Although, admittedly, while I was standing in the rain, I hadn't noticed the cold.

Oh, no.

I was very much *not cold* outside, with Hayes's arms wrapped around me, lips kissing mine, hands running all over me.

Good God, he could kiss. I remembered the kiss we shared two years ago, but everyone knew your first kiss was never the greatest. I remember it being amazing, not only because of the actual kiss, but because of the way it made me feel.

Well, kiss number one with Hayes held no candle to kiss number two.

The first time, he kissed me because he thought he'd never have another chance. But the second time, well, he kissed me because he got the chance he never thought he'd have.

I pushed thoughts of Cory out of my mind. It was maddening to think about the two of them in the same frame, as if they were mutually exclusive—which they were. I could only have one without the other. But the difference was, I kept telling myself, that Cory wasn't a choice anymore.

I let out a large sigh as I rinsed the conditioner out of my hair.

We'd kissed in the rain until Hayes had finally pulled away, running the back of his large hands over my cheeks, telling me to go inside and warm up, but that we weren't finished. I did what he asked because I had just been kissed stupid, but as I dried off and put on a pair of yoga pants and a tank top, I found myself getting nervous, wondering what he'd meant.

I walked into the living room and noticed my house was still empty. I figured Mom had stopped at Mrs. Wallace's when she got off work, and I'm sure she was planning on staying for a while since she was upset about the ring.

The ring.

I wasn't surprised that Cory had picked out a ring for me. In fact, absolutely nothing about our relationship surprised me because everything was so transparent and laid out for us. Our story had been written before either one of us could put up any kind of argument.

I grabbed my backpack and started working on the piles and piles of homework I'd gathered from school. Twenty minutes later I'd done a pretty good job of sorting work out and determining which assignments needed to be completed first. I'd always been a really good student, so I was determined to catch up quickly. The last term of senior year was not the time to fall behind.

When the front door opened and my mother walked through, followed closely by my father, I let out a relieved sigh. Time alone was making my brain run at hyper speed.

"I'm sorry we're so late, sweetie. Chelsea was a mess again."

"I know. I probably didn't help. I kind of bailed on her." I did feel badly about running out on her. She had no idea the real reason I ran, and I could only imagine how much pain she thought I was in.

My mother gave me a sad look and then her and my father sat down at the table. "Honey, we saw the ring." Her words were in the same sympathetic tone I'd grown used to, the same voice so many people had used to speak to me that day.

"Do you want to talk about it?" This came from my father, the same man who'd made me wait until I was sixteen to even go on a date or have a boyfriend. If Cory were alive and had given me a promise ring, I knew he wouldn't be sitting across from me at the table trying to have a rational conversation with me about it. Funny how death changed everything.

"I don't think there's much to say about it," I replied. "It doesn't change anything. It just kind of makes it sadder, ya know?" I dropped my pencil on the table and let out a big sigh. "He was probably really excited to give that ring to me—

whatever it meant." I paused and looked down at my hands. "But he never got the chance to give it to me. There's so much he never got to do."

"What about you?" my mother asked gently.

"What about me?" Her question confused me.

"What about everything you're missing out on?" I must have had a perplexed look on my face because she continued. "What about everything you'll never get to do with Cory? How are you feeling about that aspect of it all?"

I shrugged. "We all lost something that day. But what bothers me the most is what Cory lost. And, I suppose, what Mrs. Wallace and Hayes lost too. When I look at who all has been affected by their murder, I can't feel sorry for myself."

"You're a good kid," my dad says, still with a sad smile across his face.

"Did you get to eat dinner?" Mom asks.

"I ate with Hayes." I tried not to let my face flush at the mention of his name. I didn't really know exactly what was going on between us, but I knew no one—especially our parents—would understand.

We spent the next hour as normally as any other evening at my house. My parents ate dinner at the table while I worked on homework. My father asked about school and I explained how uncomfortable the whole day had been, but also expressed that I was optimistic it would fade with time. I did not tell my parents Hayes was my new history teacher. I knew I wouldn't be able to keep from blushing or stumbling over words and decided to avoid the topic altogether.

As if he could tell I was thinking about him, my phone pinged.

My mom is still pretty upset. Once she settles down and goes to sleep I'll come over. Will you meet me on your porch?

Sure. My parents should be in bed in about an hour. Is your mom going to be all right?

I hope so. See you soon.

There was no way to concentrate on schoolwork after his message, but I tried. I sat at the table until my parents decided to go to bed, staring at homework and feigning concentration. When they finally said their good nights, I let out a relieved sigh, feeling as though I'd gotten away with something.

I packed up my bag and went upstairs. I pulled a hoodie over my head, slipped on my Converse, made sure the bun on top of my head looked messy but not too messy, and I waited.

Finally, his message came, asking me to meet him at my front door.

My heart was cartwheeling around my chest, the thumping of its beat pulsing all the way to my fingertips. I sneaked to the front door, opening it slowly, then sliding outside into the darkness. I saw Hayes's silhouette, his back toward me, turning quickly when he heard me step outside.

There'd been a split second where I panicked about whether or not the kissing in the rain had been a mistake, worried that he'd come over to tell me what we'd done was wrong and couldn't happen again. But he hardly let those fears take root before he pulled me to him and kissed me again.

When he pulled away, it was only his lips he took from me, his arms still wrapped around me, body still pressed close.

"Hey," he said, and I could have sworn he sounded shy. Hayes. *Shy.* He'd never been anything but confident, sometimes cocky to the point of eye rolling. I couldn't believe that Hayes might have been feeling the same nerves I was, the same apprehension, asking the same questions as I was.

Was it really happening?

Could we really do this?

After all that time?

"Hey," I replied. "I can't believe you're here." My words came out as breathy whispers.

"I can't believe I can kiss you whenever I want." With that he leaned in again and pressed a quick but swoon-worthy kiss against my mouth. "God, Kenz, I waited two years between kisses, and now I can just, I don't know, kiss you. It feels surreal."

"It's surreal that you even thought about kissing me in the last two years." I couldn't help the small laugh that escaped me. At my words, his hand that was wrapped around the side of my neck gently tightened.

"I've thought about you every single day for years, Kenz."

Suddenly, a strong wave of relief rushed through me. I moved into him, pressing my cheek against his chest, loving the way his arms naturally wound around me, holding me close to him. I listened to his heartbeat, felt the warmth from his body against my face.

After a few minutes of just feeling him against me, I said something I knew needed to be addressed.

"We can't tell anyone," I whispered. "No one would understand, Hayes. It would hurt so many people." And that hurt me. We were just hours into this—whatever this was—and I already knew it was different than what I had with Cory. I'd never felt anything close to this with him. And knowing that something that felt so wonderful to me would hurt and confuse those closest to us left a dark cloud over everything.

"I know," he said softly, sounding despondent, just before pressing his lips to the top of my head. "You should probably go back inside. It's getting late."

I knew he was right, knew it was better to be inside instead of standing on my porch hugging him, but his words just brought fears I wasn't prepared for. What if we went our separate ways that night and then everything went back to the way it was the next day? What if this one night was some sort of fluke, and tomorrow we were forced back to the old Hayes and McKenzie? I didn't want to go back; didn't want to lose whatever connection we'd forged in the rain that night. I wanted him to know, for whatever it was worth, how much I wanted *us* to continue, risks and obstacles be damned.

Taking no time to worry about his response, I lifted onto my toes, reached up, and kissed him. Whatever I couldn't say, whatever feelings were too powerful to give words to, I put them into that kiss. I showed him my fears, my worries, but most of all, I showed him what I wanted.

I wanted him.

He answered my kiss with one of his own.

Finally, he pulled away again and I had to fight the urge to groan, already missing his mouth against mine.

"You need to go inside now." His voice was raspy, nearly a growl, and hearing it made everything inside me seize and then sputter back to life, but I nodded, agreeing.

"Just promise me you won't forget about me tomorrow." I hadn't meant to sound like a needy, immature girl, but I desperately needed the reassurance.

His eyes met mine again, this time both his hands cradling my face. "I couldn't if I tried."

"Okay," I whispered. He gave me one last small peck on the lips, then took a small step back, but he might as well have put a canyon between us for how far away he felt.

"I'll see you tomorrow."

I turned away from him and walked back in my house, making sure I turned the dead bolt behind me. I let out a breath I hadn't realized I was holding, and then continued to my bedroom, hoping the next day would bring a little more clarity and a little less uncertainty.

Chapter Eleven

McKenzie

The following days did nothing to quiet the uneasiness I felt about my situation with Hayes.

School was torture.

I spent the entire day peeking over my shoulder, looking down hallways, basically being paranoid and searching for his face in a crowd. I never saw him outside of class, which made sense; he wasn't a student so he wouldn't be traipsing through the halls between periods. But it almost felt as though he weren't real. That what had happened between us was simply a figment of my overactive and sadistic imagination.

Sitting in his class, however, was surprisingly easier than I had anticipated.

Because I got to look at him.

And I not only got to look at him, but I was able to *see* him.

I thought I knew Hayes, and in a big way, I did. But I hadn't met that Hayes yet. I hadn't been introduced to the guy who was passionate about history, of all things. Or the person who could make witty comments and entice laughter from a room full of sullen teenagers. I never knew the man who could engage a room full of students and make them excited about a world war or learning about it in a way that was more than just dates, names, and events. He wasn't just teaching history; he was telling us a story.

But he was also beautiful.

So I let him teach and I tried to pay attention— really, I did—but a lot of the time I was just caught up in all the new things I was learning about him and memorizing all the things about him that made him *Hayes*. He also made this very easy because not once since he'd started had he looked at me. I had my suspicions about why that was and figured he thought it was too risky for him to be looking at me at all. So it was easy to stare and get lost in him since he was never looking my way.

I wasn't dumb, and I wasn't ignorant to the situation. I knew that if anyone found out about what had happened between us, the only one who would suffer would be Hayes. So when I sat in his class every day, my body weirdly aching for him to just glance in my direction, I knew why he didn't and I was completely okay with it.

Well, for the most part.

I was having a grand old time taking him in, watching the way his body moved and stretched the shirt trying to contain his muscled arms, or how when he turned around his hair was so neatly pulled back into a bundle at the base of his neck, making his shoulders look fantastic. But I also wasn't the only one noticing how beautiful he was.

When he did turn his back to the class, I watched as all the girls looked around at each other, raising their eyebrows, their mouths forming tiny Os, their cheeks pinkening. Then the giggling started and my heartbeat pounded in my veins.

I'd never been jealous before, never had a reason to be. Every single person in our school had known Cory and I were together and no one ever tested that. But nobody could have suspected that Mr. Wallace was involved with anyone, especially not the girl in the third row who was supposedly mourning his younger brother.

I couldn't blame the girls in my class for being attracted to him, but I could blame them for pulling me aside in the hallways and asking me personal questions about him. I would dare anyone to blame me for lying to them.

He has a serious girlfriend back at college.

They live together.

He's gay.

I told them anything I could think of to get them to stop staring at him with giant pulsing cartoon hearts in their eyes.

Halfway through class on Thursday, I watched as Mr. White stood and left the room quietly, trying not to disturb Hayes's instruction. My gaze flitted to Hayes's and finally, I caught his eye. It was just a millisecond, a tiny moment, but I could see the relief flood through him. I thought it had to be stressful for him to have Mr. White and me in class at the same time, worried he would somehow slip up and give away the truth.

I gave him a small smile, trying to convey understanding, that I felt the relief too.

When class was over, my heart leapt as he spoke my name. "Miss Harris, could you stay behind a moment?"

I stilled, waiting for the other students to give me shocked glances or disapproving looks, but none came my way. I slowly packed up my belongings and as the last students left the room, I made my way to the front of the classroom.

"Hey," he said, smiling an unrestrained smile I hadn't seen in days.

"Hi," I answered, smile equally as broad, even though I made myself stop a few feet from him, keeping an appropriate distance between us. "How are you?" Every part of me ached to go to him, even if it was just to lay a hand on his arm. I wanted to feel him, to remind myself that our connection was real.

His smile faded at my question. "Last night was rough for my mom." He let out a sigh and then moved his hand absently to his forehead, looking as though he'd forgotten his hair was pulled back, trying to push his hand through it. "She's having a lot of nightmares and the sleeping pills aren't working. I called her doctor this morning and they want to see her this afternoon, so I'm taking her as soon as I leave here."

"What can I do?" My question was asked with a helplessness I'd never felt before.

"Nothing, really." He sighed. "Although I'm hoping they'll give her something strong and she'll be able to sleep. I was also hoping you'd come over later."

As soon as the words were out of his mouth my heart was back to somersaulting, but it all came crashing down with the sound of the door opening and Mr. White returning.

"If you need any help with the material, just let me know. I could suggest a study partner." Hayes's cover was expertly executed, but his eyes were wide with worry.

"Uh, thanks Mr. Wallace. I'll see you tomorrow." My response was entirely panicked. I left the classroom quickly, hiking the strap of my messenger bag further onto my shoulder. I had to practically run to make it to the bus before it left. The entire ride home I felt ill.

At dinner that evening I listened to my mom and dad discuss Mrs. Wallace and her problems, and as bad as I felt for her, knowing she was dealing with something I couldn't even comprehend, in that moment I was upset for my mother. Watching her best friend deteriorate, watching her crumble and succumb to grief was tearing my mother apart. *That* I could understand. I understood her need and want to help, only to be left helpless and unable to make a difference.

No one could help Mrs. Wallace with her pain. All we could do was be there for her and Hayes, help them through it, watch them suffer. It didn't seem like enough.

My mother took a moment to compose herself, taking a sip from the wine glass I had noticed she was drinking from more often, then turned her eyes to me.

"You've been pretty quiet lately, Kenzie. How are you holding up?"

I froze, fork midair, halfway to my mouth. I forced my hand to move the fork to my mouth, hoping the bite would give me some time to sort my thoughts. How *was* I holding up? I hadn't given it much thought lately. There was so much else going on in my brain, it was hard to focus on the sad things, easier to hone in on other people's grief.

Finally, I shrugged. "I don't really know, Mom. I'm just kind of taking each day as it comes."

"Is it getting easier to be at school?"

"I don't think it's easier to live life without Cory, I just think I'm getting used to it. I still miss him. I can still feel his absence." And that was the truest thing I'd said in days. His absence was ever-present. When I got a good grade on my math quiz, I wanted to tell Cory—he'd helped me in math since seventh grade, always the person to explain the parts I couldn't grasp on my own. When the latch on my locker had stuck the day before, I'd immediately had a rush of anger, cursing Cory under my breath for the time earlier that year when his orange juice spilled inside and jammed up the lock when it dried sticky. The anger was quickly followed by a sharp pang, wishing he had been there for me to yell at.

I forced a sad, small smile. "But I think it's getting better."

I didn't tell them that I missed my best friend, but not so much my boyfriend. I didn't think they'd understand that, and, honestly, I wasn't sure I quite did either.

"I just want to make sure you know you can talk to us when you feel sad. Or anytime. About anything." My mother was reaching out figuratively, not wanting me to slip away on a wave of depression.

"I know, Mom."

She smiled at me and took another sip of her wine and I watched as my dad reached over and placed his hand over her free one.

An hour later, as I sat on my bed trying to concentrate on my English Lit homework, I heard my phone ping.

Can you come over?

A text from Hayes. My pulse raced.

Yeah. I'll be over in a minute.

I panicked about what to tell my parents. Should I tell them I was going to Holly's to study? Then they'd expect me to take the car. I worried they might go somewhere and see it parked in Hayes's driveway. Should I tell them I was going for a walk? That wouldn't give me much time, and it would definitely throw up red flags as it wasn't something I normally did.

Shit.

I slipped on my flip-flops and found my parents watching television in the living room.

"Uh," I said, my voice shaking, sure my parents could see right through me. "I'm gonna go hang out with Hayes for a bit. I think his mom is home from the doctor and he needs someone to talk to." I held my breath, waiting for the inquisition that was surely coming my way.

"Okay, sweetie," my dad said, not even turning to look at me.

"Let me know if Chelsea needs anything, okay? Hayes too. Give them my love." At least my mom looked at me when she spoke.

Was it really going to be this easy?

"Okay, I'll call you if they need anything I can't help them with."

And that was it. I opened the door and walked to Hayes's house, just as I had one million times since I'd been old enough to make the trip alone.

It had never felt like this though.

I'd never been anxious, edgy, and excited all at the same time to see a boy. As I walked I tried to keep the goofy grin off my face, tried to remind myself that he'd had a rough couple of days—weeks really—and he needed me to be his support system, not necessarily his make-out partner. I pulled my hair up into a high bun, hoping I looked casually cool, as though I didn't put any thought into the way I looked before I left the house—which was a lie.

I knocked on his door, holding my breath, bouncing on the balls of my feet.

When he answered the door, all the air swooshed out of me, and I fell back down, flat on my feet.

He looked awful. Tired. Worn down. Sad.

Instinct had my arms around him instantly.

"You're here," he said softly as his arms slid around my waist.

"Of course I'm here."

After a moment long enough to give me a chance to take in his scent, something spicy and woodsy at the same time, he pulled away. "Come in."

The house was mostly dark aside from a lamp on a side table in the living room and the light above the stove. Everything else was dark and quiet.

"How's your mom?" I followed Hayes to the couch, sitting next to him, waiting for his answer.

"Sleeping." He leaned back, bringing his clasped hands behind his head, looking to the ceiling. "The doctor prescribed her some stronger sleeping pills, but pretty much told her he'd only give her thirty, and that to get more she'd have to go back." His hands dropped to his lap and he looked over at me. "I think he's worried she's trying to sleep through her grief."

"Is that bad?"

"I don't think it's good, but I also don't think it would be good for her to be fully here right now either. She's a mess when she's awake."

"I'm sorry if this is insensitive, and I'm only asking because I don't actually know, but doesn't she have to go back to work? She's been home for a month now."

Hayes leaned his head back on the couch, but still kept his eyes on mine, not looking one bit offended by my question.

"There was a clause in my father's life insurance that paid off the mortgage when he died. That, along with the rest of the insurance money, means my mom doesn't have to go back to work for a very long time."

I thought about Mrs. Wallace, sitting in her house, all paid off, all alone, no job to go to, with no husband and no Cory. Suddenly, tears filled my eyes. "That's a terrible trade-off." The words were hardly out of my mouth before he'd pulled me into him, his arm wrapped around my shoulder, bringing me close.

"I agree," he whispered before pressing a kiss to my temple.

"How are you even functioning, Hayes? How are you making it through every day without losing your mind?" The question might have sounded a little flippant, but it was legitimate. He seemed to be the opposite of his mother: trudging through each day, working hard, keeping his mind occupied, but was he just pushing grief aside as well? I pulled away just a little, wiping the one tear that had escaped, and looked at him, hoping for a genuine answer.

"Honestly?" he asked with raised eyebrows.

"Yeah," I said with a breath.

He let out a loud breath, ran his hand through his now-free hair, but then found my eyes again. "When your dad called me that night and told me I needed to come home, I knew something was wrong. I had this feeling in my gut, and somehow I knew my dad was gone. I had to pull over three times because I couldn't see through the tears."

My heart cracked open at his words. I could picture him, all too well, alone in his car, crying, sobbing, trying to make it home to his family, not knowing who was left. I reached over and took his hand, threading my fingers in the space between his, knowing I had nothing to offer him that could make the pain go away.

"When I got here, I saw my mom and the relief that came with that was overwhelming." He paused for another moment and I watched as his Adam's apple dipped, certain he was swallowing to keep his emotions down. "She told me what happened, and I think she was still in shock. She was still a mom, worried about having to tell her son something he should never have to hear. And I was just a kid who'd lost his father and brother. We sat at that table and we cried together. It's still all kind of a blur. But after a while, when there wasn't anything else to absorb and all that was left to do was try to figure out how to live without them, I found you in my bed."

He took in a quick breath before he continued.

"I saw you lying there, and I was so relieved. No one had mentioned you and it hadn't occurred to me that you could have been there with them until I saw you."

His words were trembling out of his mouth as he looked down at our intertwined hands. I moved as close to him as I could and reached around with my free arm, my hand slowly pulling his cheek so he would look at me. His eyes darted back and forth between mine as he said his next words.

"You were here, and you were safe, and even though I'd lost so much, I hadn't lost everything."

As if his words hadn't been forthcoming enough, his eyes were telling me so much more. They were deep and I was drowning. He was asking me for nothing and everything at the same time, and I feared I had nothing to give him, nothing worthy of the affection filling his eyes. He leaned forward, slowly moving closer, his face angling to just the right tilt so that his mouth would softly brush against mine, and I could do absolutely nothing to stop him.

Not even if I wanted to.

It felt as though he were trying to convince me of something with the kiss. The push and pull of his lips, the way his tongue so tentatively swept through my mouth, gently coaxing me, trying to persuade me of something.

On one hand I wanted to pull away and tell him he had nothing to prove to me, that he didn't have to kiss me like I was going somewhere.

But on the other hand, Hayes kissing me like he was desperate for me wasn't something I'd ever experienced before and I wasn't about to end it before it really began. I'd come to his house to make him feel better, to get his mind off the things that were plaguing him.

I wanted to be closer, needed to feel more of him pressed against me. Carefully, without breaking our kiss, I swiveled to one knee and straddled him, then slowly sank down to rest on his lap. My breath hitched when he released my hand, only to land both of his on my thighs, smoothing his hands up high near my hips, and then back down again.

My palms gently landed on his chest, then glided up and over his shoulders, up his neck, and then my fingers threaded through his soft hair. His hands were aggressive but his kiss was gentle, almost as if he were savoring my mouth and our connection, like it was a balm to his wounds.

His hands gripped my hips, pulling me down onto him, the sensation rocketing through my body and causing a moan to slip from my mouth into his. Suddenly, wherever his hands touched was aflame, and I wanted him to burn me everywhere. I wanted the flames to lick my skin, the heat to eat me up, I wanted him to light me on fire and then smother the inferno, only to start all over again.

Another whimper broke free from me and it was as if something inside of Hayes that had been tightly wound, snapped. One arm wrapped tightly around my waist, the other hand cradled my neck, and the next instant I was being picked up then laid back down on the couch.

This was new. *Lying* with Hayes. Having his body leveled entirely along mine, having his weight press down on me, holding me in place; it was intoxicating. My knees instinctively fell to the sides, allowing him even closer to the core of me, and there was no pretense about it. I wanted the most private and sacred parts of me as close to him as possible, to feel all of him, to be as open to him as I possibly could be. It was a new feeling, a new revelation, to *want* someone that way. To want to be close to him, to give him unadulterated access. It's not something I'd offered to anyone else. Ever.

Our bodies took over.

His lips were still pressed against mine, but they wandered down my neck, over my shoulder, against my collarbone, only to return. His hands roamed over my clothed body, trembling fingers smoothing over my stomach, my arms, my breasts, my hips. Every part of my body he touched completely ignited.

Then he ground his hips into mine and whatever I thought I knew about chemistry, about combustion, was thrown away. There simply wasn't anything that existed before this. Before Hayes and his body touching mine, his body making mine feel so entirely electric.

I'd had an orgasm before, but the few times it had occurred I'd been alone. What was happening on that couch was more than I'd ever felt before. More frantic. More needy. More *full*. Every part of me was brimming with emotions and sensations I couldn't process before a new wave hit me. With every grind of his hips, every pass of his lips, every sweep of his tongue, I was closer and closer to the edge of a cliff I knew would kill me to fall from. It was the biggest internal battle of my life. I wanted him to continue, feeling as though if he stopped touching me, stopped pressing all the hardness against me, I'd cease to exist. But I also knew if I didn't stop him, I was going to come in a wildly unrestrained way I'd never experienced, and that was enough to make me stop him.

All it took was the palms of my hands against his chest with the slightest of pressure and he lifted off me, panting.

"I'm sorry," I said immediately, realizing I was embarrassed that I'd let it get that far, that I'd brought him to that point then pushed him away.

"What?" His voice was full of confusion. "What are you apologizing for?" His face was far enough away from mine that I could see his eyebrows pulling together, watch his hair puff out every time he exhaled, still winded. I opened my mouth to provide an answer, but I couldn't find the words. I was too embarrassed. "Hey," he said, bringing one of his hands to my cheek. "If you tell me to stop, I'm going to stop. Every time. It doesn't matter why, and it doesn't matter when. You tell me to stop, you push me away, I'll *always* respect that."

His eyes were sparkling with sincerity, and I felt even dumber.

"I'm sorry" was the only thing I could say back, this time apologizing for not having an answer for why I was apologizing.

"Babe, stop it."

If I hadn't already been burning up, he'd have noticed the flush to my cheeks at the nickname.

"Tell me what's going on in there," he said, nodding toward my head, still hovering above me. I got the feeling he wasn't planning on going anywhere, or letting the issue drop, before I answered him.

"Um," I stammered, trying to find the least embarrassing way to explain my situation. "It's just never felt... or I mean... never been that, uh, *intense* before," I said, and cringed as soon as the words left my mouth.

"You've never had an orgasm before?" His question wasn't to tease or patronize me; he asked the question with so much earnestness, it nearly made me cry.

"I think I have, just, uh, not with anyone else around." He nodded at my response. "It was just overwhelming, and your mom's upstairs, and I just...."

"You don't have to give me a reason, Kenz. I'm glad you gave an explanation as to how you were feeling, I want to know those things about you, but you never have to explain why you want to slow down or stop." He leaned down and pressed a gentle kiss against my lips. I appreciated his understanding, but the soft kiss only made me miss the hungry ones I'd put a stop to.

"Okay," I whispered.

"Can you stay for a while and just watch a movie with me?"

"Yeah."

He pressed another small kiss to my lips, then rolled to the side, squishing himself between me and the back of the couch, his front to my back. He reached for the remote, switched on the TV, then draped his arm over my waist. I relaxed into him, not caring what he picked to watch, just content to be cocooned by his warmth and let my body come down from the new high I'd found with him.

Chapter Twelve

Hayes

I startled awake to the sound of my phone alarm, but I was instantly aware that I wasn't in my bed. I was also instantly aware of McKenzie's body against mine, the slow rise and fall of her shoulders with her breath, the soft sounds of sleep coming from her. I moved slowly, reaching over her to grab my phone from the table, and couldn't keep the smile from my face.

I'd spent an entire night holding McKenzie Harris. Only in my wildest and most sadistic dreams had I allowed myself the privilege of thinking about what I never imagined was possible. And then I was gifted with the pleasure of something so breathtaking—watching McKenzie Harris slowly wake. She stretched, a low moan escaping her as her arms stretched awake. Her eyes fluttered, slowly opening, and after a short moment, they met mine.

I was propped up on an elbow, looking down on her in all her messy-haired-but-impossibly-beautiful glory.

Fucking gorgeous.

"Morning," I said, lifting my hand to her shoulder and running it down her arm.

"Morning," she responded, obviously confused.

"We fell asleep."

"Oh."

"C'mere," I said as I rolled her toward me. When she was facing me, her arms crossed between us, I pushed her crazy hair out of her face and kissed her. Nothing crazy, just the simple good-morning kiss I never thought I'd be able to give her. The joy of being able to kiss her was only surmounted by the fact that she kissed me back. When she pulled away she wore a sleepy, dreamy look on her face that left me feeling proud.

"What time is it?" she rasped.

"Six thirty."

"Six thirty?" she exclaimed, shooting off the couch like a rocket. "My parents are awake already. They're going to wonder where the hell I am." She ran around the living room searching for her shoes then grabbed her phone, which I assumed was dead by the look on her face when she tried to turn it on.

"Didn't you tell them where you were?"

"Well, yeah, but what am I supposed to say? 'Sorry, I fell asleep on the couch with my new boyfriend after he nearly had me coming harder than I ever have'? They'll take that really well."

"I'm your boyfriend?" My question made her stop in her tracks, a newly panicked look coming over her face. "And that would have been the hardest you *ever* came?" The second question made the panic retreat while irritation stole over the sexy features of her face.

"Hayes, stop it. I'm being serious."

"So, seriously, I'm your boyfriend?" I'd never needed the title like I did with McKenzie. I was unused to feeling vulnerable with girls. I was never in a situation where the girl had the upper hand, never put myself in that position. But with McKenzie, I'd give her just about anything, including my ego, if she could provide just a little bit of reassurance.

She must have sensed my insecurity. She walked back over to the couch, straddled my lap, wrapped her arms around my shoulders, and pressed her face into my neck. I heard her inhale then felt her body melt into mine. I held her close, trying to enjoy the moment before it was over, before I had to let her go again for another day of pretending I wasn't acutely tuned in to her every move. When she pulled away her hands moved to cradle my face.

"Are you worried about whatever's going on between us?"

I shrugged. "I'm not worried, per se. It just didn't sound horrible when you called me your boyfriend."

"And you think boyfriend is an appropriate title?" The side of her mouth quirked up.

"What would you recommend?" I smoothed my hand down her back, then let it continue over the curve of her ass.

"Hmmm," she played, tapping a finger against her lips. "How about 'Hot Guy I Let Kiss Me'?"

I gave her ass a sharp slap.

"Ow," she said, laughing, but forcing an insulted expression across her face. Her face softened and she leaned forward, kissing me gently, then whispering, "I have to go, boyfriend."

"See you in class."

"Yes, Mr. Wallace," she said, just before she winked at me.

She climbed off me, smiled, and walked out the door.

Thirty minutes later, after I'd reluctantly showered and washed away the scent of Kenzie's shampoo or perfume that had bonded itself to my skin overnight, I quietly opened my mother's bedroom door. I hadn't heard anything from her since the night before, and that was unusual.

She was still in bed and I could tell by the rhythmic way her chest was moving up and down she was still asleep. I let out a relieved sigh, thankful she'd gotten a full night's rest for the first time in weeks.

I debated with myself about whether or not to wake her, to see if she needed anything before I left, but eventually decided to let her sleep. I could call her on my lunch break.

All week I'd been nervous at the high school, worried that somehow everything would come crumbling down around McKenzie and me. I was afraid to even be in the same room with her, let alone stop and talk to her in the hallway. I didn't trust myself to not reach out and touch her, or look at her in such a way that everyone around us would see how I really felt. But as I drove to the school that morning, I almost felt invincible.

After holding McKenzie all night, everything else seemed like cake. Bring on the world; I was ready.

I spent my days at the high school observing Mr. White and working on the final project I would turn in to my advisors to obtain my master's degree. I also worked on curriculum and lesson planning. I'd been in the same high school for the first two terms of the year, working closely with a teacher who taught me a lot and gave me a lot of support, and I'd had time to create lesson plans that fit in to his plans for the class. But once I took over Mr. White's class, I had to start over again from scratch, and fast.

I was there to teach, but I was also there to learn, so I observed Mr. White whenever I could, and hoped, as the term progressed, I could reach out to some other teachers in the building to ask if I could observe their classes as well.

That day, Mr. White was exceptionally distracted. He seemed scatterbrained and ill prepared for the day. I had learned early on it wasn't unusual for teachers to be running around at the last minute to prepare for class—they weren't allotted nearly enough time to do the jobs expected of them. So, when he asked me midway through third period to make copies of the test for the next class, I gladly agreed. I owed a lot to Mr. White, and I definitely wasn't above making copies.

I walked down the quiet hallway of the high school I thought I'd left far behind me. I hadn't had a terrible high school experience, but once I left town I realized there was so much more outside of my world I had yet to experience. That was part of the reason I liked studying history—in the grand scale of things, very little history had happened here. The real stories were all set somewhere far away, somewhere I'd never been, and I grabbed on to those stories hoping one day I'd care about something deeply enough to fight for it as so many had in the past. There'd always been that little voice in the back of my mind reminding me that Kenzie was that one thing, the one thing I'd go to war for, the only thing I'd fight to the death for.

I turned down another empty hallway; only the sound of my footsteps and the soft murmuring of voices behind doors could be heard. Until McKenzie turned down the same hallway.

She was at the far end, walking toward me. She was looking down, watching her feet, unaware of me for a moment, until her head tilted up and her eyes met mine. Her hair was down, bouncing gently with each step as she reached up and tucked some behind an ear. The shy smile that bloomed on her face was both adorable and sexy.

I was suddenly jealous of every lucky bastard who got to see this image every day; all the eighteen-year-old punks who got to look at her and take their fill. She was stunning and she had no idea.

She walked toward me and it might as well have been in slow motion. The way her hips swayed, the way her eyes dipped as she tucked her hair behind her ear, the slow emersion of her teeth behind her smile—I could have watched it a million times.

The closer she got to me, the pinker her cheeks became. We didn't say anything to each other, couldn't risk it, but just as she passed me I reached out my finger to trail it across the back of her hand. I felt more in just that one run of my skin along hers than I had in any of the encounters I'd had with women in the last four years.

I'd never touched anyone the way I touched Kenzie. I touched her with delicate pressure, with intention, to try and give her some measure of how much I cared about her. There were no ulterior motives, no hopes that one touch would lead to many. Most of the time I felt as though if I never touched her again, I could live off the memory of my hands on her, of her lips on mine. That wouldn't stop me from reaching out to her though, from daring to touch her in an untouchable place, where everything I'd worked so hard for could be stripped away from me.

She didn't stop, she didn't say anything, and she didn't tense at my touch—she took it, claimed it, and continued down the hall. I knew in that moment, although it was probably already a foregone conclusion, that McKenzie Harris had taken a piece of me I'd never get back.

That evening when I arrived home I found my mom asleep on the couch. I was both glad she'd gotten out of bed, but a little worried that she was still sleeping.

"Mom," I said, gently shaking her shoulder. "Mom," I repeated softly. Finally, after a few nudges, she started to rouse.

"Hey, sweetie," she said just after opening her eyes.

"You're out of bed," I said as she sat up.

"I woke up and you were gone, so I decided to try and watch some TV. You know, to keep my mind occupied."

Well, it could have been worse. She could have wandered into Cory's room. I'd found her there a few times over the last month, sitting on his bed and staring off into space, or clutching his pillow and sobbing. She swore she could still smell him on it. I took her word for it.

"How are you feeling?" A shadow fell over her face.

"It's hard to be awake." Her voice was almost as frail as her body.

"I know, Mom," I whispered. "Can I make you something to eat?"

She gave me a smile that was just a shattered shell of what it used to be. "Sure, sweetie. That sounds good." She stood at the same time I did, just ten times slower, and started heading back toward her room. "I'm just going to take a shower first."

"Okay." I started gathering what I'd need to make her dinner, but when I heard the shower start and the unmistakable sounds of her under the water, I went in her room to change her sheets.

Chapter Thirteen

McKenzie

The morning I woke up in Hayes's arms was, well, perfect. I'd never felt as cherished as I did with him, never wondered whether my heart was going to beat right out of my chest, or if my cheeks were just going to melt away from the heat.

Being in his class got easier because after that morning I no longer worried about what we were doing or what we were to each other. I knew he wanted it just as much as I did, so it was easier to be around him. The ache to touch him was still there, and my eyes still roamed over his body like they owned him, but it wasn't the agony it had been at first.

I don't know if my friends noticed some difference in me and my demeanor, but they started treating me differently as well. They no longer coddled me or handled me with gloves. They joked around with me, teased me, hugged me without sadness, and that, too, was better. I was in the midst of beginning to *remember* Cory, instead of constantly being reminded that he was gone. Holly and Becca no longer avoided topics for fear of bringing him up and making me sad. Instead, we talked about him, we laughed over our memories, and even if just a little bit, the guilt eased.

I smiled when I opened my locker and saw his picture. I laughed when Todd retold the story of the time Cory took his clothes and tossed them downriver once when we'd all gone skinny dipping. Things were getting *better*, and I wanted to cling to that, to bring it with me all the time just to show everyone, to say "Look! I miss him, but I didn't end with him. We have to keep moving, in part, because he can't."

Along with all the joys of living again, there also came the fear of what would happen when it all came crashing down. Someday, if Hayes and I continued, everyone would find out about us, and they would all have an opinion about it. There were moments I couldn't care less what other people thought, but then I'd think of our parents, of Mrs. Wallace specifically, and I'd feel nauseous. I didn't want to have to explain to her how I'd been in love with Hayes for two years, but still stayed with Cory because I loved him too, just not in the same way.

Thinking about it gave me headaches.

However, watching Hayes lightly tapping a pile of papers into a neat stack was more than enough to ease those fears. The bell hadn't rung yet and students were still trickling into the classroom. The desk next to me, Cory's old desk, had remained eerily empty. We didn't have assigned seats, people could sit wherever they wanted, but no one had taken the desk Cory had claimed as his own, right next to me. So, when a body slid into it I startled, my gaze pulled from Hayes and landing on Nathan Patterson.

"Hey, McKenzie," he said with an easy smile.

"Hi, Nate." I was a little confused. Nathan had never spoken to me before and he definitely hadn't ever sat next to me in class.

"We don't have school on Friday. District in-service, or something like that."

"Yeah, three-day weekend," I replied, still unsure as to why he was speaking to me.

"Well, Thursday night everyone is going over to Ryan Holstater's house. You've been there before, right?"

"Yeah." Ryan's house was the same place Cory and I had gone camping. Where the picture in my locker was taken.

"Well, I'm officially inviting you." He said the words as if I should have been grateful to him for the invitation.

"Oh," I stammered, unused to boys I didn't know inviting me to go places.

"Yeah, it's no big deal, just bring a tent, or, ya know, share one." He winked at me and I had to hold back a grimace.

"Can Holly, Becca, and Todd come too?"

He shrugged. "The more the merrier. Just make sure if you guys want to drink anything, you bring your own. BYOB."

"Mr. Patterson, I need you to go back to your seat. I'd like to start class." Hayes's voice was authoritative and stern. Nate just leaned back in his seat, getting comfortable.

"I'm good here, Mr. Wallace."

The room fell silent as a hush spread through, everyone waiting to see how Hayes handled his first insubordinate student. I watched as Hayes practically burned a hole through Nate with his gaze, the muscle in his jaw twitching. A few seconds felt like forever, but finally Hayes responded.

"Suit yourself, but the side conversations end now."

With that, the class began, and we all got our first taste of Mr. Wallace in a bad mood. He was short-tempered, snappy, and not the easygoing, playful teacher we'd enjoyed for almost two weeks.

When the bell rang the students practically jumped out of their seats, trying to get out of his classroom as soon as possible for fear he'd assign extra homework for stragglers. I packed up my bag and could feel the heat of his eyes on my back, knew he was watching me, and when I was just about to walk out the door I caught his gaze.

He looked angry, but not at me. He looked angry with himself.

I hurried to my locker and just as I was about to close it Ryan Holstater leaned his shoulder against the locker next to mine.

"Hey, McKenzie," he said with a bright and friendly smile.

"Ryan, hi." I closed my locker and gripped the shoulder strap of my messenger bag, trying to look as though I was ready to leave.

"I just wanted to invite you to my house tomorrow night. I'm having another campout and wanted to make sure you knew you were invited. I know you usually came with Cory, because he was on the team, but...."

His words faded away and so did my apprehension. Ryan was obviously trying to show me I was still a part of the group, still accepted by Cory's friends, even though he was gone.

"Thanks, Ryan. That's really nice of you. Nate just invited me last period too."

Ryan rolled his eyes. "Don't let Nate keep you away. That guy, if he wasn't on the swim team, I'd totally kick his ass."

I laughed, thankful that I wasn't the only one who wasn't impressed by him. "Do you think I could bring Holly, Becca, and Todd, too? They came with Cory and me to the last one, we all had fun."

"Definitely," he said, again with a friendly smile.

"Okay," I replied brightly. "I'll ask them if they want to go. Thanks for the invite."

"No problem, it'd be great to have you there." His words sounded sincere and friendly, nothing like Nate's invitation.

I waved to him as I walked toward the doors leading outside, trying to hurry.

"Kenzie!" I heard Holly's voice from behind me and turned to see her jogging down the hall, dodging between people, weaving her way through the crowded hallway. "Hey," she said, out of breath from the sprint.

"Hey, is something wrong?"

She shook her head and let out a breathy, "No." Then she took a deep breath and continued. "I just wanted to catch you before you left. What are you doing tomorrow night?"

"I don't know yet, why?"

"Todd and I got invited to Ryan Holstater's house. I wanted to know if you wanted to go with us."

I laughed. "Man, this must be one awesome party. Ryan just invited me too." Nothing spread faster through our high school than news of parties.

"Yeah, and Jacob Matthews just invited Becca." Her eyes were wide, a fantastic smile on her face, and eyes sparkling.

"He did not," I deadpanned, truly shocked. Becca had been crushing on Jacob Matthews since the middle of last year but had only been brave enough to ask him to dance at our winter formal a few months before. The fact that he'd invited her was huge news in our little circle of friends.

"He did. So we need a total intervention before the party tomorrow. We have to go to Becca's house and do her hair, her makeup, make sure she's wearing the right outfit. This is her shot, Kenz."

"This is huge." I was still a little shocked.

"I know!" Holly squealed. "So, you're in? She's gonna need all the backup she can get."

"I'm totally in."

"Okay," she said, slowly walking backward away from me. "Tomorrow after school we go to Becca's. I'll pick you up at four thirty." She waved and I waved back.

"See you tomorrow."

And just like that, normality smacked me right in the face. Crushes, parties, wardrobe decisions. It was all so familiar. I took just a moment to feel it, to let the emotions wash over me, but then I ran down the hall hoping to still catch my bus.

I made it to the parking lot just in time to see the last bus pull out of the parking lot.

"Damn it," I said to no one but myself. I reached into my bag and pulled out my phone, thumbing a text to Hayes.

I feel like a second grader telling you this, but I missed my bus. Any chance you can give me a ride?

I wandered back inside, hoping maybe I'd run into Holly again. I did a lap around the entire school and hadn't seen anyone I could catch a ride from when my phone buzzed in my hand.

You know where the equipment room is? Down the arts hall, by the practice rooms?

Yeah.

Meet me in there in a half hour. I have a few things to finish up and I don't think it's a good idea for you to wait here with me. Sorry.

No problem. See you there. And thanks.

I sighed, but then decided to head to the library to get some work done while I waited.

Thirty-five minutes later I was silently cursing myself for losing track of time while doing my homework, and I turned the corner heading down the hallway to the equipment room.

I'd taken band my freshman year, my mother still clinging to her dream of my future career as a flute player, so I'd been inside the room which stored all the marching band outfits—tall black hats and all. The hallway had multiple doors, all of which had tiny windows. Some of them were covered with paper so you couldn't see inside, and some of them were left uncovered. Beside the equipment room there were a few practice rooms. They were meant for band or choir students to use to rehearse, but I knew they got much more use as a place to hide while you skipped class, or a dark room to make out in during lunch.

The window to the equipment room was uncovered and I could see it was dark inside. I let out a relieved sigh, glad Hayes wasn't waiting around for me. I opened the door and stepped inside, my hand immediately reaching for the light switch, but another warm hand stopped me.

I yelped in surprise, even as I was being pulled all the way into the room, then pressed against the wall right beside the door.

"Shhhh," Hayes whispered. "I don't want anyone to know we're in here."

"You scared the crap out of me," I panted while trying to slow my heart rate.

"I'm sorry." His words were sincere and coupled with a warm palm cradling the side of my face. "I missed you, and I just wanted a quiet minute alone before I have to drop you off and pretend like you're not mine."

His words both broke my heart and stole it away. Before I could respond, his lips pressed softly against mine. We'd not had much time together since the night on his couch the week before. He'd been working a lot, trying to take care of his mom, and the few times I'd tried to go see him, my mom had come along. So when he kissed me, I kissed him right back.

Both of his hands moved to rest against the wall above my head, allowing his body to bow into mine, pressing me harder against the wall, the front of him firmly pressed into me. My arm went slack, allowing my messenger bag to drop to the floor with a loud thump, but then my hands wound around his waist, moving up the center of his back, holding him to me.

My hands moved up, over his shoulder, and *oh, God,* biceps. Without warning, he pulled his mouth from mine, just far enough to utter breathy, clipped words.

"I can't stand seeing you every day and not being able to touch you." The words barely made it from his mouth before it was assaulting mine again. I understood exactly what he was saying, was feeling exactly the same way he was feeling, but I didn't want to pull my mouth from his to tell him so. I just wanted to feel him. To soak in the connection and chemistry that I shared only with him, to bask in the way my body ignited around him, for him.

His hands came down from the wall, which pressed his torso and hips even closer to me. I felt gentle fingertips roam down the side of my body, but then his firm grasp was on my rear, gripping me, pulling my leg up and holding it behind the knee around his hip.

When his mouth moved from my lips to my neck, I sucked in a dragging breath.

"Hayes, we can't do this here," I whispered, even though I really wanted to do whatever came after that. His tongue was tracing lazy circles on my collarbone, then gently biting; it was maddening. "Oh, God, that feels good." My fingers went to his nape, but his hair was tied back so I didn't get the silky strands I was looking for. He grunted at my touch, moving his lips back to my mouth. The kiss slowed and he lowered my leg, eventually just wrapping his arms around my waist.

When he finally pulled away, he rested his forehead against mine as we caught our breath.

"You're not going to that party with Nathan Patterson, are you?"

"What?" My voice was high-pitched and incredulous. Suddenly, everything became clear. "No. I would never." I couldn't see him very well, but I knew he was looking in my eyes, trying to see something that wasn't there, perhaps trying to figure out if I was telling the truth or not. "Is that why you dragged me in here? You're trying to mark your territory?"

"It kills me to watch every guy you pass check you out. Then that Nathan prick just sat down next to you and invited you to a party, and I just had to stand there and fucking take it."

"Take what? You don't have to take anything, Hayes." I reached my hands up to cup his cheeks and make sure I had his attention. "Nathan invited me to a party, but I'm not going with him. He's not going to be my date."

"But you're going?" His voice registered somewhere between hurt and angry.

"I'm going with my *friends*. To a party." I tried to calm him by gently rubbing my thumbs across his cheeks. "I'm not going with Nathan. I'm just going to try and do normal stuff, like I used to." I could feel him nodding, as if he were attempting to understand my position.

"I've just spent so much time watching you with Cory, or imagining you two together because it was too painful to come home and see it with my own eyes. But now, we're still not together, not really. I can't stop that asshole from swooping in and trying for his shot with you. And it kills me."

"Hey," I said more forcefully. "You're acting like I'm up for grabs, like being with anyone else is even a consideration for me. I've thought about you just as much as you have me in the last two years. Imagining you up at college, with older girls, girls who have more experience, who are smarter, who can, I don't know, drink an alcoholic beverage with you." I let out an exasperated sigh. "What I'm trying to say, unsuccessfully, is that no one is going to swoop in and take me away. The best parts of me, the parts that matter, are already with you. Always. No one is going to change that."

"I'm going back to Bellingham tomorrow."

His words might as well have been an arrow shot directly into my lungs for all the breath I lost, for all the air I couldn't take in, and all the burning in my chest.

"What do you mean?"

"I have to go back every two weeks for a meeting. Thursdays. I was going to tell you, hoping you would come with me."

I instantly sagged with relief, my forehead falling against his chest.

"What's the matter?" he asked, clueless.

"I thought you meant you were leaving, like, for good."

"No, just for the night. I'll be back Friday." He paused, his hands running slowly up and down my back. "Come with me," he whispered.

I was tempted. Oh, how I was tempted. But it didn't feel right. Tomorrow I needed to be at a high school party with my two best friends, and I needed Hayes to understand that, to let me have that part of my life back.

"Becca really needs me to be there for her tomorrow. And I really need to be there too. I need to take these seemingly insignificant steps back toward normalcy."

There was silence between us, hanging from us, dripping like fat raindrops from green leaves.

"I'm not going to lie to you, Kenz. I'm afraid that every step you take back toward normalcy will only take you in the opposite direction of me."

I didn't know how to respond to that, couldn't really argue with him because I could understand how he felt that way. I could see his point of view and see how doing normal high school senior things could make me think I no longer wanted what he and I shared, would only highlight the gap between us. I wanted to ask him to have faith in me, to trust that I only wanted him, only us.

But I didn't have words powerful enough. So I kissed him instead.

When he pulled away minutes later, nothing felt resolved. In fact, for the first time since he kissed me in the rain, everything felt fragile. Like watching a plate fall to the floor, knowing it would crack into a million pieces when it finally hit. We were in slow motion, hurtling toward our epic fracture.

I just prayed something would break our fall.

Chapter Fourteen

McKenzie

School on Thursday sucked. I didn't have any better words to describe it. People were buzzing about the party, making plans, and for some reason, the fact that I was even going was big news.

Big.

Stupid.

News.

At least five different guys asked me if I had a date to the party and all seemed very disappointed when I told them I wasn't taking a date, that I was going with my friends. Halfway through the day I'd almost told Holly and Becca I wasn't going to go. Thoughts of sneaking away with Hayes ran through my mind, and I second-guessed myself to the point of madness.

But then Becca looked at me with big blue eyes and asked me to help her choose an outfit, and I knew I had to go. I had to be her crutch for the evening. Besides, if things went south with Jacob, I couldn't just leave her there with Holly and Todd, then she'd be the third wheel *and* depressed. No, I needed to go to be her backup. So, I'd be the fifth wheel. And I was mostly okay with that.

Until I got to History and spent the entire period trying to reassure Hayes with my eyes that everything between us was fine.

I did, however, fail to hold in a snicker when at the beginning of the period he announced a new seating chart. I was completely surrounded by girls.

Hayes wouldn't be home before I left with Holly, and the idea that I wouldn't get to tell him good-bye before he left for Bellingham bothered me. I pictured him sitting at a fancy coffee shop, full of overeducated people, a particularly smart blonde across from him, gazing into his green eyes. I didn't want to think about what could happen. And I knew I was driving myself crazy with the same insecurities that were making him crazy as well. I would just have to trust him, and trust myself to believe enough in what I felt for him, to believe in *us* enough to know everything would turn out all right.

But for some reason, Hayes and I spending this one night in different cities felt more important than it should have. It was foreboding. It was a bigger divide than even I was comfortable with, but I thought it was important, for so many reasons.

When Holly came to pick me up, I'd replaced all my homework in my bag with an extra change of clothes, and I'd managed to find our two-person tent in the garage, along with a sleeping bag. I didn't know if Becca would be sharing my tent or not, so I brought an extra bag just in case. We loaded Holly's car—lucky for us her parents had gotten her a small SUV when she turned seventeen—and we headed to Becca's, where we spent more time than we should have getting her ready for her party date.

"You look great," I said for the millionth time, with forced enthusiasm. The truth was, she looked amazing, but she always did. The last ten outfits she'd put on had looked awesome, but she and Holly hadn't been satisfied. She was wearing black leggings with a short denim skirt, and a loose purple sweater that hung off one of her shoulders. They'd originally tried the outfit without the leggings, but then I reminded them that we were, indeed, going to be outside all night, sitting on low logs, climbing in and out of tents. So, they'd added the leggings even though it covered up what Becca thought was her best asset.

Holly and I were in traditional campout wardrobe: Jeans, t-shirts, and hoodies. I had no one to impress and Todd would take Holly in a paper sack, so she wasn't worried about her outfit either.

"Are you sure?" Becca asked, her voice nervous.

"Becca, he's going to think you look awesome. And you don't want to look out of place, you know, like you're trying too hard. You can't exactly wear a clubbing dress to a campout," I offered, trying to make her see reason.

"She's right," Holly agreed. "Plus, if you take too long getting ready, we'll be more than fashionably late."

"Okay, okay," Becca said, convincing herself she looked all right. She was crazy. Jacob would lose his mind when he saw her hair and the way the loose sweater draped over her frame, hinting at what lay beneath without being revealing or scandalous. I thought her outfit was perfect.

"Time to go," I shouted.

We grabbed all our belongings and headed downstairs and out the door.

I sat on a log taking a wide sweep of my surroundings. The Holstater compound was enormous, and essentially out in the middle of nowhere. There was no cell service, no electricity, and no bathrooms. If you were looking for a four-star resort, the Holstater compound was not your place. But, for a bunch of teenagers, it was perfect. Ryan had met us at his house, where there were no less than thirty cars parked in the field right next door, and pointed us toward the path leading down to the campsite.

It was about a half-mile hike, all downhill, only accessible by the quads Ryan and his friend were operating, hauling down everyone's belongings. At the bottom of the trail was a large open area, almost like a sandy meadow, surrounded by trees on three sides, the fourth side being a river. Swimming wasn't really a thing, because, well, gators, but it was always nice to listen to the rushing of the water when you were trying to fall asleep in your tent.

The warmth of the fire kept me content on the log, watching as my friends enjoyed themselves. Becca and Jacob were on the other side of the fire, sitting close on a log, knees touching, their faces smiling and animated as they laughed with Holly and Todd. Holly was sitting on Todd's lap, and he was in heaven. Holly carried Todd's world in the palm of her hand, and he didn't want it any other way. I watched as he would absentmindedly run his hand down her back, wrap a hand around her waist, touching her without thinking about it. It was sweet and I smiled knowing Holly had a true kind of love, something tangible, something fulfilling.

I felt the log shake and dip, then heard the grunt of someone landing next to me.

"Hey, McKenzie, glad you could make it."

Nathan's words were delivered with a slimy tone, as if I were there for some reason besides to hang out with my friends. I chose not to respond and instead, brought the red plastic cup in my hand to my mouth, taking a long, slow, drink.

"Whatcha drinking?" His words were slurred slightly, which made me want to roll my eyes.

"The same thing everyone else with a red cup is drinking."

"You mean that jungle juice shit?" He scoffed. "I've got some good stuff in my tent if you'd rather drink something that doesn't taste like lighter fluid."

"I'm fine."

"Why the hell did you even come if you're just going to sit around by yourself and be a bitch?"

I finally turned my head and looked at him, noticing the bottle in his hand covered with a brown paper bag. "I'm not sitting here by myself," I said, motioning to the fifteen people sitting around the big bonfire. "But I definitely didn't come to the party to be hauled off to your date rape tent."

"You've always been a stuck-up bitch. I thought, maybe, since your boyfriend got shot, you'd be looking to relax a little."

His words caught me completely off guard, shocked me like a bomb had gone off right in my face, I nearly fell backward from the force of his words. Before I could recover, I heard Todd's angry voice from right beside me.

"Leave her alone, Nathan."

I was being pulled to my feet by Holly and Becca, while Jacob went to stand beside Todd.

"Oh, you guys are going to come to her rescue? Good luck, she's a frigid tease. Everyone knows Cory never got anything from you. He was probably glad to be killed to get out of having to put up with your shit."

"What's your problem, man? You got nothing better to do than harass girls at a party? Go back to your booze tent and get bent." Jacob's voice was just as angry as Todd's. I was on the other side of the bonfire, watching as the orange flames licked the images of all three boys. Then Ryan walked into the scene, taking sides with Todd and Jacob.

"Man, I let you come because I didn't want to deal with keeping you away, but you can't be a dick. Either shut up, or we'll drive your ass back up the hill."

I watched as Nathan stared down the trio of guys. Then, in a literal flash, he threw his bottle of liquor into the fire. The loud explosion and burst of flames made Holly, Becca, and I scream, clinging to each other, and everyone else around the fire scattered. Without even a moment's hesitation, Ryan and the other two guys grabbed Nathan and dragged him back to where the quads were waiting. We could hear Nathan yelling and swearing all the way up the hill.

I collapsed back onto the log, hands covering my face, trying to hide the tears that had escaped and were trailing down my cheeks. Holly and Becca both took seats on either side of me, one of them with her arm around me, the other rubbing my knee tenderly. I wasn't sure which was which, but it didn't matter. They were there, trying to comfort me.

"Kenzie, don't let that asshole get into your head. Cory loved you. He would have kicked his ass if he were here."

Those words were true. Cory never would have let anyone talk to me that way, say those horrible things about me. He'd always protected me. Even back in third grade when Ray Samuels would chase me around the playground and pull my pigtails. Cory pushed him down and told him to leave me alone. He'd always looked out for me.

"I know," I said through a sniffle.

"And don't believe what he said about you. Just because you never had sex with him doesn't mean you're frigid or a tease."

"Holly!" Becca exclaimed. "Damn it, don't say shit like that to her right now."

"I'm just trying to help."

"Guys, I'm fine," I said, wiping my cheeks with the palm of my hand. "Nathan is a jerk. And he doesn't know what he's talking about. I was just caught off guard by his words. I didn't expect to be verbally assaulted around the campfire."

"Kenz," Becca said softly, her hand rubbing a small circle near the top of my back. "It's okay if you're not fine. He said some pretty horrible shit."

"Listen, Cory was a normal seventeen-year-old guy. He wanted to have sex," I said, my voice dropping to a whisper at the end of the sentence. "But he never pressured me, and he never expected it. Can we just drop it now?"

"Sure," Holly said.

"I'm going to go for a walk."

"We'll come with you," Becca said, standing with me and Holly following suit. I sighed, really wanting to be alone, but I knew the woods at night in the middle of nowhere wasn't a smart place to find some alone time.

We walked down the riverbed, keeping about ten feet between us and the water because, gators, and also we didn't want our feet getting wet. Holly and Becca were talking, dissecting every word Jacob had said to Becca, every move he made, and searching for evidence to substantiate the fact that he was totally crazy for her. I heard their words, their voices floating over the sounds of the water rushing by, and let myself get a little lost in the darkness of my mind.

My thoughts were centered on Cory. Nathan's words had stirred a proverbial pot I'd been happy to let rest for the last two weeks, but I couldn't ignore the wave of thoughts and emotions that were flowing through me.

If Cory and his father hadn't been killed that night, my life would be so different in that moment. I couldn't help but think about what would have happened that night, that week, the rest of the year, if Cory were still here. All of it was good, I wanted a life for Cory, wanted him here with me, but now, looking back, I don't want him in that same capacity. I wanted to grab a hold of aspects of him, tiny slivers of the friend I had in him, and remember those parts best. But he was also my boyfriend. That part caused me the most trouble.

It was late, the moon was hiding behind some clouds and trees, and there were no lights besides the sparkling stars that managed to peek out from behind those clouds. Darkness was simply everywhere. I could hardly see the ground in front of me, and that notion was mirrored in my mind—darkness. My life with Cory would have been dark in some ways, in the best ways and the worst. I didn't want to live in that world, and I would never know if I would have had the courage to end it, to tell Cory I wasn't in love with him and would never be.

The weight of my thoughts pressed down on me, slowed me down, and I heard my friends' voices drifting farther and farther away.

With troubling thoughts trampling through my brain, heartbeat racing and pounding through me, hands shaking, breath hitching, I finally just collapsed to the ground, panic taking over. I pulled up my knees, wrapped my arms around them, and dropped my head into the crook created there. I focused on breathing, trying to tame the flow of thoughts.

It only took a few moments for Holly and Becca to realize I wasn't with them anymore, and I heard them coming back.

"McKenzie, what is it?" Becca asked, kneeling down next to me. "Holly, call someone."

"I don't have any service," she replied frantically.

"Kenz, what's wrong?" Now Becca sounded scared too.

"I'm okay, I just need a minute," I managed, a hoarse whisper croaking from me.

"Are you freaking out because Nate wanted to get you drunk and molest you?"

Becca screamed, "Holly!" and the very same time I let out an enormous laugh. I laughed until I cried. Holly was a handful sometimes, but I never wanted her to have a filter installed. The thoughts and words that came out of her sometimes were the best parts of my day. Like right then.

"Holly, oh my God, you're just so wacked," I said through the sputtering end of my laughter.

"What?" she asked innocently, because she had no idea why her question was inappropriate. "Besides, you're the one on the ground having a breakdown."

Her words weren't as unkind as they seemed, I knew her well enough to realize she wasn't trying to be rude. And anyway, she had a point.

"Why *are* you on the ground having a breakdown?" Becca asked, sitting down next to me, probably ruining her favorite denim skirt.

I didn't know what to tell them. My heart was telling me to just be honest. Or, as honest as I could be.

"What would you guys say if I told you...." My heart thundered in my chest.

"Whatever it is, Kenz, you can tell us," Holly said softly from her seat next to me on the ground, redeeming herself.

"Yeah, you're scaring me. Just spit it out," Becca demanded.

"I was never in love with Cory." I said the words, finally said the words to someone besides Hayes. The truth was heavy when you tried to keep it inside. And although I wasn't completely weightless, the words definitely took some pressure off. I let out a loud sigh, immediately glad I'd let the truth out.

"Wait. What?" Becca asked.

"I was never in love with him. I had nothing beyond really affectionate, friendly feelings toward him. He was my very, very best friend, but I wasn't in love with him."

"But...," Becca stammered. "But you were with him for two years. You guys, like, *did* stuff."

I shrugged, even though I knew they couldn't see me very well. "I know. I'll probably never be able to fully explain our relationship, but I never wanted to hurt him, and I thought maybe, someday, I'd fall in love with him. I thought maybe I was a late bloomer."

"You were just going to be with him until, when? Forever? Because you hoped you'd one day, maybe, eventually fall in love with him?" This came from Becca, and I was a little surprised at how upset she sounded.

"I wasn't 100 percent aware of how I felt until he was gone, Becca. I loved him, I did. So much. More than anything. But I can't explain the amount of relief that came with his death. I'll never be able to forgive myself for that, but it happened."

"Wow," Holly whispered. "That must be really hard for you."

I nodded, once again wiping away a tear rolling over my cheek. "I was never untrue to him, and I never stayed with him for any reason other than, well, because I *wanted* to be in love with him. I hoped every day that I would wake up and that one piece that was missing would just fall into place. But it never did." A sob broke free and my head dropped back into my little hiding spot. "I would never have hurt him on purpose."

"God, Kenz, this is crazy. We all thought you guys were the real deal. Like, house, kids, dogs. The forever kind of thing."

"I know." Everything she said was everything I'd tried to give Cory. I'd wanted him to have whatever he wanted, even if I couldn't love him the way he loved me. I'd have done anything for him. "If he hadn't died, that's what would have happened, Becca. I would have been with him forever. Half of me thinks I would have been okay with that. But now, the other part of me who realizes fully what was going on, the terrible part of my brain, is actually *thankful* he died." I let out a cry as more sobs broke free. I hadn't cried this hard since the first night we lost him.

"Oh, Kenzie," Holly said, wrapping her arm around me and putting her mouth right next to my ear. "You're not thankful he died, that's ridiculous. You're thankful that you don't have to force yourself to live a lie anymore, and that's understandable. You loved Cory, we all know that. No one could deny that. But just because you can imagine a life without him doesn't mean you're glad he's gone."

"I'm not glad he's gone," I said quietly, knowing it was the truth. But I couldn't help but question whether I wanted to go back to how it was before. Knowing what life could be like with Hayes, what just a glance from him could make me feel, I wasn't sure I could have gone back to the life I had with Cory. I was also glad, in a terrible, terrible way, that I didn't have that choice. I didn't have to choose between Cory and Hayes and I would probably forever be grateful for that.

Chapter Fifteen

Hayes

The meeting with my cohorts was exactly as I expected, and was very similar to all the meetings we'd had since the beginning of the program. The only difference was, this was the first one I'd been able to attend since Cory and my father were killed. I'd missed a couple and thankfully my advisor was very accommodating, but it was nice to have something to do back in Bellingham, nice to go back to a physical place that didn't hold any bad or confusing memories.

As I'd expected, my advisor, Donna Hunter, had explained my situation to the other cohorts, so when I approached the table at the café we always met at, I was received with a lot of sympathetic expressions. Everyone expressed their condolences, and once they were convinced I wasn't going to break down and cry, the meeting moved along as all the others had before it.

Aside from Donna, there were five other students in my group, all of us at the same point in the process of obtaining our master's in education and our teaching license. The meetings served as a way for us students to talk about our in-classroom experiences, bounce ideas off each other, and decompress if needed. I'd been pretty lucky to be grouped with five pretty awesome students, and

Donna was probably the best advisor I could have asked for.

After the official meeting was over, Donna asked me to stay behind. I said good-bye to all my fellow students and waited for Donna to dive into whatever she wanted to discuss.

"I hope you didn't mind me telling the others about your situation." Her words were compassionate and worried.

"It's fine. I'm sure everyone was wondering why I'd been gone for so long, missed so many meetings."

She nodded. "They were. But they were also glad when I told them you wanted to continue with the program despite the tragedy. How is your classroom going? Are you handling everything all right?"

I shrugged. "I think it's going well. Mr. White has been really helpful, a great resource, the class is great, and I've been able to adopt the curriculum to work with my thesis topic."

"That's great," she said, but the tone of her voice indicated she wasn't convinced. "What about the emotional aspect of the assignment? How are you faring working in the same class your brother used to attend? That must be difficult."

"I guess I'm really lucky that Cory and I were four years apart. I never went to high school when he was there, so I don't really have that connotation. When I go in that building it feels weird, but only because it's where I went, not because Cory was there."

"Well, that's a good thing, I suppose."

"I think so."

"I know Mrs. Anderson and Mr. White already explained this to you, but I wanted to reiterate: If this assignment proves to be too difficult, or you realize, at any point, that it is not in your best interest to be at that school, in that classroom, the university and I are willing to let you take an incomplete. You can come back at any point and pick up right where you left off. There will be no detriment to your GPA, or your licensure status."

"Except that I won't actually *be* licensed. I'll have to wait another six months at the very least."

Donna folded her hands on the table, threading her fingers together, giving me a sad look. "It wouldn't be the end of the world." She sounded like my mother, before she lost her husband, son, and mind. Before she fell apart, with good reason. I knew Donna was just expressing concern for me, but it made me uncomfortable. I wasn't used to people, especially in academia, questioning my capabilities. She let out a breath, her shoulders loosening, slumping forward just a bit. "Promise me you won't hang on to an unhealthy situation. Please, promise me you'll let us know if you need to walk away. We'll all understand, Hayes."

"I promise if I feel I need to leave the classroom, I will." It would take wild horses to drag me away from the one hour a day I got to be in the same room with McKenzie.

McKenzie.

She'd gone to that party and the two-hour drive back home was only spent imagining the things that could happen there. I'd been on the Holstater compound before; I went to school with Ryan's older brother. I knew there would be alcohol and guys waiting to take advantage of drunk girls. And I also knew Nathan Patterson would be there.

I tried calling her a few times, hoping maybe she'd decided not to go after all, but when my calls went directly to voice mail, I knew she was at the compound and had no signal.

Shit.

I didn't want to be that caveman who couldn't control himself, but, damn it, I couldn't control myself. She was with her friends, but her friends were all paired off, and I didn't want to imagine what could happen to her if she were left all alone.

My foot pressed down on the accelerator and I sped up, knowing I should drive straight to my mom's house, but that's not where I ended up.

I could see the glowing embers of what used to be a pretty large bonfire, and I shook my head at the teenagers who couldn't even properly put out a fire before they abandoned it. Although, it was providing a little light, which I was thankful for.

I'd parked in the lot with all the others, not surprised at how easily my memory returned and took me right to it. I'd wrestled with the decision to use my cell phone as a flashlight, knowing that if anyone saw me it would be really difficult to explain the situation without raising some red flags. So, I'd used it until I got close to the end of the path, then I'd waited a few yards away from the main campsite, in the dark, behind some trees, watching to see if anyone was still up.

There was a group of ten or so kids near the slowly dying fire, but just moments after I'd spotted them, one yelled, "Who's up for skinny dipping?"

There were a bunch of cheers and then they all ran down the beach toward the river. I couldn't see another person anywhere, so I stepped out from the trees, walked past the fire, and headed toward the meadow where I knew all the tents would be.

"Kenzie," I whispered loudly, the screen of my cell phone lighting the path. I passed seven tents before one caught my eye. I knelt down next to the tent, near the door that was zipped closed, and took a deep breath. I was about 80 percent sure it was McKenzie's tent, but I had no idea if she was in there, let alone in there by herself. What if one of her friends were in the tent? How would I explain my being there at all? What could I possibly say that would excuse me, a teacher, unzipping a student's tent in the middle of the night? Never mind the thoughts racing through my brain at what I'd like to do to said student.

I was possibly making the biggest mistake of my life, unzipping that tent.

I didn't care.

The zipper moved smoothly over the tines, quieter than expected, and I opened the tent just enough to pull the nylon fabric back and look inside. There I saw McKenzie, alone, sleeping. I let out a relieved sigh, then opened the tent enough for me to climb in, trying to be as quiet as possible. She started to stir as I was closing the tent back up.

"Becca?" she asked, groggily.

"No, babe, it's me." There was a second sleeping bag laid out next to her, I assumed for Becca, so I stretched out on my side, facing her.

"Hayes?" There was shock in her voice, confusion as well. "What are you doing here?" She pushed up on one hand, her hair falling from her face. I couldn't stop the hand that reached out and tucked some of her crazy hair behind her ear.

"I wanted to see you," I replied honestly, even if my urge to see her was more complicated than that.

Her eyes softened at my words. "I want to see you too, but if anyone else sees you, you'll get in so much trouble."

"No one saw me. Promise. C'mere." I motioned for her to lie with me and loved the fact that she came without reservation. I opened my arms to her and she came to me immediately. Fitting herself against my side, her arm draped over my stomach and her head rested on my chest. After a few moments of content silence, she tilted her head to look up at me.

"I thought you were spending the night in Bellingham."

"I was planning on it, but the longer I stayed there, away from you, the more I needed to come back." Her eyes never left mine as I spoke. "I was kind of a dick about you coming to this party, but only because I know what high school guys are like, especially when a beautiful girl who was previously unavailable is back on the market."

"I didn't come to the party to look for guys. I came because it's what normal high school students do. It's what I would have done before Cory died. I just wanted to do something ordinary."

"I know." When I lost her eyes I knew there was something she wasn't telling me. "What is it?" I used my finger to bring her eyes back to mine.

"You weren't entirely wrong." Her words were whispered, as if she were afraid to say them. "There was one, um, situation."

"What happened?" I left my finger at the bottom of her chin, the gentle pressure there not changing, but I could feel the tension in my body growing, my muscles tightening, the adrenaline coursing through me.

"It was Nate." At his name, my blood ran hot and fast. "He tried to get me to go back to his tent with him, to get me drunk. But the guys stopped him and kicked him out of the party."

"I'm going to kick his ass." I let go of her chin, but only to run my hand through my hair, itching to punch a wall and angry there wasn't something firmer than the nylon tent around.

"No, you're not. Hayes, look at me." This time it was her hand pulling my cheek around to look back at her. "You can't let him get to you. He's a douche bag who thought he had a chance with me, but he doesn't. No one does. But you. Until we're able to be out in the open with our relationship, you're just going to have to trust that I'll never let the Nates of the world come between us."

I took real issue with the fact that I had to trust a bunch of high school guys to keep my girl safe at a party. It sucked that I couldn't just walk into that party holding her hand, making sure every guy knew she was mine. But all that was my fault. I was the one who'd put us in that situation, and there wasn't much I could do about it.

"I want to be the one to protect you." Her eyes went soft at my words, and her body relaxed into mine. I rolled toward her just slightly, letting my lips find hers, loving the way her breath pulled in quickly at the touch. She kissed me back, her hands moving around my neck, up into my hair. I continued until I was over her completely, my legs straddling her sleeping bag, instantly frustrated with the thick and puffy layer between us.

180 | Anie Michaels

As I kissed her, I fumbled for the zipper, found it, then unzipped the bag as far as I could without pulling my lips from hers. Once the sleeping bag was open, my hands reached for her, but all I felt were more layers.

"What the hell are you wearing?" I whispered as a laugh escaped me.

"I didn't want to get cold," she answered by way of explanation. I squinted in the dark and looked down at an oversized hoodie, a pair of sweatpants, and peeking just above the waistband of those, was the waistband of a pair of jeans.

"Are you seriously wearing two pairs of pants?" More snickers.

"I get cold easily." She pouted and I wanted to kiss her lips so fucking bad. So I did.

I sucked her bottom lip into my mouth, biting gently, hands gently resting on either side of her neck. I released her lip only to ask, "Mind if I remove a few layers? I promise to keep you warm." She nodded slightly, then reached down and pulled her hoodie over her head. Then she reached down again and I smiled as she pulled the long-sleeved t-shirt over her head, only to reveal a tank top. She threw both her tops in the corner of the tent, so I stripped off my own jacket, tossing it in the same corner. Then I moved down and pulled the sweatpants over her hips. She helped, lifting up so I could get them down her legs.

I wanted to take everything off, wanted access to all of her, but I knew we needed to take it slow. I also knew, no matter how much I wanted her in that moment, I didn't want our first time together to be in a tent at a high school party. But I did want part of her, just a tiny piece to tuck away, something between us.

I leaned back down, one hand resting on the ground beside her head, the other on her waist, and put my mouth to her neck. I heard her gasp, felt her stomach muscles tighten beneath me, and it only spurred me on. I trailed wet, hard kisses up the column of her throat, only to move back down again. Her body started moving beneath me, breaths quickening, hips rolling. My hand moved up her waist, her tank top bunching up, moving with my hand, until I felt the swell of her breast. She arched into me and I knew she wanted me to touch her there.

I slipped my fingers beneath the hem of her thin tank, stopped kissing her, and breathed out a rough, "Is this all right?"

"Yes," she replied instantly.

My fingers dipped under her shirt and moved to cover her breast. I felt the lace of her bra and palmed her, while my mouth moved over her jaw and back to her lips. She fit perfectly in my hand, and that small fact wasn't lost on me. In fact, every single part of her fit perfectly against me. I stopped kissing her just long enough to pull her tank top over her head, but she surprised me when she sat up, forcing me to also, then climbing onto my lap. Her legs wrapped around my waist and her hands gripped the bottom of my shirt and brought it up slowly, tugging it off me. Her eyes found mine, and without words, she reached behind her back, unclasped her bra, and tossed it in the corner with the rest of our clothes.

My heart was thundering in my chest, and I tried to keep my eyes on hers, tried hard not to be *that guy* who is distracted by boobs, but I couldn't help it. I loved her, all of her, and this was the first time she was showing me a part of herself that was sacred. My eyes lowered.

Fuck.

She was perfect.

I always knew she would be.

My hands went to her, gently cupping both her breasts, and I saw her chest shake with a shattering breath, goose bumps breaking out over her sensitive flesh. I dragged my thumb over her perfectly pink-brown nipple, and even in the dark of the tent I could see it stretch and stiffen, reacting to my touch.

"Christ, Kenz, you're gorgeous."

"Hayes," she whispered, wrapping her legs tighter around me as her hands gripped the back of my neck. My arms instinctively moved to wrap around her waist, and then we were pressed together, skin to skin, and I almost couldn't believe it was real.

She was softer than I imagined, her hair silkier, skin warmer. Everything about her was *more*.

Our mouths devoured each other, my hands trying to feel every bit of her exposed to me, and *fuck*, when she started rocking her hips against me I lost it. I lifted her, laid her back down on the sleeping bag, and pulled my mouth from hers.

"You stop me if you're not comfortable, Kenz. I swear, just tell me no, and I'll back off, but right now, my mouth wants to taste more of you." She nodded, biting her bottom lip, and I started pressing open kisses down her throat, over her collarbone, and across the swell of her breasts. I used one hand to palm her, squeezing her, loving the whimpers that came from her mouth. Then I slowly moved my mouth to her other breast, using my tongue to circle her, watching her eyes roll back in her head, then taking her fully in my mouth. I sucked gently at first, wanting to watch her react to my mouth, but when she rolled up, making the most beautiful sounds of pleasure, I couldn't help but draw her even further in, sucking hard, all while pinching her other nipple between my fingers.

"Baby, you have to be quiet," I murmured around her breast after she let out a low, guttural moan. I thought about someone hearing her cry out, and that alone made me uneasy—I didn't want anyone to hear her but me. Her sounds were for me alone. But if someone heard her, they'd know she was with someone, and we didn't need that kind of talk.

"I'm trying," she gasped. "Oh, God...," she cried softly as I pulled her nipple back in my mouth. "Please, Hayes," she started.

"What, Kenzie? Tell me what you need."

"I don't know...."

I moved my hands to the side, trailing lightly over her ribs, and placed a line of small kisses down the center of her. I paid special attention to her navel, but all that got me was more panting and low moaning. When I made it to the closure on her jeans, I met her eyes, silently asking her if she wanted me to stop. She gave me a small nod, and I swear I'd never felt luckier in my life.

I unbuttoned her jeans, pulled the zipper down, then tugged them off her legs, watching her lift and wiggle her hips to assist. It was dark, but I could see the stark white of her underwear and the sweet lace that lined the edges. I let out my own groan as I trailed my nose across her belly just above the soft edge of lace. I wanted to do so many things with her, to her, but I tried to rein myself in.

I pressed my lips against her skin again, moving up to her mouth, kissing her, feeling her bare legs wrap around me again. She used her feet to pull me down to her and, *Jesus, fuck,* she ground her hips up into me. Something inside me snapped and the thread of sanity I was so desperately gripping slid right through my fingers. My hand rested on her hip, then slid to her knee, holding her to me, then I thrust against her, watching as her eyes fluttered closed and her mouth fell open, only a soft moan coming from her.

So many countless nights I'd dreamed of being with her, of watching her underneath me, this was all too surreal, and so much better than I imagined.

Suddenly I felt her hand at the button of my jeans and I stilled, closing my hand around hers. "Kenzie, we can't." My forehead was pressed against hers, my breaths panting out of me at a rapid pace.

"I want to touch you." Her voice was raspy, deep, drowsy almost. And sexy as fuck. Her hand wriggled free from mine and she unbuttoned my pants. I lost the will to stop her. "We don't have to have sex, but I at least want to feel you." I opened my eyes to find her staring right at me, paused, waiting for permission. Suddenly, our roles were reversed, and she was the one taking cues from me.

I would deny her nothing.

I finished unzipping my pants and pushed them over my hips, kicking them off, then rolling off Kenzie so we were facing each other. I reached up, pressed my hand to her cheek, then slid it back into her hair, pulling her lips to mine. I felt her hand tremble as it grazed my stomach, her fingers tentatively pulling on the elastic of my boxer briefs. I lost my breath as her hand slid in and wrapped around me. Our lips were just a breath apart, both of us panting, her fingers moving gingerly over the most sensitive part of me.

She started at the base, squeezed, then moved to the tip, her hand becoming slick once she moved over the top.

"Jesus, McKenzie," I whispered, unable to even move my lips from hers before I uttered the words.

"Am I doing it wrong?"

"What?" I pulled back, looking her in the eye. "No, it's better than I ever thought it could be."

Her hand started pumping up and down again, and I tried to focus on her, but I was losing control. "Hayes, please, touch me too."

Without a second thought my hand slid down the softness of her stomach, pressed under the lace of her underwear, and I found her wet and warm. "Christ, you're perfect," I managed, even though I could hardly put the words together.

Minutes seemed like hours as we moved our hands over one another. It might have lasted days, I had no idea. She was moving her hand up and down my shaft so perfectly, and I was glorying in the feel of her, so tight and ready for me. I slipped one finger inside and smiled softy when I felt all her muscles contract, even the ones in her jaw. We had so much time ahead of us to figure it out, to make sure we were always in tune, but this first time—that first touch—it was so much more than I could have asked for.

We were all hands and mouths and bodies rubbing against each other. Eventually I lost the ability to care whether anyone could hear us because I was so lost in her. We were panted breaths, and bitten shoulders, and *Yes*es and *Oh Gods*.

I focused the pads of my fingers on her clit, rubbing gentle yet quick circles, and I matched her pace. My fingers followed the crescendo of her hand against me, and finally, we both found release together.

It was not lost on me how incredible or rare it was to come with someone simultaneously. It had never happened to me before, and I simply couldn't wrap my mind around how connected I already felt to McKenzie.

"Wow," she whispered after a few moments, both of us lying still, catching our breath. "That was... perfect." She said the words and before I could even agree, she backpedaled. "I mean, it was for me. I know it probably wasn't great for you. I'm sorry."

"What are you talking about?" I said the words as I pulled her face to look me in the eye. "You've got to stop doing that. What we just did? It was incredible." I pressed a soft kiss against her lips, trying to reassure her. "Stop doubting yourself."

I lost her eyes for just a moment as she looked away, but she brought them back and said, "I just feel really inexperienced with you."

"Inexperienced?"

She let out a small huff. "Can we not talk about it? I'm sorry I brought it up." Her hand came to cradle my face. "I'm just overwhelmed is all." I watched her eyes, trying to figure out how to respond, when her face lit up suddenly. "Oh, don't move." She pulled out of my arms and reached into the corner of the tent that held all our clothes and pulled her purse from the bottom of the pile. She reached inside and pulled out a travel-sized container of Kleenex. I watched as she gingerly cleaned me up, then threw the tissue toward the foot of the tent.

I watched as she searched for her tank top, then pulled it on. I groaned inwardly, sad I was losing the beauty of her bared to me. But as she was doing that, I remade the bed of her tent, zipping the two bags together, making it one bag and big enough for both of us. She climbed back in, her sweatpants back on, but not the full garb she'd had on earlier, and I pulled my t-shirt back on.

When we finally settled, she didn't hesitate to curl into my side and rest her head on my chest again.

"Can I ask you a question?" she whispered.

"Of course."

"How many people have you slept with?"

"Five," I answered immediately.

I heard a long pause, silence, then "Oh."

"Oh?"

I felt her shrug. "It's just a lot."

"Is it?"

"It's more than me."

"I'm four years older than you."

Another silent pause. "Yeah."

"Babe, I don't want you to worry about how many people I've been with, or how you compare to any of them. You don't. Or, they don't, actually. None of them compare to you. They can't. They started in your shadow and none of them ever managed to get out of it. The other girls, they were just, like, road bumps."

"Okay," she whispered, but she did not sound convinced.

"Listen, it goes both ways. If I spend our whole relationship worrying about how I compare—to Cory of all people—it wouldn't be fair to *us*. I don't want to think about you with other guys. It's not good."

Another silent pause, longer this time. I thought maybe she'd fallen asleep, but then, "There's no one to compare you to. I've never been with anyone else."

"You mean, besides Cory?"

"No," she said softly. "I mean, I've never *been* with anyone."

One day I'll be glad the tent was pitch-black in that moment so McKenzie couldn't see my face twist up in confusion, or my jaw drop at her words.

But the darkness couldn't hide the words I said, unfortunately. "You never had sex with Cory?"

"Can we just take him out of the equation? Can we just talk about my lack of experience in a general way?" she asked with exasperation.

"Sure," I said, even though I would never be able to pretend Cory wasn't the guy she'd been with before me. Ever. "So, you've never had sex? With anyone?"

"No."

"How is that possible?" I heard the words come out of my mouth and then realized they probably weren't the best choice. "What I mean is... um... I guess I'm just surprised. You were with your last boyfriend for a long time. And you're eighteen. I guess I just assumed...." I rubbed my hand up and down her arm, trying to smooth over any aggravation I might have caused with my words. "I'm sorry. I'm saying all the wrong things."

"Is that okay with you? I mean, I'm not very knowledgeable in the bedroom department."

I pressed my lips into her temple, kissing her gently. "You know your way around a tent pretty well."

She laughed, which was exactly what I was going for, but then she also slapped my arm, which I also took since she was still laughing. Her laughter died off slowly and I made a point to take all the humor out of my voice before I asked, "So, can I ask what you *have* done?"

"Well," she started, her voice a little shy and shaky, "everything I did to you tonight, I've done before. But that's as far as I've gone. But...." Her voice trailed off and I could feel her muscles tensing.

"You don't have to tell me right now, Kenz. But you should tell me eventually. This is important, you know, if we're going to be together."

"The last person I was with, um, he'd seen me without my top, but he'd only ever touched me over my clothes between my legs." She said the words fast, as if she was trying to get them out before she lost her nerve. Like ripping off a Band-Aid.

"I wish you had told me sooner."

"Why?"

"I think I might have handled the last hour of my life a little differently."

"What do you mean?"

"If I'd known no one had ever touched you, I might have been a little gentler. I would have taken a little more time. I'm sorry."

"No, don't be. Everything was perfect."

I agreed, but I still felt terrible for it. "I just need you to promise me if I ever hurt you, you'll tell me. If anything is ever uncomfortable, I need you to say something."

192 | Anie Michaels

"Have you ever taken someone's virginity?" she asked, her voice even quieter and soft.

"Freshman year of college. Her name was Allison. We dated for almost a year."

We were both quiet for a while, then finally she asked, "Will you stay the night with me?"

"I don't want to be anywhere else."

Chapter Sixteen

McKenzie

I woke to the sound of a zipper going down. You'd have thought thunder and lightning had stuck outside my tent for how fast I sat up, realizing that someone was trying to come in my tent, the tent that currently held a sleeping Hayes. I threw the sleeping bag over his face and crawled to the opening, still panicking, when Becca's face appeared in the hole she'd created.

"Hey," she whispered. I could tell by the amount of light it was still early. "I have to go to the bathroom." She stared at me expectantly.

"And that involves me how?"

"I'm not about to walk out in the trees to pee by myself. Where's your sisterly solidarity? There could be creatures out there."

"Fine," I conceded. "Just give me a minute to get dressed."

"Hurry, please," she said, making me laugh as she did a little dance. I zipped the door closed again and turned around to see Hayes peek out from under the sleeping bag. I held my finger up to my mouth, making sure he didn't say anything. I didn't want Becca to hear him.

He gave me a stupidly cute smile and crooked a finger at me. His eyes were sparkling and his hair was absolutely all over the place, and his gorgeous

194 | Anie Michaels

lips were tipped up, smiling for me. I crawled toward him, and when I got close enough, he reached out and wrapped his hand around my neck, pulling me the rest of the distance until our lips met. He kissed me as his hands slid around my waist, dangerously close to my ass, until I pulled away.

I used my thumb to point to the door of the tent and he nodded. Then he gave me one last kiss before he buried himself in the sleeping bag again. I made sure all his belongings were out of sight, pulled on my sweatshirt and shoes, then unzipped the tent just enough for my body to slip out. Then I made sure to zip it up all the way before I walked with Becca to find a place for her to pee.

We walked in silence until she felt she was far enough from the tents and found a large bush, copping a squat. She'd come prepared with a roll of toilet paper. That fact made me giggle. I was not, however, too proud to ask to use it. On the way back to the tents, she led me closer to the water and started talking about her evening with Jacob.

"I stayed in his tent all night." She said the words with a wince, as if she were afraid I would judge her for it.

"I figured, seeing as how you didn't spend the night in my tent." I gave her a smile, trying to show her that I wasn't going to tease her or judge her for spending the evening with a guy. "Did you have a good time?"

She let out a dreamy sigh, and I think I saw little love birds flying around her head. "He's so sweet, Kenz. He held my hand and it felt like I was fourteen again, holding a boy's hand for the first time. He kissed me but didn't pressure me to do anything else. We were just talking in the tent, not even, like, making out or anything, and he just held me until I fell asleep." She let out another lovesick sigh. "Best night ever."

I couldn't disagree. But I also couldn't tell her why my night was so exciting. "So, do you think you guys are going to start dating, like, exclusively?" I watched a blush come over her face in a wave, starting at her neck and moving up to her cheeks.

"He asked me to be his girlfriend last night."

"Oh, God, you're in trouble," I said through a laugh. "You guys are gonna be the cutest and most barf-inducing couple ever."

"I know!" she whisper-squealed, jumping up and down and quietly clapping her hands. After she calmed down a bit, she turned to me, both her hands wrapping around my forearm. "Nate was such an asshole last night, but you have to admit, watching Jacob, Ryan, and Todd get all alpha male on him was pretty hot."

"Hot? I don't know. It was nice of them...."

"Come on, Kenzie, Ryan's been crushing on you for years. You can't tell me that him kicking Nate out of his party for you wasn't flattering in the least."

Oh, no. The last thing I needed were rumors started about me and a guy. I wanted to fly low, under everyone's radar. Eventually, if things worked out with Hayes and me, my friends would find out. But now was not the time.

"He threw Nate out of the party because he was being a poor excuse for a human being, not because he was trying to flatter me."

"I don't know," she sang.

"Even if you're right, even if he's had a crush on me for years, I'm not looking to date anyone right now."

"I know. You're right. I'm sorry. Cory's only been gone six weeks. Of course you're not ready yet." She sounded honestly contrite.

Even though it felt terrible, I had to let her believe that was the reason I didn't want to pursue anything with Ryan. "Thanks for understanding," I said as I shot her the guiltiest smile.

We made plans to pack up camp in an hour or so and try to beat the rush of all the other kids, who would inevitably be hungover and grumpy, up the hill. Becca said she'd get Holly, hoping she and Todd were asleep, not wanting to "get an earful." Not that they were big exhibitionists, but it was early in the morning and they were alone in a tent. I understood her hesitance. Pancakes were on our agenda.

When I made it back to my tent I was almost giddy with the excitement of seeing Hayes again, getting the chance to kiss him again before he left, but I was sadly disappointed to find he was already gone. In the back of my mind I knew it was smart of him to leave early, lessening the chance of being seen by anyone, but after such an intense night, of feeling so connected to him, I was able to admit it hurt he hadn't said good-bye.

He was gone. His shoes were gone. His clothes. I felt his absence in a scary way, as if an actual part of me were missing. I crawled back into my now-too-big sleeping bag and let out a heavy sigh, silently chiding myself for being so silly. But when I inhaled, I smiled.

Hayes.

I could smell him on my pillow.

Two hours later, Becca, Jacob, Holly, Todd, and I all sat in a booth at our favorite breakfast spot. Ryan had driven us and our gear up the hill and looked a little dismayed that he couldn't come with us. Holly invited him no less than ten times. She obviously couldn't see me shooting her an angry look that said, "Shut up!" He'd declined every invitation, telling us he needed to stay behind and help everyone get up from the campsite. I waved and gave him a quick, "Good-bye," before getting in the car.

I'd been wearing a ridiculous smile for the last half hour. As soon as we'd made it up the hill and off the compound, back into civilization and cell service, my phone pinged with a text.

I took the opportunity to sneak out of camp while you were with Becca. Last night was amazing. Call me when you get home.

It had taken me ten minutes to finally come up with a reply.

I missed you when I came back. I'll call you later.

I didn't want to seem needy or clingy, but I couldn't contain the overwhelming feelings within me, all the emotions the night before had brought up. The decision to tell him I'd missed him was something I debated with myself over, but finally I decided to take the leap. I *had* missed him. I'd been disappointed to find him gone. I thought, if anything, maybe he needed the reassurance just as much as me.

"So, what do you guys want to do today?" Holly asked, just before she took a dainty bite of pancake.

"We could hit the mall?" This came from Jacob. He wasn't exactly a stranger, but he was a new addition to our group—a welcome addition—but new nonetheless. I admired the way he didn't seem intimidated by us and all of our long-standing friendships. He just kind of fit right in.

For the tiniest moment it occurred to me that there'd been a spot to fill. The one Cory had left

199 |Instead of You

open. But I pushed the thought aside, telling myself that Jacob would be there regardless. He was by no means trying to fill a role.

"I need to shower and change first," Becca said, making a disgusted expression as she reached up and palmed her bun. All three of us girls were sporting the messy bun. Not out of choice, but out of necessity. We truly looked like we'd all spent the night sleeping on the ground.

"I think you look amazing," Jacob said without one ounce of insincerity. The two of them locked gazes. Becca blushed, I rolled my eyes, and Holly and Todd continued to steal food from each other's plates.

"Well, you guys have fun. I still have so much work to catch up on, I've got to go home."

"What? No. Kenz, come with us. You can do homework tomorrow," Becca begged, her voice whiney but sincere.

I hadn't been to the mall with my friends in weeks, and part of me thought it would be fun, but then I thought about being the fifth wheel, especially to Becca and Jacob's budding romance, and I knew it would just be awkward and uncomfortable. "No, really, I shouldn't have even gone to the party last night." I bit off a piece of my bacon, and watched my friends make plans for their afternoon.

The girls dropped me off at my house, and I used the side door to sneak into the garage, putting my camping gear away, a smile slipping across my face as I placed the sleeping bags back on their shelf, remembering Hayes's fingers playing with the strands of my hair as we laid in them. When I went back around to the front of the house and opened the door, I found my mom and dad sitting in the living room. My dad was watching TV, reclined and relaxed, and my mom had her Kindle, reading while she lay on the couch.

When I came in they both turned to look at me and I took the obligatory moment to gauge their faces to see if they had realized I wasn't where I said I'd be last night. My mom smiled so I let out a small breath of relief, knowing they hadn't caught on.

"Hey, sweetie. Have fun with the girls last night?"

"I always do." I returned her smile, but then headed toward my room. I stopped at the mouth of the hall when she kept talking.

"What are your plans for the rest of the day?"

"Just homework," I said with a shrug, feeling the weight of everything I still had to do pressing down on my shoulders. "I'm still pretty far behind. I shouldn't have even gone out last night."

"Don't put too much pressure on yourself, McKenzie." This came from my father, who kicked the foot of his recliner down and spun around so he could face me. "Your teachers all gave you ample time to make up your work.

There's no need to cause yourself stress to finish it all in one week. Take it easy."

My father's concern warmed me. I found it impossible to not be a daddy's girl, especially since I was an only child. His fatherly love and devotion was concentrated on me, and I loved it. Bloomed under it.

"Okay, Daddy. I'll try." He winked at me, spun back around. I looked to my mom. "Are you going to check on Mrs. Wallace today?" I knew my mom had been the one to stay with her until late last night because Hayes was supposed to be in Bellingham until today.

"I was going to head over there later. Hayes called me this morning and said he'd come home early, so I haven't been there yet today."

"I can go over there if you want, if you need a break." I had both selfish reasons for offering to go, but also because my mom truly deserved some time away. She'd never say it, but caring for Mrs. Wallace was emotionally draining for her. I knew it chewed her up inside to see her best friend in such a fragile state, barely holding on to her sanity.

"How about we go together?" Her face was filled with affection, as if my offering to go for her was a gift.

"Sounds good." I turned and continued down the hall to my room. I took a shower, both glad and sad to rinse the night away. Even though my instincts told me my nights with Hayes had just begun, I couldn't help but slip the memory into the little folder of my mind labeled Best Night Ever.

Sitting down at my desk, my homework in front of me, piles formed based on which assignments were most important or due first, was just a little overwhelming. I knew if I took it one piece at a time it would be easy, but the stacks intimidated me. I picked up my phone and called Hayes.

"Hey," he answered, the sound of his voice, just one word, making some of my stress float away. "You get home okay?"

"Yeah, the girls dropped me off a little while ago." I stood from my desk and walked to my bed, lying down and looking out the window. "Did your mom do all right while you were gone?"

"I think so. Actually, she got out of bed a little while ago and ate breakfast." His voice sounded optimistic and happy.

"That's amazing."

"She ate, then took a shower, and now she's in the living room. She's just sitting there watching TV, but she's not in bed, so I say it's a win." The hope in his voice broke my heart. I wanted that for him, for his mother to get better. Not only for Mrs. Wallace's sake, but equally for Hayes's.

"It's a good day, then."

"The best," he replied, voice lower and raspy, making the hairs on my arms stand up. "It killed me to leave you this morning."

"Well, it killed me to come back to the tent and see you were gone. But I understand why you left. It was smart, actually. We're lucky no one saw you."

"Yeah."

"I'm going to come over later with my mom."

"And the day just gets better and better."

"Do you think it's going to get harder to be around our parents? To pretend like nothing is happening between us?"

"Probably," he said, the honesty vibrating in his voice. "Does that bother you?"

I shrugged and then realized he couldn't see me. "I don't know. It just sucks that something that makes me so happy has the potential to hurt so many people."

"Just promise me something, Kenz."

"What?"

"Promise me the moment you aren't happy anymore, you'll tell me."

His voice told me he was thinking about all the time I spent with Cory. All the years I convinced myself the feelings would come eventually. I didn't have the words to explain to him how being unhappy with him seemed like an impossibility.

"You're not him, Hayes. And I'm not the same person I was when I was with him, either. I'll tell you how I know the difference."

"How?"

"My feelings for you were never a question. I never once had to think about how I felt. I've known all along it was you, I was just too afraid to believe it." I waited, listening to his soft breaths through the phone, wanting to hear any kind of response.

"You shouldn't say things like that to me over the phone," he murmured, so quietly I almost couldn't hear him.

"Why?" I whispered.

"Because I can't kiss you through the phone."

His words had the same effect as a kiss: my head became light, my mouth turned up in a shy smile, and my pulse raced. "Oh," was my breathy response.

"I'll find a way to kiss you later."

Oh, God.

My body reacted immediately to his words, my core clenching, breath hitching. I didn't know if he meant he'd find an opportunity to kiss me, or he'd kiss me in a way I'd only imagined someone kissing me—his mouth on unfamiliar parts of my body.

"All right." I wasn't sure he heard me; my voice was just a whoosh of air, my lungs simply giving up on functioning correctly.

"I'll see you when you get here."

"Okay."

He hung up and if I weren't already lying down, I would have collapsed onto my bed. I didn't know if I was going to be able to keep up with Hayes; he obviously had an advantage in the sexual prowess department. Something told me even if he left me in the dust, I'd regret not taking the ride.

Chapter Seventeen

McKenzie

It was dinnertime and Mom and I were headed to see Mrs. Wallace and Hayes. My dad stayed behind, telling us he had things to work on at home. Mom kissed his cheek, her hand reverently on his face, and told him she loved him before we left the house.

Mark had been my dad's best friend. Introduced to each other through my mom and Mrs. Wallace, they'd become fast friends. Twenty years of friendship had been built between them, and I knew my dad was taking Mark's loss hard. Not in an unhealthy way, but still in a gut-wrenching way. I knew going to Mark's house made him uncomfortable—he did it, but he sometimes tried to stay away. That evening seemed to be one of those times.

My mother carried two pizza boxes down the street while I kept pace beside her. She'd decided she was too lazy to cook, so it became a pizza night.

"I hope Chelsea doesn't mind the pizza."

"Mom, you know she won't."

"Part of me kind of wishes she would. I'd love to see the feisty side of Chelsea, love to see her get worked up over something. *Anything.* "

"She'll come around." I tried to sound confident in my words, but the truth was, I had no idea. I could hope, just as much as anyone, that eventually she'd be all right, but I knew there was no guarantee.

Just like it'd been for over twenty years, my mom pushed open the door to the Wallace household without knocking. We stepped in, but I stopped suddenly when I collided with my mother's back. I was not even a foot inside the house and my mother was stalled. I followed her gaze and my eyes landed on Mrs. Wallace, sitting on the couch, showered, and looking tired but completely lucid.

She looked more alive than she had in weeks.

"Chels," my mom breathed. I placed both my hands on my mother's arms, near her shoulders, my heart nearly breaking at the sound of my mother's unbelieving words, as if she were seeing a ghost.

"Hey, Luce." She smiled and my mother's shoulders started to shake, moving with a mixture of laughter and tears. Even I was surprised by the transformation. Mrs. Wallace looked almost normal. She still had dark circles under her eyes, and she'd lost a lot of weight, but the distant, faraway look in her eyes was practically gone.

Mrs. Wallace stood from the couch, pushing up on the cushion with force to lift herself, weak from weeks of not using her muscles, but she made it. Then she slowly walked toward us. I put gentle pressure on my mother's back, urging her into the house. She shuffled forward and I was able to enter and close the door behind me.

I'd been so wrapped up in Mrs. Wallace, I hadn't noticed Hayes in the kitchen, but my eyes swung to him as he walked to my mother, taking the pizza boxes from her just in time for Mrs. Wallace to wrap my mother in a hug.

"It's good to see you," Mrs. Wallace whispered, still hugging my mother tightly.

"You, too."

Both of them had silent tears streaking their faces, and I wiped away one of my own. A light touch caressed my arm and I looked over to see Hayes with his hand wrapped around my elbow, steering me toward the kitchen. I followed him and we started setting the table and getting dinner ready, giving our mothers a moment alone.

A minute later they broke apart, both laughing lightly, wiping beneath their eyes, Mrs. Wallace's smile tinted with sadness still. I wondered if I'd ever see her again without the shroud of grief. Probably not.

"Shall we eat?" Hayes's question caught their attention and I watched his mother's gaze soften when her eyes fell on him.

"It's just pizza," my mom said, defending the meal we'd brought.

"It's perfect," Mrs. Wallace said with a smile.

We all sat at the table, Hayes taking the seat next to mine, making me hide a smile. Our mothers held light conversation, never venturing into any

209 | Instead of You

heavy topics, and I was content to sit and listen. I knew the conversation was good for Mrs. Wallace, that she was taking a big step in moving forward, but it was also good for my mom; she'd missed her best friend.

When a foot hooked around my ankle beneath the table, I tried not to react, but couldn't help it when my eyes stole away to Hayes. He wasn't looking at me, but I saw his smile anyhow. He brought my foot toward him, captured it really, and then held it hostage between his own. Every few moments I felt his toes move up my calf, making it impossible for me to eat without looking like I was trying to keep a secret.

"McKenzie's been a big help around here, Luce. I really appreciate her." My name from Mrs. Wallace's mouth caught my attention. "I shouldn't have leaned on her as much as I did, but in some ways, she's all I have left of Cory."

My stomach plummeted all the way to my knees. Warmth drained from my face and I'm sure all my color went with it. I shrugged. "I haven't done anything. Just brought over some food and stuff." Mrs. Wallace reached her hand over and placed it on mine, squeezing it gently.

"Just having you here helps, McKenzie. When I lost Cory, I knew I'd lost you too, in a way. You're the closest thing to a daughter I've ever had, and I was looking forward to the day I could call you mine officially."

Oh, God, no. My eyes flitted to my mother's and she looked like a combination of sad for her friend and worried about me. Mrs. Wallace's words were landing on my shoulders like boulders, pinning me down in a way I hadn't felt in weeks. Hayes's foot unhooked from mine and it was as though he'd cut the rope to my life raft, sending me out to sea to fend for myself.

"Mom," he said, his voice soft but rough.

"Oh, sweetie," she said, waving one hand, dismissing him, while the other wiped a tear from her face. "I know you'll marry someone one day, but it won't be the same. McKenzie and Cory were meant to be, from day one."

All the oxygen in the room was being sucked out by her words, my lungs shriveling in my chest, aching for air.

"Chelsea," my mom whispered, slowly shaking her head. Mrs. Wallace looked at her, then seemed to wake up a little, as if her mind had been somewhere else. She looked around the table, probably taking in my stunned expression and Hayes's face, which looked like a cross between angry and murderous.

"I'm sorry," she whispered, her eyes darting back and forth between Hayes and me. "I think," she started, but stopped, looking at my mom. "I think I want to get some fresh air. Will you go for a walk with me?"

Everyone was silent. Besides doctor's appointments for sleeping pills, Mrs. Wallace hadn't left the house since the funeral. For her to ask to leave, to offer to go for a walk, was surprising. I was floating somewhere between being happy for the milestone and relieved she was leaving and giving my mind and body a chance to deal with the effect of her words.

Hayes and I both sat in silence while our mothers pulled on their jackets, tied their shoes, and left the house.

I had no words, so I was glad when Hayes spoke first.

"She doesn't understand what she's saying." His voice was still low and raspy, like his throat was doing everything it could to hold back his screams. It was the kind of control that you knew was just seconds away from being lost, like he could snap at any moment. "She's drowning, Kenz. In grief. She can't understand the effect her words are having. You can't take what she says to heart."

I sat in my chair, mouth tightly shut, hands clasped tightly around each other in my lap, jaw tense, with emotion simply squeezing me to the point of rupture. I was trying to hold it all in, trying to let the wave of anger and sadness pass over me, to feel it crest and wane, but it just kept building until I couldn't take it any longer.

My elbows came to the table, my face went into my hands, and I erupted in cries. It was not even two seconds before Hayes had his arms around me, holding me, his hand running soft circles on my back. And I simply cried. The very last thing I needed in that moment was for Mrs. Wallace to walk in on her *other son* touching me in a way that indicated anything more than friendship.

I stood up quickly, my chair scraping against the linoleum floor, and I ran to the bathroom. I shut the door behind me, locked it, and didn't even bother with the light. I didn't particularly want to look at myself in that moment anyhow.

I was the worst kind of person.

Again, not two seconds after I'd made it into the bathroom, Hayes was on the other side of the door, pounding on it.

"Kenzie, don't do this. Don't push me away. We have to stick together." His words were punctuated by thumping on the door. I could picture him on the other side, breathing hard, waiting for me to open the door, to open myself up to him again.

It was so easy to forget that what we were doing was wrong. So easy. I let the way I felt around him, the way every part of me cried out for him, overshadow the fact that there's no way for our relationship to be *right*.

He was my boyfriend's brother. The brother of my boyfriend who died thinking I loved him, thinking that I would spend the rest of my life with him. And he was my History teacher. I couldn't think of one single other person who I could choose to start a relationship with that could cause as much destruction as Hayes and I could if anyone found out about us.

"You don't have to mourn him the way other people think you should, Kenz. You don't have to stay home, you don't have to be single forever, you don't have to *act* any certain way. My mom wants you to be sad without him forever, because that's how she thinks she's going to feel. Sad. Forever. But that's not true. And it's not how you have to feel either."

I turned my back to the mirror I couldn't see, rested my rear against the counter, and ran my fingertips under my eyes, wiping away the wetness.

"Please, baby, let me in." Those words were whispered, and I thought I heard fear in them as well. I reached out and turned the lock. He must have heard it because the door slowly opened, light streaking into the bathroom. He opened it just far enough to get his body through, and then he closed it. When I heard the lock turn again, my breath caught in my lungs.

It was dark in the bathroom but I could still see him move to stand right in front of me, see his shadowed form come to a stop. His hand reached out and gripped my hip, my eyes closing at his touch even though I could see barely anything. I'd never experienced such conflicting emotions before. On one hand, I desperately wanted him to touch me, to soothe the ache inside of me, force me to focus on what his touch made me feel as opposed to the pain currently ripping through me. On the other hand, I knew, on some level, he shouldn't have been touching me at all. I should push him away. I should tell him we couldn't do whatever it was we were doing anymore.

But I simply wasn't strong enough.

When I didn't push away his first touch, he reached out with his other hand, both hands now on my waist. Slowly they moved toward my back, pulling me into him.

And I went.

Because I was weak.

We'd all lost so much, and losing Hayes would have been too much to bear.

When I was pressed against him, my hands wound around his waist, his hands moving into my hair, the tears didn't stop and neither did the thoughts. So I spoke them. I let them have a voice.

"Our being together is going to hurt everyone around us, Hayes. If they ever found out, if your mom ever knew, it would break her. It's *wrong*, Hayes. We're wrong."

"I know," he whispered after a long pause. "But nothing has ever felt so right."

I couldn't argue with him.

His hands moved from my hair, down to the sides of my neck, and he leaned away from me. I opened my eyes and all I could see was the outline of his face, feel the warmth of his hands on my throat, the gentle stroking of his thumbs over my cheeks, still wet from tears. When his lips feathered over mine I didn't try to pull away. I knew it was wrong, but that wasn't reason enough to stop him. The way he kissed me, as if I could fall apart at any moment, as if he didn't know whether his kiss would shatter me or hold me together, it made me love him that much more.

Good, bad, wrong, or right, I needed him to know.

"I love you," I said against his lips between kisses. For seconds, the only thing I heard was the thundering of my pulse in my ears. "I don't care if it's wrong, it doesn't make it *feel* any less real, any less true." He was still quiet, his hands frozen in place on the sides of my face. Then they were quickly moved to my hips where he gripped me, picked me up, and placed me on the counter. My knees instinctively opened, and he immediately moved in between them. He was still so much taller than me, and even though it was pitch black, I still tilted my head up to look at him, knowing without a doubt he was looking down at me.

"You love me?" he asked, quickly followed by, "or you're in love with me?"

I understood why he was asking, why he needed the clarification, and I wanted nothing more in that moment than to reassure him.

"Every part of me is in love with you." The words left my mouth just before his lips descended. The kiss was soft and slow, lingering, as if he wanted it to be branded there, to last forever, to mark me. My hands lifted to his stomach, sliding around, pulling him closer to me. With every second of the kiss that elapsed, the panic within me rose. His kisses, unlike any kiss I'd ever received, were limited. We had an expiration date, I could feel it. There was no way for this to last. Something would pull us apart, wedge between us, crack the foundation we were standing on, which was already broken when we climbed atop it. I pulled away just as a sob ripped out of me, climbing out of my chest.

"You know I'm in love with you, Kenzie. I love you so fucking much," he said, holding my face to his chest as I cried. His hands pulled me into him, moving rapidly to make sure he got hold of all of me.

I didn't answer him, couldn't vocalize what I was thinking. *It doesn't matter how much we love each other; it's all doomed anyway.*

Chapter Eighteen

Hayes

Sitting at my desk, I looked over the assignment in front of me, the one I was supposed to be grading. I'd read the first paragraph four times already, each time losing interest and my mind wandering. I dropped the paper, exhaling loudly, running my hands over my face. It had been almost a week since McKenzie had told me she loved me, that she was *in love* with me. It wasn't at all how I'd imagined those words passing our lips for the first time—in a dark bathroom, her crying, the words sounding more like a good-bye than the promise of a future together.

That night she'd wiped her eyes, dried her tears, pulled away from me—in so many ways—and gone home. She didn't wait for her mother, didn't kiss me good-bye, said practically nothing before leaving my house. It killed me. And since then she'd been distant, hardly speaking a word to me, answering my texts with short, one-word replies, and definitely not touching me. In fact, it seemed as though she was going to extra lengths to stay as far away from me as possible. She'd been late to class all week, coming in just after the bell, making it impossible for me to say anything to her in private, practically running for the door as soon as the period was over, and she'd stopped coming to my house with her mom.

That fact I couldn't really blame her for, not after what my mother had said to her.

The door to the classroom opened with more force than usual, causing my eyes to dart in that direction. Mr. White strode in, his steps quick, a somewhat panicked look on his face.

"Mr. Wallace, I'm glad you're here. There's been somewhat of an emergency with my daughter, and I have to leave. Mrs. Anderson has given the okay for you to cover the rest of my classes, if you're okay with that." His statement was a question.

"Of course, I hope everything will be all right."

"My daughter was in her PE class at the middle school, playing soccer, and they're afraid she's broken her leg. They already took her to the hospital by ambulance, so I'm headed there now. My wife is meeting me there."

"Well, that sucks," I said, running my hand through my hair, which I'd decided not to tie back that day. "Is there anything in particular you'd like me to cover? In your classes?"

"Oh, um," he said distractedly as he patted all his pockets, finally pulling his car keys out of the front left one. "You know what? Just give the kids a study period. I'll catch up tomorrow, or whenever I get back."

I didn't bother mentioning that tomorrow would be Saturday. I just nodded and watched as he gathered his belongings in a somewhat frantic manner.

"Don't worry about anything here. I've got it covered."

He gave me a very weak smile. "Thanks, Hayes."

He left and I let out a sigh, pushing the paper I obviously couldn't focus on away. I sat in silence for a few minutes, trying to find a solution to all my problems, to find that path that was obviously eluding me. When no answers came to me, I picked up my phone to text McKenzie.

Come to my classroom during your lunch.

It took a while for her to text back, which made sense since she was currently in class.

You know that's not a good idea.

Mr. White left for the day. The room will be empty.

It wasn't lost on me that I needed a convincing argument to get my girlfriend to come have lunch with me. Everything felt wrong, like it was slipping through my fingers and all I could do was grasp at the remaining pieces of what I thought we had together.

Please, Kenzie. I need to see you.

Apparently I wasn't above begging.

All right.

Students started filing into the classroom, so I tossed my phone into my desk drawer and prepared to try and make it through two more periods before I saw McKenzie.

When she walked into my classroom a few hours later I was ready for her. I waited until she was all the way in, closed the door behind her, and then turned the lock. Her eyes flitted down, watching my fingers essentially block everyone else out of the room, out of our lives, even if it was just for a few moments.

She didn't have anything with her besides her messenger bag, no lunch, which made me think she hadn't come to enjoy a meal with me. Instead she'd come with armor, her shield so firmly in place, even if it was invisible.

"How are you?" I asked, trying to open some sort of communication between us. It wasn't the real question I wanted to ask her. I wanted to know why she was pulling away, what I could do to keep her close, if she really loved me the way she'd said she did just a week ago, but I know those questions would only make her shield go up even farther, put more of a wall between us.

I watched her face as she battled to answer the question. Her eyes were welling and I let a string of curse words run rampant in my mind. I was so fucking tired of watching her cry. She quickly wiped a tear away and said, "I've been better."

"Yeah," I said on a breath. "Me too."

"Why did you ask me to come here, Hayes? You know if someone sees me in here, you could get in a lot of trouble."

"I just wanted to talk to you. You've been avoiding me. At least here we can talk in private."

She didn't say anything in reply. Just wiped away another tear.

"Why are you crying?" I asked softly.

"This *hurts*, Hayes." Her words were accusatory, like I was trying to hurt her on purpose.

"Tell me what I can do to make it hurt less?" I took a step toward her, feeling so much relief when she didn't move farther away.

She just shook her head, looking at me, begging me with her eyes to make the pain go away. *Fuck it.* I walked to her, took her hand, and pulled her to the one corner of the room hidden from the window. She came willingly, let me lead her. I grabbed the rolling chair from my desk, sat in the corner, then pulled her onto my lap, her legs straddling mine. I pulled her into me, letting her face rest against my chest, and wrapped my arms around her, trying to comfort her.

Minutes passed, just her sitting on my lap, crying. I didn't know what else to do, so I just held her. Eventually, she spoke.

"I'm so confused, Hayes. The whole time I was with Cory I knew what we had wasn't right. I knew he wasn't it for me, but I hoped, because I loved him, I was wrong." She lifted her head to look me in the eye, her face wet from tears. "But now, with you, it's *right*, I know it is. You're it. There will never be anyone else who makes the world as colorful as you, who makes me smile as much as you, who loves me like you do. But it's all still so wrong. So, tell me how I'm supposed to ignore the part of my brain that screams at me every day, that reminds me of who we're hurting and who we're lying to, and just *be*."

My hands cradled her face, eyes darting between hers, trying to find the right words, the words that would keep her with me.

"I know this, us, isn't ideal. Trust me, I want to shout to the world and tell everyone how much I love you, how long I've waited for you to even look at me with the tiniest spark of interest." My thumbs rub just under her eyes, catching the tears that just keep falling. "And I know the odds are stacked against us, Kenz. I do. But none of that outweighs my need to be with you. None of the consequences are worth living without the hope of us. Does that make sense?"

She stared at me, eyes vacant, and all I could see was worry and hurt. *Fuck.*

"Okay, let's try something different. You tell me what you're worried about, and I'll explain why it doesn't fucking matter."

Underneath the sadness I swear I saw just the hint of a smile, and it was just as though someone had lit a fucking fuse inside me, hope sizzling through my limbs. She was still in there, my McKenzie, and I could still keep her. I just had to show her there was nothing that could come between us.

"What if your mom finds out?" I knew this was her biggest concern, and frankly, it was mine too. My mother wasn't exactly stable.

"Listen, I'll agree that if my mom were to find out about us, oh, tomorrow, it would probably be a shock to her, and might upset her, but eventually she will come around. She's dealing with a lot right now. You can't make yourself unhappy to save my mother. She needs to deal with her own emotions."

"What if us being together causes tension between our mothers? What if my mom takes my side, and your mom is mad at me, and they stop being friends?"

"What if an asteroid hits the earth tomorrow?" I blink at her, trying to make her understand that we can't deal with what-ifs. Then, *then*, she smiled and slapped my shoulder, laughing while still crying a little.

"What about my friends? Cory's friends? They'll hate me."

"If they're really your friends, they won't," I say, pushing a lock of hair behind her ear. My hand splayed on her cheek and she leaned into it, her tears finally stopping. "Do you really love me?" She nodded, eyes locked on mine. "Then trust me to take care of you." She didn't respond, but she kept her eyes on mine, so I took a chance. I leaned in, waited for her to tell me no, and when she didn't, I kissed her.

It had been almost a week since I'd had my mouth on her, and it was too damn long. I kissed her softly, trying to soothe her, take some of the worry away. It was an innocent kiss, even though she was straddling me. I pulled away just far enough to say, "I've missed you. Please don't avoid me when you're upset."

She pressed her forehead against mine, her fingers playing with a button on my shirt. "What are we going to do when you're done here? After I graduate?"

I threaded my fingers through the hair at her nape, silently asking for her eyes, which she gave me. "What do you mean?"

"You're going to be a teacher, and I'm going to go to college. How will that work?"

"Are you planning on going to college in the United States?"

"Yeah," she said with a laugh, and I could tell she wanted to slap my arm again.

"Well, that's fortunate, because my license will transfer to almost any other state."

"Hayes." She said my name like she was tired of my shit, and I smiled, thinking I could listen to her saying my name that way forever.

"Wherever you go to college, I'll apply for jobs there. That's my plan. I don't expect us to live together. You still get to be a college student, but I'd like to be close."

"I'd like that too," she whispered and I finally saw the McKenzie smile I loved. The shy one, where one side of her mouth tipped up just slightly higher than the other. "But all the colleges I applied to are here, in Florida."

"Even more perfect. Less paperwork." I leaned in and kissed her again. I had just used my teeth to trap her bottom lip, my hands on her hips pulling her into me, when I heard the door handle jiggle. She must have heard it too because she jumped from my lap, wiping her mouth with her palm, eyes wide, definitely starting to panic.

I stood up and put my hands on her shoulders. "Kenz," I whispered, getting her attention. "Let me handle this."

She nodded, eyes still wide and scared.

I wiped my own mouth and headed toward the door.

When I stepped close enough to see through the window, my heart rate sped up. Mrs. Anderson was waiting on the other side. I smiled at her, trying to look carefree, then unlocked the door, and opened it wide, hoping she'd think I had nothing to hide. She stepped inside and I watched as her eyes swept the room, landing on McKenzie.

"Mr. Wallace, I came to check in with you to make sure Mr. White's classes were going according to plan. May I ask why you have a student in your room, alone, with the door locked?"

"Miss Harris is having a rough day and she stopped by to talk. She was upset, so I locked the door, hoping to spare her the embarrassment of other students walking in on her."

Mrs. Anderson's eyes were like a pendulum, swinging back and forth between McKenzie and me. When they finally landed and stayed on Kenz, I held my breath.

"Is everything all right, Miss Harris? Did you seek out Mr. Wallace to talk with him?"

"He's the only person who understands what I'm going through," she said on a raspy whisper, and I could tell by the look on her face that using Cory as an excuse, to use his death as a cover story, made her ill.

Mrs. Anderson considered her words for a moment, and then I watched with relief as her expression softened and I knew she'd bought our story. "If you need to talk with someone, McKenzie, our counselors are trained to deal with loss and grief. I am sympathetic to your unique situation," she said to both McKenzie and me, "but we still need to maintain student and teacher boundaries."

"It won't happen again," I said immediately.

"I'm sorry," McKenzie whispered, and I wanted so badly to reach out to her, because I knew she was beating herself up. We'd taken two steps forward and then faltered with four steps back. I watched as McKenzie grabbed her messenger bag off the floor and hurried out of the room. I ran my hand through my hair again, letting out a sigh, then met Mrs. Anderson's eyes again.

"It is your responsibility as the teacher to impose the boundaries, Mr. Wallace. I know you have a history with Miss Harris, but you can't let the lines between you blur."

"It's a unique situation and I agree, I didn't handle it well. It will not happen again." I maintained eye contact, giving her no reason to think I was deceiving her. After a very long moment, she finally nodded.

"Are things otherwise going all right? Mr. White's classes going as planned?"

"Everything is under control." I gave her a tight smile.

"Very well." She turned on her heel and left the room. I let out a large sigh, combing both hands through my hair, walked back to my chair, and collapsed.

It was then I noticed a button on my shirt was undone.

Chapter Nineteen

McKenzie

I walked into what I thought would be an empty house. Mom and Dad were usually still at work when I got home from school. Mom surprised me by standing at the kitchen counter, coffee mug in hand, seemingly waiting for me.

"What are you doing home? Is everything all right?" I asked as I dropped my bag on my usual chair at the table.

She gave a one-shoulder shrug. "I thought it would be good for us to talk. Things have been pretty crazy and after what happened at Chelsea's house last week, I just wanted to check in."

"Oh." This caught me completely off guard. "Um, okay."

"Sit down, baby," she said, motioning to the table. I moved my bag off my seat, hung it on the back of the chair, and sat down. "I just wanted to make sure we're on the same page. I want to know how you feel about everything."

"Everything? Meaning what?" I could feel my eyebrows pinching in the middle of my face.

"Well, about losing Cory, and what that means in regard to your future."

"I feel like I miss Cory." It was definitely a statement, but it came out more like a question. "I mean, I miss Cory," I said with more assertion. "I miss him and it's really sad that he's gone and won't get to do all the stuff my friends and I will get to."

"Like what?"

"I don't know, Mom. College, jobs, marriage, *life*. Stuff. He's gone, ya know? But he's still here, kind of? So, we're all just sort of leaving him behind, and that's sad."

Her hand reached out for mine, gently stroking the top of it. "It's totally normal to be sad for a while when you lose your boyfriend." She paused, looking at me with mom eyes, like she knew something and wanted confirmation. "Or even just a best friend," she finished, her voice soft and knowing.

"What do you mean?" I whispered.

"No matter what Chelsea says about you and Cory, I want you to know that you were the light of that boy's life. You made his life beautiful, and you were an angel to him. And you've done your time. You do not need to mourn him forever, Kenz. And moving on, getting on with your life and doing all the things Cory will never get to do is your *right*. You can't sacrifice parts of your life for someone who's passed, sweetie. Do you understand?"

"I think so. I just don't understand why we're talking about it. Did I do something wrong?"

"No, baby. No. I just see you going through the motions. I know you're still adjusting to life without him, but I don't want Chelsea's words to take root. She's in a very different space than you. She lost so much more than you did. It's not fair for her to want you to suffer like she is. She's entitled to mourn in whatever way she chooses, and so are you."

"You mean, like, dating other boys, or going to dances, and stuff?"

"I mean *living*. You don't have to run out and date the first boy who asks, but if you feel like you want to, then, yeah. Go on a date."

I looked down at my hands, noticing all my cuticles were practically gone thanks to my nervous habit of picking at them. "Why did you say Cory was just my best friend?"

"Listen, ever since Cory died, your father and I have been keeping a watchful eye." Her words made my heart speed up and worry crashed through me, panic settling in. "And it's okay if I'm totally off base here, and I'm sorry if this upsets you, but your dad and I just noticed that you've been mourning the Cory you've known for the last eighteen years, but not the Cory who you might have spent the rest of your life with."

Again, my eyebrows drew together. "What does that mean?" My voice was a whisper again.

"It means that we see you missing the boy you grew up with, the one who teased you, protected you, played with you, but we haven't seen you mourn the future you lost with him. The marriage, the children, the life." She must have noticed the realization come over my face, the proof that I was taking in her words and putting them together, and that I knew she'd figured out my true feelings for Cory. "McKenzie," she said soothingly, "it's *okay*. You don't have to say anything, do anything, or act a certain way. The truth is, whatever you had with Cory, it doesn't matter anymore. But I don't want you to be trapped in this vision you have of what your grief is supposed to look like. There's no timetable for moving forward. No manual. No instructions. As long as you're still the smart, sweet, bright, and caring girl we raised, your father and I will stand behind you. We just want to make sure you *live*, mostly because Cory can't. And he'd want you to."

"Okay," I said, only because I had no idea how else to respond.

"And until Chelsea is back on her feet and a little more stable, I think it's best if you don't go over there."

"What?" I asked with more force than I intended. "What do you mean?"

"Baby, I just don't want Chelsea to say things to you that she shouldn't. I just know one day she'll feel terrible for the pressure she's putting on you about all this. And I want to spare both of you the pain of going through all that. And honestly, sometimes I think seeing you sets her back."

"Really?" I hadn't thought of that, but looking back on all our interactions over the last month or so, I could totally see what my mom was talking about. "I don't want to hurt her."

"Oh, we know, honey. We know. Daddy and I just want you to be healthy and happy, and right now, the Wallace house isn't a good place for you to be."

"But what about Hayes?"

"You know Hayes is welcome at our house any time."

"But he needs me. I'm the only friend he has here."

My mother held my gaze, staring intently into my eyes, and I never wavered.

"Okay, a compromise. Hayes can come here to visit you if he needs to, and you may go to his house *only* if your father or I go with you."

I thought about all the potential time lost with Hayes if I couldn't go over alone, but then I saw the concern and love written all over my mom's face and I knew I had no reason to argue.

"Okay."

She smiled at me, patted my hand, and then went to the refrigerator, starting to prepare dinner, and it was like the last ten minutes never happened.

Later that evening, alone in my room, I called Hayes. There was so much to talk about, so much to tell him.

"Hey, babe," he answered, the phone only ringing a few times.

"Hey."

"You okay?" It was impossible to hide anything from him it seemed.

"My mom was waiting for me when I got home, and she says she doesn't think I should be at your house until your mom is a little better off than she is now." He was silent for a moment, too long of a moment, but when he finally spoke, it surprised me.

"I agree. The things she said to you were out of line. You already know how I feel about it."

"So, how are we supposed to see each other if I can't come to your house and we can't be seen in public together?"

"I can always come over there?" He sounded unsure of his answer.

"Hayes, you know I love you, but hanging out with you and my parents isn't really the experience I was looking for. This is exactly what I was talking about—this isn't how relationships are supposed to be."

"That's the first time you've told me you loved me in a flippant kind of way." His words were lit up with a smile I couldn't see, but knew was there regardless. The memory of his smile made my heart flutter a little. "It makes me really happy."

And I was a McKenzie puddle.

"You want to go on a date?" He sounded serious, which just made me groan.

"You know we can't go on a date."

"We can in Bellingham."

"Hayes, this isn't funny."

"I'm not joking." Suddenly he was excited, as if the idea was blooming in his mind and he couldn't contain his enthusiasm. "Seriously, have Holly or Becca cover for you, tell your parents you're spending the night with them, and come to Bellingham with me. We can leave tonight and come back tomorrow."

"What about your mom?"

"My mom's been doing okay all week. Still sleeping late, but getting up in the afternoons. She even made dinner last night. She'll be fine for one night."

"I don't know."

"Listen, I'll make up some excuse, and ask your mom to check on her. It's no big deal, really, she's doing better."

His plan sounded a little crazy, a little too sneaky, too dishonest, but my mind grabbed hold of the idea of one whole night with Hayes, and suddenly the need to be with him outweighed the risk.

"Okay," I whispered.

"Okay? You'll go?"

"I'll go."

An hour later we were driving down the interstate in Hayes's Mustang and I couldn't help but feel as though I were a criminal running from the law. I was sure someone was going to catch on to us, see us, or simply put two and two together. Becca had been easy enough to convince to cover for me, although I'd had to promise to tell her why I needed an alibi on Monday. I agreed, knowing I'd have a whole weekend to figure out what to tell her. Part of me wanted to tell her the truth, wanted just *somebody* to know what was going on between Hayes and me. It didn't feel real otherwise.

He'd told me we were going to meet up with a few of his friends and that terrified me. Especially since he said we were meeting up with them at a bar. He'd assured me that they never checked IDs, but I was still a nervous wreck thinking about sneaking around with my boyfriend who I was certainly not supposed to be dating, but also sneaking into a bar when I was completely, 100 percent underage. But I'd also learned from that conversation that I would apparently follow Hayes anywhere and somewhere deep inside of me, I was perfectly okay with that. I knew, on some base level, that he'd take care of me, that I would be safe with him.

He turned his head, looking at me quickly, then turned his eyes back to the road. His hand, which had been firmly planted on my bare thigh the instant we got on the freeway, gave me a gentle squeeze. "You look like you're zoning out on me." He squeezed my thigh again and I figured he knew every time he did that, little bolts of electricity shot through me, causing my lungs to stop functioning and my brain to go muddy.

"No, I'm not. I'm just thinking."

"About what?"

"About how secure you make me feel." His head turned and his gaze caught mine for just a few moments before turning away again. "It's not something I ever really considered before, or ever thought I wanted from someone, until you gave it to me." I shrugged, looking away, my cheeks heating with the embarrassment of letting my words run away with me. "I don't know, it's silly I guess."

"It's not, babe. I'm glad I make you feel that way. I'd never let anything happen to you."

My hand reached for his far cheek as I leaned over the console, and kissed him just below his jawbone. Then, because I could feel the way his heart started thumping and the way his Adam's apple bobbed, I moved my mouth lower.

"Kenz," he squeaked as I slowly moved my mouth over his neck, noticing how great he smelled

238 | Anie Michaels

there. "Babe, seriously, I just vowed to keep you safe, so you can't do this to me while I'm driving a car."

He had a point, so I pulled away. The rest of the drive was spent with some part of him touching me, and I couldn't complain.

We headed straight to the bar and my nerves were bouncing through my body. I wasn't sure if I was going to barf or not from the adrenaline. Surely the bouncer at this bar would take one look at me and either realize I was way too young to drink, or see that I was shaking and hyperventilating and become suspicious.

But there was no bouncer. In fact, there was no one at the door at all. Hayes just opened it and led me inside, his hand wrapped around mine. We walked through a little area that looked like it might have been a coat room, but was now simply covered with papers stapled to every open space. People looking for roommates, furniture for sale, textbooks for sale—a paper stapled to the wall for almost anything you could think of. He pushed through a second door and I was accosted by a wave of loud music. The bass was so loud it thumped my chest, sending vibrations through me.

Hayes didn't stop, he made his way through the bar like he'd been there a thousand times, his hand still firmly gripping mine, and we headed toward the back corner. We had to weave through people because the place was packed. It made sense though, once I thought about it—it was a Friday night in a college town. He pulled me all the way across the dance floor, squeezing between people who were in every state imaginable between respectfully dancing and having sex with clothes on. He brought me all the way to the back of the bar to a table with four people already sitting around it, smiling, laughing, and drinking.

A blonde girl who didn't look a day older than me gave Hayes a wide smile when she saw him.

"Hayes! Oh my gosh, I'm so glad you decided to come down." She hopped off her stool and I was surprised by how tiny she was. Her short blonde hair made her look like a tiny pixie. She moved to hug Hayes and he wrapped his free arm around her, not letting my hand go. The other girl at the table followed suit, a brunette who was much taller and much curvier, and hugged him. Both girls returned to their seats and I noticed their eyes roaming over me. The two guys at the table stood and they all exchanged handshakes followed by back slaps.

"Guys, this is McKenzie, my girlfriend."

Surprise shot through me at his introduction, but I tried to hide it. The last thing I needed was Hayes's friends watching me freak out. I *was* his girlfriend, but I hadn't expected him to come out and tell his friends about us so openly.

"Kenz, this is Alice, Kristen, Bryan, and David."

I waved with my free hand and then shouted, "Hi," in order to be heard over the music.

"David is my roommate," he said pointing to the guy in the middle who had his arm wrapped around the brunette. "He's with Kristen," he said pointing to her. "Bryan majored in history with David and me, and Alice was the barista at the coffee shop we used to always invade."

"Nice to meet you all," I said loudly, still trying to combat the music.

"Sit!" Alice yelled. Hayes let go of my hand and pulled up two chairs that had been abandoned at nearby tables. The table was high and so was the chair. Hayes held out his hand and helped me up and once I was settled he kissed my temple before climbing up onto his chair. When I turned back to the table all four of his friends were looking at us like we'd grown third arms.

"So," Kristen said, her eyes darting between us. "How've you been?" She asked the question expectantly, but not unkindly.

"Good. You know, just taking everything day by day." He reached out to me, threading his fingers between mine.

"How's the teaching going? I know you were worried about having to start over." Alice stirred her pink, fancy-looking drink as she asked the question, her eyes centered on Hayes, seeming to be genuinely interested in his answer.

He shrugged. "It was a little rough at first, trying to work a new concept into my thesis, a new topic essentially, but luckily my anatomy theory can be molded to fit any shape. I just took everything I was using here and applied it to the host teacher's curriculum topic." He laughed and then ran his hand through his hair. "You guys don't want to hear about this stuff."

"You're right," David said without hesitation. "We want to know why you've shown up with a girlfriend none of us have ever heard of."

"Yes," Kristen let out on a loud exhale, while Bryan took a long drink from his beer, looking as though he didn't want to get pulled into the conversation, but was eager to know the answer. Hayes laughed again, a true, sincere laugh, as though his friend's question didn't strike him as rather abrupt like it had me. Hayes obviously thought David's question was funny.

"I've known McKenzie my whole life, but it's just never worked out before now." He looked over at me as he said the words and I was a little dumbstruck by how much love I saw reflected in his eyes, by how much affection the words held. And like he was reading my mind he leaned over to me, wrapped his free hand around the back of my neck, and pulled me into him for a kiss. It wasn't a chaste kiss by any means, but it wasn't obnoxiously inappropriate either. It was slow and soft and completely out in the open. Any person in that bar could have seen him kiss me, and the weight that lifted off me in that moment was heavier than I remembered it being as I carried it around the last month of my life.

He pulled away, smiled at me, and then tucked a piece of my hair behind my ear before turning back to his friends.

"Well, I think I speak for everyone when I say that was ridiculously cute and also it's about freaking time, Wallace." This came from Alice, who was all smiles. Looking at me she continued, "I was afraid he was going to be a bachelor forever. He never really seemed interested in anyone since freshman year."

I thought about the girl, Allison, he said he'd been with. I didn't really know how to respond, so I just smiled.

"Do you want a drink?" Hayes asked, whispering in my ear, making a shiver float down my spine.

"Water?" I wasn't brave enough to drink alcohol. Not that night. Not when it was our first together out in the open. I wanted to be in the moment, even if I was terrified down to my bones to be around his friends, in his environment. I wanted desperately to fit in, to feel as though I could slip right into his life and be a part of it. But I didn't want to drink.

"Sure, I'll be right back." He looked around the table. "Anyone else need a refill?" Both David and Bryan held up their beer bottles, but both girls shook their heads. I watched as Hayes headed toward the bar, then turned back to the group, plastering a smile on my face.

"So, how do you know Hayes?" This came from Bryan, the first words I'd heard from him that night, and they were friendly.

"His mom and my mom have been friends forever. Hayes grew up just down the street from me."

"Oh," Kristen said sadly, "so you knew Cory then? And their dad?"

I nodded. "Cory was my best friend." I didn't add any more information. For once, these people didn't know all the intricate lines drawn between Hayes and me. So I didn't share.

"We're so sorry," Alice said solemnly.

"Thank you." I gave them a small smile, but then tried to redirect the conversation. "So, you guys had classes with Hayes?"

"Well, we had *some* classes with Hayes, but he took them so damn fast that after sophomore year he'd already passed us. But we'd claimed him by then, and we've just never really let him make any other friends," David said with a laugh.

"No joke," Bryan added, "Hayes kicked our asses at learning." Both guys laughed and I found myself laughing too.

"And you two are together?" I pointed between David and Kristen. She immediately held out her left hand and wiggled her fingers at me, one of which held a very pretty diamond engagement ring.

"We're getting married after graduation," Kristen practically squealed.

"Congratulations," I said, with genuine enthusiasm.

"So, what do you do?" Alice asked. My blood froze in my veins. Hayes and I hadn't really discussed what we were going to tell his friends about me, my age, or that I was his student. So, I decided to be vague.

"I'm in school."

"Oh, yeah? What's your major?" she asked, leaning in, truly interested in my answer.

"Uh, I'm undeclared still. I have a few years left." I wanted desperately to get the focus off me and my age. "Are you in school? What's your major?"

"I'm going for my BFA—fine arts." She shrugged like it wasn't a big deal, brushing it off like it meant nothing.

"What does that entail?"

"I'm focused on the visual arts, so painting, ceramics, photography, stuff like that."

"That's so amazing. I'm so not creative in any way." I shook my head, wishing there was something I was good at.

"She's being modest. She's amazing. Her paintings are going for a grand at a studio downtown." Kristen was obviously very proud of her friend.

"That's amazing," I replied, honestly impressed. I'd never met a painter before.

"See?" Kristen said, bumping her shoulder into Alice's. "It's amazing."

"Shut up." Alice smiled then took a sip of her drink.

"So you guys have known Hayes for a few years, then, right?" I asked.

"Pretty much since the beginning," David said.

"He left for college and I never really saw him much. There's a whole side of him I don't really even know." I found myself leaning forward toward Hayes's friends, feeling comfortable, wanting them to give me a little tiny piece of him I could tuck away, something new and special.

"I guess you could say the same thing about us. He never talks about home, and even though he only lived two hours away, he never took any of us there to meet his family," Bryan said, all this while spinning his empty beer bottle on the table. "But that never really bothered us because Hayes is pretty much the best guy we'd ever met. He's loyal, smart, fun, but he's also the one person you know you can always count on. He'd sacrifice everything for someone he cared about."

That I knew. I loved that about him. I nodded, giving them a smile that probably said, "Gosh, what a nice thing to say about my boyfriend." But I felt more like, *his greatest attribute might be his downfall.* He'd sacrificed so much already.

As if on cue, Hayes returned to our table with three beer bottles and my water. He handed them out, took a pull off his own, then sat down next to me, and took my hand in his again. This time it was I who leaned over and kissed him. I was the one who showed him, in front of his friends and the whole world, that I had him, finally.

A few hours later when we made it to his apartment, I was incredibly nervous. We'd spent two nights together, but I knew that night was going to be different. In the timeline of our relationship, a big fat circle would mark this night as important, and I was trying to prepare myself for that.

He held my hand as we walked through the parking lot of his apartment complex, and something about being there with him made him seem older, or me younger. I couldn't quite figure it out, but I definitely felt a shift in the dynamic between us. I was letting him lead, letting him be the one to teach me something new.

"So, you share this apartment with David?"

"Yeah. We moved here last year after a horrible apartment on the other side of town the year before. This place is cool, though. A little far from campus, but that also means there's less loud college students out here."

"And you guys aren't loud college students?" I asked, bumping my shoulder against his.

"Not really anymore. I mean, sure, freshman and sophomore year we might have been a little reckless and rowdy, but that gets old after a while. David calmed down a lot when he and Kristen got together, and I was happy to leave the party life behind." I thought immediately about how he was a whole year ahead in his schooling, how he was focused and driven, which probably left little time for cutting loose and getting loud.

He led me up a staircase to the second floor and stopped at a door toward the back of the building. He let go of my hand to unlock his door, then when it opened he motioned for me to enter first. I dropped my overnight bag inside the door and when he flipped on the light I was instantly transported into a weird alternate reality where Hayes Wallace was an actual adult, with couches and dining room tables and big-screen TVs. I'd never really tried to imagine where he lived because, in truth, I tried not to think much about him at all for self-preservation purposes, but the living space I was looking at in that moment was not how I would have pictured his apartment.

The living room, dining room, and kitchen could all be seen from the doorway, and all three rooms were tidy and clean. The furniture was used but nice looking, it all matched, and there was that same feeling of adultness. I turned to him.

"You're like a real-life grown-up."

He shrugged and gave a shy smile, shutting the door behind him, and turning the lock. He took my hand again as he walked past me, taking me on a grand tour.

"This is the living room, dining room, and kitchen, although I'm not sure how stocked the fridge is, so don't yell at me if I'm out of everything. We'll probably have to go out for breakfast tomorrow." He led me down the short hallway, motioning to the first door on the right. "This is David's room. He's staying with Kristen tonight, so we probably won't see him again before we go back."

He let the words hang in the air and I immediately grabbed hold of them, turning them around in my mind and realizing what he was saying: we were alone for the night.

"Oh," was my incredibly adult response.

His hand squeezed mine, but then he tugged gently and led me to the next door, opening it, and again motioning me in before him. When I walked through the door I knew I was entering Hayes's room immediately because the smell of him moved over me. It was his own scent, nothing I'd ever smelled before, something dark and spicy, but not heavy. Just Hayes. The light came on and I took my time looking around, taking in this new Hayes's room.

There was a desk in the corner that looked a little cluttered, but only because it appeared to be frequently used. There was a bookshelf that held what looked like a mix of textbooks and also books he might read for pleasure in his spare time. There was a closet I imagined you could just barely walk into and turn in a circle, and another door that I could see led to a bathroom.

And then there was his bed.

His headboard was made of wooden slats and they stretched horizontally along the entire king-sized frame. It was a dark mahogany color with a solid footboard that matched. He had a dark gray blanket with the fluffiest pillows I'd ever seen. It looked manly and comfortable all at the same time. I wanted to climb atop it and snuggle down, but I also knew I would have a hard time sleeping a wink in Hayes's bed.

He pressed his body into mine—his front against my back—and rested his chin on my shoulder, his hands on my waist. His words were whispered next to my ear, the breath of them caressing me and making the hairs on my arm stand on end and the swallows in my stomach take flight.

"We don't have to both sleep in my bed, Kenz. I can sleep in David's room if you're uncomfortable. There's no rush or expectation here."

His offer, to sleep away from me, made my heart hurt. The very last thing I wanted was to be apart from him, especially during this one night where we had, what seemed like, a finite amount of time to pretend like we were carefree, like we were normal. I was definitely some messed-up version of Cinderella, and sooner or later, my coach was going to turn back into a pumpkin.

I turned slowly in his arms, my hands automatically coming to his chest, and I looked up at him.

"I would be uncomfortable if you were anywhere but next to me."

He leaned down and I was expecting a kiss, but his mouth went directly to where my neck met my shoulder and he breathed me in. It was a tender moment, a moment in which I felt as though he was treasuring me, committing the two of us together in his room to memory. A moment in which, possibly, he was memorizing what it was like to hold me because he was afraid one day he wouldn't be able to. Or maybe it was me who was doing that.

He walked me backward slowly until the back of my thighs ran into the mattress. He pulled his mouth from me, only to bring his hands to my face, eyes peering into mine.

"You're in charge, Kenzie. We'll take this as far as you want to go. You tell me if you want me to stop."

"I won't want you to stop," I whispered, pressing up on my toes to capture his mouth. He groaned against my lips as soon as our mouths met, and I reached down to pull his shirt over his head. I didn't necessarily want the experience to happen quickly, but I did want to feel his skin pressed against mine as soon as possible. He apparently shared my view on the matter because my shirt was being lifted over my head next. My skirt was pulled down my legs, his pants were kicked off his feet, and we were tumbling together onto his monstrous bed. He was kissing me and I was scooting back, trying to reach the head of the bed, when I suddenly started laughing.

"Your bed is enormous." I finally gave up and flopped down right where I lay. He was leaning over me, hands on either side of my head, holding himself up, gazing down at me. And he was smiling at me as if I were his whole world.

"I love you," I blurted out, the words rising up in me like lava, spilling out, sprouting wings and flying away. "I love you more than anything."

His smile softened, almost disappeared, only to be replaced with the most intense expression of love. I knew how much I loved him, could feel it in every cell of my body, but I also realized his love for me went even deeper. No matter how hard I tried, I'd never be able to love him as much as he loved me.

His elbows bent slightly, and his forehead rested against mine as he let out a soft sigh. "I've always loved you," he said, then pressed a kiss to my throat right below my ear. "I love you now." His next kiss landed just below my other ear. My body arched up into his, just the sensation of his lips on me making all my synapses fire. "And I'll love you forever," he said just before his lips met mine.

Oh, God. He was so much better at love than I was.

He kissed me just as his arm wrapped around my waist, picked me up, and pulled me until my head rested against his fluffy pillows. My knees parted and he settled between them, one hand holding him above me, while the other took its time grazing over my bare skin.

I reached around him, my hands splayed wide over his shoulder blades, moving down, my fingers trailing through the valley of his spine, feeling all the contour of the muscles, the map of his body, until I came to his narrow waist. The elastic band of his boxer briefs slipped easily over my fingers as I explored lower. Both of my hands gripped his rear and he reacted by grinding into me.

"Hayes," I panted between kisses. I'd gone from nervous to completely lovesick to downright needy in the span of minutes. I was reeling from all the emotions. He pressed his hardness into me again, the ridge of him grinding into the most sensitive part of me, and I nearly lost my composure at that very moment.

His mouth moved from mine, down my throat, over my collarbone to the swell of my breast. I lifted up, unhooked my bra, and threw it across the room faster than I ever had before. He didn't waste any time either, as his mouth immediately found my breast. I gasped, lost in the sensation, only spurred on when his hand palmed the other. Everything I was feeling I was familiar with, it was just more intense than ever before. The pulsing, the hot and constant throbbing between my legs, the feeling of stretched-tight rubber bands from my nipples to my core, the way my breasts felt hot and heavy. It was the perfect storm of lust.

His mouth moved from my nipple, kissing down the center of my stomach, looking to me for permission when his lips met the top of my underwear. I nodded and rolled my hips toward him, catching a glimpse of a smile as he pulled my underwear down my thighs.

Hayes pulled the last article of clothing off me and I resisted the urge to cover myself, to hide the parts of me no one had seen before, the parts I was most self-conscious about, but the expression on his face was one of awe and adoration. I realized then, Hayes was the very first person to see me that way; laid bare and completely naked in every way.

"You're beautiful," he whispered, his eyes moving slowly over the expanse of my pale skin that never got any sunlight, a drastic contrast to the parts of me that were tanned from days on the beach. When his mouth landed just below my belly button, my breath caught in my throat and my whole body shuddered. "I want to do so many things to you, McKenzie. But this has to be slow and gentle. I don't want to hurt you any more than necessary." He moved north a smidge and kissed me again, repeating the pattern until his mouth was back to mine.

When his face was back up to mine, my hand reached out for him.

"You're shaking," he observed, taking my hand in his own and bringing it to his mouth, kissing my fingers. "We don't have to do this."

"I'm not shaking because I don't want to, I'm shaking because I do. So badly. I'm just nervous."

"What are you nervous about?" His question was sincere and soft, his eyes still looking into mine.

"I'm nervous that it will hurt. I'm nervous I won't do it right. I'm nervous you won't like it." The truths were spilling from me, and it felt good to speak them, as though some of the tension was released from my chest and I could breathe a little easier for saying them. "I'm worried we'll do it, and then everything will change between us."

He ran the back of his hand down my cheek, a small smile playing on his face.

"Everything will change, but it will only be good. It's hard to explain, but once you've shared your body with someone, it makes everything better."

I tried not to let the jealousy take over knowing he'd shared his body with someone else. I was both angry and happy he'd been with someone before me. At least one of us knew what we were doing.

"I can't tell you if it will hurt or not. But I can tell you if it does, it won't last too long or be too uncomfortable. But," he continued, bringing his hand to cup the back of my neck and lowering his face to mine, our mouths just inches apart. "There's no wrong way to do it, and there's not a chance in hell I won't like it." He kissed me then, softly, one hand still gripping the back of my neck. It was a slow, lingering kiss, and when he pulled away I wasn't ready for it. "This will be a first for me too," he said, resting his forehead against mine. He must have felt my eyebrows bunch together in confusion. "I've never been with someone I was in love with."

His words melted me, absolutely dissolved the worries and fears that had been building up inside me. When he kissed me next, I wasn't the bumbling virgin. I was the McKenzie who'd been in love with Hayes from afar for years, who was finally going to be able to give herself over to him in every way. He kissed me and I pushed his pants down his legs, needing us both to be completely bare. I got them as far as I could and then he finished the job, his mouth never leaving mine.

When it was finally just us, no barriers between our bodies, I pulled away. I let my eyes drift down between us, taking in the sight of him, worried about the logistics and how in the whole wide world *that* was supposed to fit inside of me.

"Hey, look at me," he said, using his fingers to pull my face back up to him. "I promise it'll be all right." He pressed one more kiss to my lips just as gentle fingers grazed my nipple. I gasped, the feather-soft touch causing every nerve ending to come to attention. His hand smoothed over the skin of my stomach and continued until it was between my legs.

He trailed one finger down, parting me, pressing gently in just as his mouth covered the same nipple he'd just teased. With his tongue swirling around me and his finger circling, my eyes fluttered closed and tried to let myself just feel. The way his tongue mirrored his finger, the way his small sounds vibrated against my breast, the way his hand gripped the hair at my nape.

Suddenly his teeth nipped me as he pressed two fingers deep. My back arched, fingers reaching out, trying to find something to hold on to, while a moan ripped out of me. One hand found the sheet at my side and the other threaded through his hair.

His fingers pumped in and out while his palm ground against my clit. His speed built and the tension between my legs was overwhelming. Hot and slick, I was unable to keep still and found my hips moving to his rhythm. He let my breast fall from his mouth and dragged his lips up my chest and throat, breathing heavily against my damp skin.

"Oh, God," I moaned as his mouth landed on my neck, sucking and licking in time with the movements of his hand. "Hayes," I breathed. Each movement between my legs was like an archer pulling the string back on his bow. The tension built. Inch by inch, stroke by stroke, until it was just his fingers that were holding me back from flying.

I came. I soared. I flew.

All while Hayes's forehead pressed to mine and his arm pulled me closer to him. I shuddered, I quaked, but I was never unaware of him or his skin touching mine. He was so close, and I couldn't wait to be closer.

As I floated back down, tremors still making my hands and legs shake slightly, his mouth hit mine. It was a deep kiss, but quick, and then he was gone. I watched as he leaned over to his nightstand and pulled a condom out of the top drawer. My heart, still trying to recover from my orgasm, tripped and then sped forward as my mind processed that this was all really going to happen.

I watched with curiosity and fascination as he knelt between my spread legs, opened the foil wrapper, and rolled the condom down his shaft. It was strange, but watching him handle himself with his strong hands was more erotic than I would have ever imagined. I was still staring at his cock when his mouth met mine again. I blushed, a little embarrassed at my level of fascination but then I remembered what we were doing, why he'd put a condom on to begin with, and a wave of anxiety rolled through me.

His mouth was on mine, one of his hands on the mattress next to my head, his other palming my breast, all the while I could feel him hard, hot, and thick resting against me. I broke the kiss, pulling my face away, simply trying to breathe.

"Tell me you still want this," he whispered, his mouth right next to my ear.

It took a moment, but eventually I nodded, the nerves starting to take over.

"Kenz," he said as his hand cupped my cheek, his face appearing before mine. "You need to say the words, baby. I need to hear you tell me you want this."

His sincerity and gentleness crashed over me and I suddenly remembered why I loved him so much, and why being with him was exactly what I wanted.

"I want this," I said on a breath. "I want you."

He smiled, not the big happy smile, but the soft one that was all too sexy. Then he kissed me. While our lips touched, I felt him position right at my entrance. My heart pounded and I pulled my lips from his, unable to concentrate on kissing him at that particularly life-altering moment. He pushed in a little and I instinctively braced myself for the pain I knew was coming, making every muscle tense.

"Kenzie, try to relax, baby."

"I'm trying," I lied.

He pushed in a little further and I took in a deep breath. There wasn't enough oxygen in the room to fill my lungs.

"Are you all right?" he asked, concern written across his face.

"I'm not trying to be rude, but I just want this part over with." Not only did I want the painful part behind me, I wanted to finally have that connection with him, that bond I'd never forged with anyone else. "I'll be okay," I whispered.

His eyes stayed on mine for a moment longer, but then he pushed in slowly. I wrapped my arms around his shoulders and pulled him down, burying my face in his neck, not wanting him to look at me.

"Breathe, baby," he whispered, and when I took in a deep breath, he pushed the rest of the way in.

There was a stinging sensation at first, and Hayes didn't move even a little, letting me adjust to everything. After a few moments, the most painful part eased, leaving me with only a feeling of being uncomfortably stretched. Finally, after a few deep breaths, I found my voice.

"Hayes?"

He lifted his head and his eyes found mine. "Hey."

"Hey," I said, unable to keep a small laugh from escaping. Here we were, in a monumental moment, and he was making jokes. But I knew it was for my benefit and so the laughter bubbled out of me.

"Are you all right?" he asked, brushing a strand of hair off my face.

"I'll be fine, but I think I need you to move."

"Your wish," he said before kissing me just under my jaw. "Is my command." He followed the words by pressing his face into my neck and then slowly pulling out of me. I gasped, unfamiliar with the sensation, but then he pushed back in, and a different sound broke free from me. A guttural moan, one I hadn't anticipated. It was still slightly uncomfortable—I was very aware it was my first time—but there was pleasure too.

Everything started soft and gentle. He spoiled me with kisses, his hands running tenderly over my body, but slowly the intensity picked up. He was holding back, trying to be gentle, and I both loved and hated it. I wanted, more than anything, for him to enjoy being with me. Before I could voice my concerns, or try to figure out a way to make him come apart just as I had, his voice pulled me out of my head.

"It's everything, Kenz. Everything I've ever dreamed it would be. You feel so fucking perfect." His words were punctuated by his thrusts and his lips kissing various parts of me between them. My hands went to his waist and then smoothed around his back, pulling him closer. My knees opened wider, pulled up higher, and he went deeper. The pain was subsiding, although not gone altogether, but the other sensations were taking over.

The most private part of me, a part that had been unnoticeably empty all along, was now so full of him that I wondered how I'd ever feel whole again. It occurred to me I wouldn't, that I'd forever be empty without him, in more ways than just physically. I'd given him a part of myself that I never wanted back.

We continued the dance and I followed his lead. He made adjustments to my body—moving a leg there or lifting my ass—all the while seeming as though he could never get enough of me. I did what I could, trying to find the things that made him breathless—raising my hips up to meet him, scratching my nails down his ribcage, reveling in watching him fall apart piece by piece.

When he came, it was with one of my legs thrown over his shoulder and his mouth pressed to mine. I'd seen him come before, but this time it wasn't in a dark tent and neither of us were trying to keep our voices down. The sounds he made, the words he used, were enough to make me want to try it all over again. There was a certain level of satisfaction and pride, hearing him grunt out swear words and praise, knowing it was my body he was worshipping. *Me.*

He caught his breath and then he kissed me, deep and long. As if we hadn't just made love. As if he missed me already.

Chapter Twenty

Hayes

It took me a moment to remember where I was when I finally woke up. The bed felt familiar, and I knew before I even opened my eyes it was McKenzie's body I was wrapped around. Then the whole night came back to me. Snapshots filtered through my mind, every one making me smile into her hair. Her laughing. Her dancing with Alice and Kristen. My hand resting on her thigh as we drove to my apartment. Her eyes looking up at me from my bed. Her hair falling around us while she lay on top of me.

It was all so much more than I ever could have hoped for. More than I deserved, I was sure.

I took a deep breath, loving the way her hair smelled mixed with the scent of me on her. I wanted her to smell like me all the time. She stirred, her body moving against mine, and I watched the moment she realized what I had: that we were together. She smiled and then rolled over to face me.

"Hey," she whispered, smiling that brilliant fucking smile I loved, the sunlight painting her shoulders.

"Hey," I replied before leaning forward and kissing her. "How do you feel?"

She shrugged, blushed, and then said, "Wonderful."

My heart leapt at her word, but I wanted a real answer. "How do you really feel?" I asked, running my nose along the bridge of hers.

"I haven't moved much, so I'm not sure. For now, I'm okay. Thank you." She pulled away slightly and I watched as her eyes drifted down to my chest. "Last night was so perfect, Hayes. No matter what happens, or where we go from here, I just want you to know that. It was everything I hoped it would be."

I used my finger to tip her chin back up to me. "Kenz, baby, I'm glad you enjoyed it." I grimaced at my own words, stroking my finger behind her ear to capture some of her hair. *Enjoyed* was a terrible word to use to describe what we'd shared. I hadn't *enjoyed* being with McKenzie—I was whole, for the first time in my entire life. I hadn't even realized I'd been walking around with a part of myself missing, but I had. Being with her was like beginning again. Everything was new. The feel of her skin against mine was like nothing I'd ever experienced. The gratitude I felt for the gift she'd given me was overwhelming. *Everything* was different. "But this isn't the end. This is just the beginning." She smiled at my words then pressed in close again.

We'd never bothered to put our clothes back on and there was something soothing about lying naked with McKenzie while the morning sun filtered in through the window. I trailed my hand up and down her spine, and eventually I fell asleep again.

When I woke McKenzie was missing from my bed, but I heard the shower running. I rolled over, stretching, feeling the strain of a few muscles I hadn't used in a while, groaning about the use of them the night before. I wanted nothing more than to sneak into the shower with her, but the need to protect her overruled my wants. I didn't want to hurt her.

Instead, I snuck into David's room to use his bathroom, and then started a pot of coffee. Coffee was just about all there was in the house. David always spent a lot of time at Kristen's, and since I'd been gone, the fridge was bare.

When Kenzie emerged from the hall with only a towel draped around her, it was all I could do to continue sipping from my mug and not throw her over my shoulder and march back into my bedroom. She walked straight toward me, stopping only when our chests were pressed together. I put my mug down on the counter and placed my hands on either side of her neck while her arms wrapped around my waist.

"Hey," she said, a dreamy smile on her face.

"Hey." I let my thumbs smooth a trail over her jaw.

"I love you." Her words were soft and it looked as though saying them made her almost as happy as hearing them made me.

"I love you too." She moved in closer, resting her cheek on my chest, so I wrapped my arms around her and pressed a kiss to her hair, which smelled like my shampoo. Then I pictured her in my shower, using my shampoo, and I knew we had to get moving or else I really would drag her back to my bed. "Feel like grabbing some breakfast somewhere and then heading back home?"

She tilted her head back to meet my eyes. "Do we have to go back?" Her lips moved into a pout and I'm sure she didn't mean it as such, but it was sexy as hell.

"Unfortunately." My mind wandered to my mom and I hoped she was doing okay with Mrs. Harris. "We can come back soon. We'll figure something out."

She sighed and then rested her face against me once more. "I can't wait until we can just be open about everything. I hate having to hide from everyone. I love you too much to keep it to myself."

I cupped my hands around her face, making sure her eyes were looking into mine when I spoke. "In a few months, when I'm done teaching here, and you're out of high school, and my mom's better, we'll be able to act just like any other couple. It's complicated now, but I wouldn't trade last night for the world, McKenzie. Maybe we had to drive two hours away, and maybe we had to bend the truth to a few people, but being able to hold you in public, to kiss you, dance with you, to take you home to my apartment and make love to you, that was worth everything to me."

"Just a few more months?"

"Then it'll be different," I promised.

"Okay," she whispered. I kissed her, softly but deeply, and then we both got ready to head back to reality.

Still not wanting to be apart, we figured her mom wouldn't be too suspicious if we told her McKenzie had called and asked me for a ride home from her sleepover. And we were all prepared to tell her mom our fabricated story when we got to my house, but instead we were met with a worried Mrs. Harris.

"I'm glad you're home," she said as soon as I put my bag down by the door. "I was just about to call you."

"What's wrong?" I asked, my panic striking fast and hot.

"Everything was good overnight. We even played some cards and watched a movie. We went to bed and I thought we'd had a good time. But now, I went to check on her and she won't talk to me. Won't even acknowledge me. I don't know what happened."

I looked back at McKenzie, who'd stopped just inside the door, hoping to get some invisible strength from her. She looked just as worried as I felt and I wanted to feel her arms wrapped around me, her voice whispering in my ear that everything was going to be all right. Instead, I turned and walked down the hallway toward my mother's bedroom.

I knocked gently on her door, but then pushed it open. She was sitting in the rocking chair she'd placed by the bay window when my brother had been born. We'd heard the stories a million times about how he was a terrible sleeper, so she'd rocked him in that chair all night sometimes, because it was the only place he would sleep.

"Mom?"

If she heard me, she didn't respond. She was just rocking back and forth, staring out the window, eyes lost and unfocused. My eyes scanned the room, looking for any hint as to why she'd had such a drastic setback in just a few short hours. On my father's side of the bed, atop the things he'd usually left there but would never come back for, lay a piece of paper with creases in it, as if it had been folded and inside an envelope. I walked over to it, picked it up, and started reading. I'd only made it one sentence in when it all became clear.

Dear Cory Wallace,

Congratulations! On behalf of the faculty and staff at Central Florida University, it is with great pleasure that we inform you of your admission....

268 |Anie Michaels

I didn't need to read any more.

Kneeling down next to her, I placed my hand on her knee, hoping to break whatever trance she was in. It didn't. In fact, for the next twelve hours my mother seemed nearly catatonic. She rocked in her chair, but wouldn't talk, wouldn't acknowledge anyone else in the room. When the sun went down, I'd gone to check on her and found her in her bed, still awake, but still silent.

McKenzie and Mrs. Harris eventually left. I think McKenzie wanted to stay, to help me with my mother, but Mrs. Harris told her, "Everyone needs some space." I didn't want to think about what would happen if she had caught on to us—if she'd somehow figured out we'd spent the night away together—but those words stuck with me, lodged themselves in the back of my mind, just something else to worry about. When she left, McKenzie wrapped her arms around my neck, hugging me, and I tried to hug her back in the most platonic way possible, knowing her mom was watching us, examining us. But what I wouldn't have given for five minutes alone with her. Just five minutes to feel her and let her comfort me. To just hold her.

Over the next few days, it felt as though we were back at square one. We were on a cyclical loop of mom sleeping, eating, and then sleeping some more. In the middle of the night I'd hear her crying, and I'd check on her. But there was nothing I could do. I'd lost her to the grief again. Everyone was worried, but we were hoping she'd pull out of it again, just like she had before. We just didn't need any more setbacks.

Unfortunately, each night got progressively worse.

Chapter Twenty-One

McKenzie

It was lunchtime, Tuesday, and I hadn't had a moment alone with Hayes since we got back from Bellingham. He'd been dealing with his mom, and my parents both kept me away, afraid that in her grief Mrs. Wallace would lash out at me again.

I looked over my shoulder, stupidly paranoid that someone would see me walking toward the practice rooms and become suspicious. I made it into the equipment room, fairly confident no one had seen me enter, and stood next to the door with the lights off. I pulled out my phone to send a text to Hayes.

Can you meet me in the equipment room? *

It took an agonizing three minutes before he responded.

**I'll be there in a few. **

Time stood still until I heard footsteps coming down the hall. I held my breath when the door opened. It would be easy enough to explain why I'd be in the room with the lights off; I could tell whoever it was I had a headache. But I was a terrible liar, so I hoped it was Hayes.

I saw the silhouette of his broad shoulders and long hair and let out a sigh of relief.

"Kenz?" he whispered.

"I'm here," I replied quietly, standing but not moving. I wanted the door closed tightly behind him before I even attempted to move. The sliver of light that had leaked into the room disappeared as the door clicked closed, and I was immediately pulled into his arms. My hands twined in his hair that was hanging loose that day and I pressed my nose into his neck.

"God, I've missed you," he said, his voice raspy, full of emotion. "These past few days," he started, but paused, squeezing me tighter. "All I've wanted was to have you by my side."

His words shattered my already fractured heart. It pained me to be away from him, especially when I knew he was struggling, but it was obviously hurting him as well. "What can I do?" There was almost nothing to my voice; it was a strangled sound, like fear, anger, and regret squeezed through a funnel.

He pulled back at my words, his hands leaving my back and coming to my face. "You're doing it. Right now. Just by being near me." He brought his lips to mine, and even though the room was dark, my eyes closed. He walked me back until I was pressed against the wall, his tongue gently sweeping into my mouth, his hands sliding down my chest.

It had been a few days since we'd had sex, and I would have been lying if I'd said I hadn't thought about it nearly every second since, but the way Hayes was kissing me in that darkened room was nothing like the way he'd kissed me in his bed.

Before, he'd wanted to share something with me, to show me how much he loved me. But in that equipment room, with the lights off, and the sound of shoes on the linoleum just outside the door, it felt as though he were using me for a distraction. It took me only a moment to come to the conclusion that I was all right with it, that I was happy, even, to let him use me and my body to take his mind off everything else in his world that was troubling him.

I wasn't sure if he could feel my acquiescence, or if he just didn't care that we were just feet away from the very people who could turn his world upside down, but suddenly he became unapologetically intense. His kisses were harder, his hands groped with more force, and I found myself right in the middle of a storm of lust I'd never experienced before.

His knee pushed between my own, pressing my legs apart, while his hands continued to roam my body.

"Did you wear this for me?" he asked as his hand slid over the curve of my ass, right to the edge of the denim skirt I'd put on that morning. Of course, when I'd dressed I'd considered whether or not Hayes might like my outfit, but I never imagined this would be happening. However, that wasn't the answer Hayes was looking for.

"Yes," I breathed. His lips smiled against mine, but I gasped when his hand yanked on the crook of my knee, hauling my leg up and over his hip. He rolled his pelvis into me, his hardness rubbing against my clit, the roughness of his denim no match for the cotton of my panties. I whimpered into his mouth, trying hard to be as silent as possible.

"At night, I lie in my bed and imagine you underneath me again, think of all the ways I can explore your body, and it kills me that you're not there when I wake up." His hand disappeared from my breast and I jumped when I felt it between my legs, slowly moving my panties aside, and gently pushing into me. I didn't have his mouth to swallow my cries, so I bit my bottom lip, hoping to contain the screams wanting to break free. His movements were a strange and addictive mixture of needy and loving. He touched me because he needed to, but he did it with tenderness and gratitude. I'd never felt more desired than in that moment.

My body shuddered at his touch, but my heart filled with hope for the day when waking up in Hayes's arms was a possibility. A day when we weren't hiding in equipment rooms from other teachers or students, or his mother, or my parents.

"What are you thinking, Kenz?" he asked, two fingers disappearing inside of me. I gasped at first, my body reacting to being full again, but then I managed a response.

"I'm thinking that I love you." I managed to say the words, but they were soft, quite nearly a moan. I saw his cheeks bunch slightly and knew he was smiling, but I gasped again as his thumb stroked my clit.

"That's sweet, babe, and I love you too. But my thoughts are a lot dirtier at the moment." All I could do was hold back a cry as he increased the pressure of his thumb, the depth of his fingers. His face moved and suddenly his mouth was at my ear, his words rushing past with fast breaths, making my entire body pulse. "I'm thinking about how wet you were when I slid my fingers inside of you. How you were waiting in this dark room, hoping I'd come here and touch you. You've missed me just as much as I've missed you." His words were like sandpaper scratching against me. I felt them everywhere.

"Hayes." I managed a strangled cry just before I came apart. His mouth slanted over mine, taking any noises from me, as his fingers continued to lazily dip in and out. He dropped my knee and had I not been leaning against the wall I would have toppled over. I was weak and dizzy from him. I lazily reached for his belt, wanting and needing to touch him, to give him the escape he'd given me, but the sound of voices from the hallway caught our attention. They started distant, but grew louder, one voice becoming more prominent than the others.

"I think I left a twenty in the pocket of my uniform last week. I gotta check."

Hayes's eyes became wide and mine mirrored his. Someone, it sounded like a student, was headed toward the room we were in. The room in which Hayes had just fingered me to the point of orgasm.

"Quick," he whispered, stepping away and pulling my skirt down. "Over here." He took my hand and led me to the rack that stretched along the far side of the room. It was wall-to-wall marching band uniforms. He forced me into the corner, behind the curtain of polyester. He grabbed what looked like a tuba case and placed it in front of our feet, hiding them from view, and we pressed our bodies up against the wall as far as we could. Not even two seconds later the door opened and the light switched on.

Hayes's fingers squeezed mine as I heard the footsteps move closer. The rack was probably twenty feet long, but in that moment the room was rapidly closing in on me. The clothes around us moved, and somewhere along the line of uniforms I heard the student rifling through them.

"Josh," came a new voice from the hallway, "if you need money for lunch, I'll spot you five bucks."

Josh Miller. Nice guy. Asked me out freshman year, but I wasn't allowed to date and Cory nearly gave him a black eye. I was sure he'd have loved to find me holding my History teacher's hand in a room that was dark just a few seconds ago.

"It's not lunch, bro. I'm supposed to take Kasey to a movie tomorrow and that was my movie money."

He was slowly making his way down the line. Each second and each uniform that didn't hold a twenty in the pocket brought him closer to us. Bringing Hayes and me closer to being discovered.

Please let him find his twenty.

Pocket by pocket, he slowly made his way toward our end of the room. I was breathing shallowly, hardly enough air to keep me upright, but Hayes was stone-like.

"Got it," Josh said excitedly. "Thank God they never wash our uniforms between performances." There were more rustling noises, but then the sound of footsteps in the hallway got softer and the door clicked shut. We both let out audible breaths. It was a few moments before either of us moved. I was afraid someone would come back, or some other student would wander into the room. But when Hayes's hand pulled out of mine, I knew he was upset.

He kicked the tuba case out of the way and used his arms to part the uniforms, stepping through them furiously. I stayed behind, back pressed against the wall, unable to move.

"This isn't how it's supposed to be." He paced around the room, his hand pushing back his dark brown hair, only to have it flop right back around his face. "This is one big metaphor for our entire relationship, McKenzie. Hiding. We're hiding." He stopped and faced the wall he'd previously pushed me up against. "This is bullshit!"

I was startled by his outburst, and even more taken aback when I saw his hand slam into the wall in front of him. Hayes had never been a violent person and seeing that side of him scared me, but not enough to keep me from going to him.

I pressed my front to his back, wrapping my arms around his waist. He was so much taller than me that my cheek rested right between his shoulder blades. He was practically shaking with anger and I could feel his heart thumping inside his chest.

"This part is only temporary," I whispered, trying to calm him down. "It won't always be like this. It won't always be hard."

"You deserve better than this," he rasped. "You shouldn't be in some dark room, hidden away. You should be out in the daylight, with someone who can stand next to you proudly."

I squeezed him harder. I loved him more for his words, but also hurt for him, knowing it was killing him a little to be in our situation. I turned my head and pressed a kiss into his back through his white cotton shirt. "I love you, and I'd rather be here in the dark with you than out in the light with anyone else."

He let out a sigh as one of his hands covered mine, twining his fingers through mine on his chest. "That's what I'm afraid of."

Chapter Twenty-Two

Hayes

At first it was just crying. Then it turned into screaming. By Wednesday evening it was nothing short of night terrors. She was screaming and practically nothing we could do would wake her. Thursday morning, as the sun was rising, I was rocking my mother back and forth as she came out of her dreamlike state, as she sobbed, crying for the son she'd lost. I resisted the urge to shake her, to bring her face right in front of mine and simply wake her up, to scream at her, "I'm still here! You haven't lost everyone and I still need you!" But somehow I managed to maintain my composure.

I knew she missed my father too, she had to, but most of her grief was focused on Cory. Part of me was afraid once she finally pulled out of this, she'd start all over when she realized she'd never really mourned my father.

Juggling my mother, teaching at the high school, McKenzie, and everything else that came along with a house and two deaths, had me exhausted by Thursday afternoon. I sat at my kitchen table. Mrs. Harris sat across from me, waiting for me to make a decision. I was supposed to be in Bellingham in three hours for my bi-weekly meetings with my cohorts, but I was exhausted and worried about leaving my mother alone for another night.

"I'm worried about you driving, Hayes. You look exhausted."

I scrubbed my hands over my face, trying to force some life back into me, to rouse the backup reserves I knew were stored in me somewhere. "I'll be fine. Honestly, I think I can get there all right. It might be the drive back that gives me trouble."

"So, go and stay the night. I'll be here all night anyhow."

"Don't you have to work tomorrow?"

She shrugged. "I can take a day off. It's not a big deal."

"It is a big deal," I said, looking her in the eye, trying to wrap my head around how much she'd done for my mom since my father and Cory died. She'd always been around, *always* been a surrogate aunt, the woman I saw just as much as my mom, who I knew cared just as much about me as she would someone actually related to her. And as one did with family, I'd taken her for granted. I probably still was. But I didn't want to. "Thank you."

"Tell you what," she said, reaching a hand out to mine, giving it a squeeze, then pulling away. "Why don't you take McKenzie?" My eyes snapped up to meet hers, surprise coursing through me, followed closely by panic. "She could drive you there, you could rest, and then you could both come back tomorrow morning."

She was looking at me, her eyes never wavering from mine, but it was almost as though she was trying to say more with her eyes than her words. She was smiling, just slightly, and I was utterly confused.

"You want me to take McKenzie with me?"

"I want you both safe and happy," she replied with honest sincerity.

I wasn't brave enough to ask her to confirm, but it was that moment where I suspected Mrs. Harris knew I was in love with her daughter.

"McKenzie can get you there safely, and I trust you to make her happy."

Fuck. She definitely knew. I opened my mouth to—I didn't know—explain myself? Defend our relationship? To convince her that it definitely couldn't be what she thought it was, but she held up her hand and stopped me.

"It's *okay*, Hayes," she said softly.

"We'll be back tomorrow morning," I said, trying to reassure her but I wasn't sure of what. She'd basically just told me she trusted me with her daughter, but for some reason that wasn't enough. I wanted to prove to her that I was *best* for McKenzie. That no one could love her the way I did. In that moment, something inside me snapped and no matter what happened next, I wasn't going to let her mother think any less of our relationship. "Look, I love her, Mrs. Harris. I've loved her for a long time. This isn't something either of us fell into lightly, and she was never unfaithful to Cory."

She reached her hand out to me again, but this time leaving it there, gently rubbing mine. "Sweetie, I know you and I know my daughter. Neither of you would do anything to hurt people you care about. If you love her like I think you do, then you want her to be as happy as I do, and she's happiest with you."

"You can't tell my mother."

She slowly pulled her hand away. "I agree that right now is not the best time for your mom to hear about the two of you, but when she does find out, it shouldn't be from me. You should be the one to explain to her how you feel about McKenzie, but not until she's mentally well enough to think clearly about what this all means."

"So you won't tell her?"

She shook her head. "I don't think it's best for her right now."

I let out a huge sigh of relief. Not only was it a relief to hear that she wouldn't tell my mother, but the feeling of weight lifting off my shoulders, the release of tension now that somebody knew about us, was incredible.

"Thank you," I said, and it might have been the most sincere thing I'd said to anyone. I was thankful for her compassion and her understanding, for not judging us or trying to convince us that what we were doing was wrong. "Your support means the world to me."

"Just take care of my girl. Be good for her."

I nodded. It was all I could do.

Ten minutes later I was knocking on Kenzie's bedroom door, both anxious about the night away from my mom, but also elated to have some sort of stamp of approval from her mother. Her bedroom door opened and I watched the surprise sweep over her face as I moved into her room, forcing her to step back.

"Hayes," she managed, but that was all she got out before I pulled her into me and then spun around to press her back against the door.

"Pack a bag," I said, my eyes meeting hers, my hands coming to rest on her waist. "You're coming with me to Bellingham." Her eyes went wide. "My meeting is tonight. Soon, actually, so we need to get a move on. But your mom suggested you come with me."

"My mom?" she was just as shocked as I had been at the suggestion.

"She knows," I whispered, moving my face into her neck, trying to breathe in the scent of her. "She figured it out and she's all right with it."

"*She knows?*"

I nodded my head, my nose moving along the skin of her neck, and I could feel her shiver slightly against me from the touch.

"She just told me she knows we're together and she wants you to be happy." McKenzie was silent for a few moments, so I took the time to slide my hands up her back, bringing her body flush with mine, and to press my mouth into the crook where her neck met her shoulder. "She said you could come with me. Practically insisted."

"Okay," she breathed, her hands moving slowly up my arms, over my shoulders, and threading through the hair at my nape. I moved my lips up the column of her throat, loving the way her back arched and her hips pressed into me, but I had to pull away. Even though I wanted nothing more than to bury myself in her, we had to leave, and I would have wanted more than three minutes with her had we continued.

"I'm going to finish this later," I said, kissing the underside of her chin. "But right now I need you to throw together an overnight bag." I kissed her quickly on the mouth, not nearly long or deep enough, but I didn't want to lose focus. "I'll meet you over at my house as soon as you're ready, okay?"

"All right," she said, leaning her weight back against the door, my fingertips sliding off her skin. "I'll be over in a few." She stepped away from the door, letting me pull it open, and I left her house feeling lighter than I had in days.

Chapter Twenty-Three

McKenzie

Hayes slept most of the way to Bellingham. There was something that struck me as sweet about him sleeping while I was driving. He'd started the drive with his hand on my thigh, and it had stayed there most of the trip. I'd never tire of having Hayes touch me while he slept. I kept the radio low and enjoyed the quiet drive. The soothing sounds of the music playing softly and the road whizzing by outside the window lulled me into a sense of ease I hadn't had in weeks. In the quiet there was calm.

Twenty minutes from his campus I woke Hayes up and we decided I would drop him off at his meeting and head to a coffee shop just down the street to work on some assignments I'd brought with me, and then we'd meet back up and head to his apartment.

I pulled up in front of the cafe where he had his meeting and he pressed a fast kiss to my cheek, said a hasty good-bye, then hopped out of the car and practically ran to the door. I smiled watching him, loving the fact that he seemed a little lighter too.

I found a vacant table in the corner of the coffee shop and settled in, hoping to make a dent in my work. Hayes had been busy all week trying to bring his mother back from the darkness she had fallen back into, and I hadn't really been able to see him much. The only bright side to that was I'd nearly completed all of my make-up work. The sooner I finished the last few assignments, the sooner I felt like I could close the door on that part of my life with a little more force.

I would always love Cory; of that I was sure. But I couldn't help but feel there were still parts of my life tying me back to him. And even though homework seemed inconsequential, I wanted that whole terrible period of my life behind me. I wanted desperately to look forward, to have the excitement of what was to come fill me, not the dread of the painful things that had happened in the past.

So with my papers spread out, book open wide, and earphones plugged in, I set out to finish the last few things I was tasked with. The time flew by and the focus came easily. I let out a breath and slumped back into my chair, taking a moment to look around.

What I hadn't told Hayes, what I'd kept to myself while I watched him struggle with his mother and battle the darkness right along beside her, was that the same day Cory had gotten his acceptance letter to Central Florida University so had I. So when I looked around the coffee shop, I imagined myself there in a year, in two years, three even, and I could picture myself spending countless nights at this very table. I pictured Holly and Becca with me, because they'd gotten in too, but the image of Hayes was blurry.

We'd been clinging to each other for the past few weeks, simply grasping on to each other so fiercely we'd never really loosened our hold to look around to try and see if we even really fit together.

From behind me I heard a knocking and when I turned I saw Hayes's smiling face on the other side of the window. He looked tired, but also happy. He walked to the door then headed straight for me.

"Hey," he said, a little out of breath, but bent to press a kiss to my mouth just before taking the empty seat across from me.

"Hi." I smiled at him, warmth spreading through me. Being seen in public was still a novelty, so to have him kiss me in front of other people was something I wasn't used to. It was the best.

"Get a lot of work done?"

I slammed my textbook closed for emphasis and said, "Finished."

"With everything?"

"One hundred percent caught up."

"That's amazing, Kenz."

I shrugged. "I'm just glad it's done." I watched him run a hand through his hair and he let out a sigh. "How was the meeting?" He leaned forward and rested his elbows on his knees.

"Pretty much the same as the last one. We talk about what's going well, talk about issues we have and get advice from each other."

"Sounds helpful." I had no idea what else to say. He was a graduate student and I hadn't even made it through high school yet. I had no words of wisdom on how to best approach anything he was dealing with.

"The meetings are required. At the beginning of the program it was really helpful to have a group of people tackling the same issues as you were, and an experienced mentor to help guide the way. But I kind of feel like if you don't have it by now, you were never going to get it." He shrugged as if teaching were like riding a bike, or learning how to surf. That, perhaps, it didn't take a special kind of person to stand in front of a room full of teenagers and try to make them care about something like World War II. "The best part of the meetings is when the advisor leaves to go home and the grad students all go out for a beer afterward." A smile crept over his face as he said the words and there was a flutter in my belly.

"Did you want to go meet up with them? I can just stay here, or go back to your place. Is David home? He could let me in...." I let my words trail off, hoping Hayes would jump in and tell me what he wanted.

"David won't be home tonight. I told him we were coming so he is staying with Kristen."

I felt the flush move up my neck and over my face, warmth spreading all over me. "Oh" was my only response.

"Is that okay with you? I mean, I've gotten beers with my cohorts twice a month for almost a year. I'd rather just go home and be with you."

"That's perfect." I packed up my things, trying to ignore the nervous flipping in my belly. I stood, attempting to sling my messenger bag strap over my shoulder, but Hayes took the bag from me, and then grasped my hand, his fingers twining through mine while his thumb traced circles on the back.

We walked out of the coffee shop, hand in hand, and the smile on my face had never been as wide or as embarrassingly obvious.

"Where'd you park?" he asked, looking at me. His ridiculous smile matched mine. It was hard to believe we were just walking down the street, holding hands, as if it were the easiest and most normal thing ever. And, in fact, it was. I thought for a moment about how my mother knew about us, and how we were just one step closer to being this normal couple. For just one instant, just that one flittering moment in time, I had hope. Hope for Hayes and me, that we'd have many more nights of walking down the street holding hands, not hiding from anyone, not having to tamp down our love.

"Just around the corner," I whispered, leaning into his side, wrapping my free hand around his bicep, keeping step with him. When we made it to his Mustang he led me to the passenger side and then opened the door for me. Before I climbed in, he pulled me toward him, pressing my hand wrapped in his against the small of my back, and covered my mouth with his. It was a slow and sweet kiss, but people were walking past us on the sidewalk, the streetlight above us illuminated the somewhat chaste kiss, and that was exciting.

"I missed you," he said before his lips were entirely disconnected from mine. I pressed my lips to his again, firmer, with more force. I heard him inhale sharply, then he moved into me, pressing me back against the car. I heard my bag hit the passenger seat and just after he released my hand from his, he was cupping my face. He kissed me hard, and I let him take the lead, let him give me whatever he wanted.

"I'm right here," I said between breaths, between lips and kisses and touches. He pulled away and we were both panting, clinging to each other.

"It feels so right to be with you. But it's so right, so perfect, I sometimes feel as though it's temporary. Like a bright, hot-burning star. The brighter the star, the shorter the lifespan." He rested his forehead against mine, running the back of his fingers down my cheeks and over my neck. "I'm afraid you're going to slip through my fingers."

"Then hold on to me tightly." It could have been an off-the-cuff remark, could have just been the silly reply in the heat of the moment. But, no. I begged him. My hands came up to grip his wrists. "Please, whatever you do," I said, my voice still a soft panic. "Don't let me slip away."

He kissed my forehead, breathing me in, then pulled back. "Let's go." I stared up into his eyes for a moment, then slid away from him and climbed into the car. The drive to his apartment was quiet, but his hand was wrapped in mine the whole way there. My main focus was the future. We had to have a future. We needed to make plans. I knew if we sat down and discussed what would come next, it would ease my mind a little.

Once inside his apartment, I watched as he looked through a stack of his mail then walked to his fridge. "Do you need anything? Water? I've got beer, too. Nothing else, really." He looked at me sheepishly.

"I'm fine. But, do you think we could sit and talk for a minute?"

He closed the fridge and gave me a concerned look. "Sure. Is everything all right?"

"Yeah, I just have a few things to tell you." I tried my best to give him a confident smile, but on the inside I was being torn up from all the nerves. He led me to his bedroom and we sat on the edge of his bed. I couldn't help but glance behind me, looking at the place we'd been together the last time he'd brought me here. Memories of that night flooded my brain and I could feel my cheeks blushing. His fingers gently gripped my chin and he brought his eyes level with mine.

"Don't fade out on me now, Kenz. What's up?"

I took in a deep breath and then decided to just spit the words out. "I got accepted to Central Florida University, and I just wanted you to know. I don't know exactly what your plans are for next year, or the next four, but it looks like I'll be here. I'm not expecting anything from you, but I'm hoping there's a way to make this work because I'm not ready to give you up just yet."

His fingers tightened on my chin slightly, not allowing me to look away from him. "You got your college acceptance letter? Babe, that's amazing. I'm so proud of you." He leaned in and kissed me gently, his hand moving from my chin to cup the back of my neck. "That's a big deal, McKenzie." His words were warm and sincere, and I let out a small breath of relief. "You're going to love it here."

"What does this mean for us?" I asked with more bravery than I realized I had. "Whatever your answer is, I'll accept it. But I can't sit on your bed kissing you if I don't know what's happening down the road."

"You're going to go to school here and I'm going to try to find a job here. Nothing will change, Kenzie, except that we'll be able to really be together."

"What if you can't find a job here? What if the only job you can get is far away?"

"We can't think about the what-ifs, babe. You asked me what my plans were, and the only thing I see in my future is you. I'll stay in my apartment, you'll live in the dorms with your girlfriends, and next year is going to be great. The best year of your life, I bet." He played with a loose tendril of my hair, then said, "We just have to be sure to always make our relationship a priority. You're going to get busy, and I'm definitely going to get busy, but we need to try to remember us, right now, worried we'll grow apart, and make sure it doesn't happen. "

Chapter Twenty-four

Hayes

A loud buzzing noise woke me, startling me from sleep. Kenzie's warm body was draped over mine, our legs intertwined, her face resting on my chest. It was the best way to wake up—aside from the buzzing. I gently eased out from under her limbs, trying hard not to wake her. I made it off the bed and she rolled away from me, her hair trailing across my pillow, bare back on display, blanket only covering her from the waist down. It was practically every fantasy I'd had since I was twenty— to wake up next to McKenzie Harris. To be allowed to see her uncovered and bare. The gift she gave me every time I was allowed to touch her, to be with her, was something I'd never be able to repay her for or give back to her. The simple gift of her was priceless.

I found my jeans on the floor and dug around in the pockets for my phone, the darkness not helping. When I finally got hold of it and powered up the screen, my heart immediately started pounding in my chest. Ten missed calls. Twenty-seven new text messages. Something was wrong.

Every single call and text was from Mrs. Harris. I didn't bother listening to the voice mails or reading the texts, I simply called her back. The phone rang as I stepped into the hallway, but it only rang once.

"Hayes?"

"Mrs. Harris, what's wrong?"

"Oh, Hayes," she cried. Immediately my lungs shut down and my heart skipped a million beats. "It's your mom...." Her words trailed off because she was crying too hard to continue.

"What is it? Is she all right?" I was panicking, pacing the length of my living room, but also flashing back to the night Mr. Harris had called me and told me to come home. The night Cory and Dad died. "Did she... is she...."

"She's alive, Hayes. But you need to come home. She was taken by ambulance to the hospital. I don't know if she'll...."

"I'll leave right away," I said hastily, heading back into my bedroom. "Please, promise me you'll keep me posted." I flipped on the light, sorry I had to wake McKenzie that way, but unable to move slowly. "I can't handle driving home again not knowing if she's dead or alive. Please, Mrs. Harris."

"I'll text you when I know something." Her words sounded sad, I knew she didn't want to have to tell me my mother had died. I was hoping she wouldn't have to either.

"What happened?" This came from McKenzie, who'd been woken up by the light and my voice. She sat up in the bed, her hair falling around her face, her eyebrows scrunched inward with worry. I pressed the speaker button on my phone.

"My mom was taken to the hospital," I said as I pulled on my jeans.

"McKenzie?" Mrs. Harris asked. I was definitely focused and panicked, but not enough to at least consider how odd it was that McKenzie was naked in my bed and her mother was on speakerphone. But it was a minuscule part of my brain concerned with that, and the majority worried about getting back to my mother, making it to her before something catastrophic could happen.

"I'm here, Mom," she replied, sliding off the bed and pulling on her clothes.

"I need you to drive Hayes home, sweetie. He shouldn't be driving right now."

"Mom, what happened?"

I heard Mrs. Harris take in a deep breath, could hear it shaking even through the phone, but I was relieved when she continued talking. "I checked on her around 5:00 p.m. and she was asleep. A few times throughout the night I heard her get up, but she never called for anyone or came into the living room, so I assumed she was just using the restroom or something. I didn't want to bother her because I know she's been having a hard time...." Her voice trailed off as she started crying. "I fell asleep on the couch, and when I woke up around midnight, I went to check on her."

I heard her sniffling and sobbing, and my panic started to intensify. I needed my mom to be okay. I needed to get to the hospital and see my mom sitting up in bed with a smile on her face, apologizing to everyone for scaring us. I needed her to live and thrive because I didn't think I could handle being the only person left alive.

"Mom," McKenzie said, trying to calm her mother from such a great distance. "It's okay. Everything's going to be okay."

"She was lying on her bed, but she looked strange. Her head was hanging off the edge and it looked uncomfortable. I didn't understand, I just walked in to try and help her, and that's when I saw the bottle. And the pills."

No.

No.

"Oh, my God," McKenzie said, her hand coming to cover her mouth, her eyes darting to me, wide with fear and understanding. I felt my legs give out and luckily I was near the bed, landing with a thud, my elbows coming to rest on my knees while my head fell into my hands. Immediately Kenzie's arms were around me, her face pressed into my neck, one hand running up and down my back.

"She still had a heartbeat when the paramedics took her away, Hayes."

I scrubbed my hands over my face, adrenaline pumping through me so thoroughly, I could feel my knees starting to bounce. "We have to go," I whispered.

"Okay," Kenzie said, her hand threading through the hair at the back of my neck. "Which hospital are we headed to, Mom?"

I listened as McKenzie took the lead. She gathered information, soothed her mother, brought me the rest of my clothes, hung up the phone, finished dressing herself, and then led me to my car. She drove us through the night, the two-hour drive seeming as though it were stretched out to days and days. We got four updates from McKenzie's mom, but none of them lifted the weight off me or made me feel any better.

She's still back with the doctors. Haven't heard anything.

Nurse came out to update me, said she was still unconscious, they're running blood tests.

She's finally being admitted.

She's upstairs in the ICU. Room 415. I haven't been able to see her since I'm not family.

McKenzie drove fast, not slowing down for anything, and it was amazing she never passed any cops as she would have been pulled over for sure. We were both mostly quiet, but every once in a while she'd say something to try and make me feel better.

"She's going to be fine, Hayes."

"Everything will work out. We just have to believe she'll be all right."

I said nothing. I stared at the road, watching the lines on the pavement pass us by, a steady rhythm, a pulsing that kept me grounded. If I were quiet, if I were still, I could upset nothing. Everything, my entire life, seemed to be dangling from just my fingertips, flailing over a dark abyss, and I knew if I moved, if I spoke, I risked upsetting the cosmic balance. So I stayed quiet and still, the only thing about me in motion was my brain.

When we pulled up to the hospital, McKenzie stopped at the front doors, put the car in park, and then leaned over to me.

"No matter what you learn when you walk in there, I am here, Hayes. I'm here, I love you, and I'll be here to walk with you through whatever happens next."

I turned to look at her, silently grateful for her words and simply for her. I kissed her, but still spoke no words, before I climbed out of the car and walked into the hospital, wondering if tomorrow would be the first day I'd wake up without a mother.

Chapter Twenty-Five

Hayes

The time passed just as slowly in my mother's room as it had in the car: painfully so. Each beep of the machine, each thump-thump of someone's feet as they walked past her room, each tick of the clock above the door, all the noises only intensified the fact that everything was happening in slow motion.

I'd inquired about my mother at the registration desk of the hospital. The woman behind the desk gave me instructions on how to find her, and I'd listened, but I was surprised I'd retained any of the information. I'd managed to find the ICU and the nurse there had led me to my mother's room once verifying our relationship.

I opened the door to her room and was both shocked and relieved by what I saw. My mother was sleeping—the same thing she'd been doing for weeks now. Sleeping. But this time she was sleeping in a hospital, her wrists restrained, cuffed to the side of the bed.

"That's for her own protection," the nurse had explained when she'd seen my eyes go wide. "She's been unconscious since she was brought in so we haven't been able to evaluate her mental state. We don't want her to wake up and do anything to harm herself."

I nodded because it made sense, but I wanted to cry from the logic.

My mother had swallowed enough sleeping pills to kill herself.

Enough sleeping pills to slow her heart rate to the point of near death, to cause the hospital to pump her stomach, to fill her veins full of drugs to counteract what her system had already absorbed.

The nurse explained everything she could, but then left us, telling me she'd let the doctor know I was there. "It's a waiting game now, honey," she'd said with a softness to her voice that felt a lot like pity.

When the doctor had showed up, he'd not really told me anything new or worthwhile.

Mom would pull through, but the effects of the drugs she ingested weren't the real worry. The real and immediate danger was the fact that she'd taken them to begin with. She was breathing on her own, they'd been able to get her heart rate up, she'd been intubated, but after receiving medication from the hospital, she'd quickly started breathing over the machine, so they took her off it. Now, they were just waiting for her to wake up on her own.

I sat in the uncomfortable chair just to the side of her bed, and I watched her sleep. I hoped she wasn't dreaming, hoped that she was, for just a moment, blissfully unaware of all the pain she'd obviously been living with. I hoped she was just resting. Existing. Perhaps healing. Because she'd done none of that so far.

And I was partly to blame for that.

How many times had I left her? To what? To finish a degree? To continue to live my life like nothing had happened while she obviously lost her mind? I thought back to every time I pushed my mother's problems aside, every time I passed her off to someone else, every time I told myself she'd be fine.

It was all my fault.

Eventually I fell asleep in that uncomfortable chair, and when I woke up, it was to my mother's frail voice calling my name.

"Hayes," she whispered, obviously afraid, sounding terrified. "Hayes."

I sat up and moved the chair to her bed, as close as I could get, and rested my hand over hers still strapped to the bed.

"Hey, Mom," I said, my voice wavering, throat tightening, and eyes welling. "I'm glad you're awake."

"Where am I?" Her eyes were flitting around the room with panic.

"You're in the ICU at the hospital. Mrs. Harris found you unconscious last night, so she called an ambulance." I watched as my mother tried to mentally piece together what I was saying. I reached forward and pressed the button on the side of her bed and in just a few seconds a voice rang out.

"Nurse's station, can I help you?"

"Yes, my mom has woken up. Can someone please let her doctor know?"

"Of course."

I grasped my mother's hand and felt her try to grasp mine in return, but her grip was weak. "Someone will be here soon to explain everything, Mom. But I promise, everything is going to be okay. You don't have to worry about that. Trust me."

She nodded silently, obviously still petrified, and I couldn't help but feel like our roles were more reversed in that moment than ever before. I was her caretaker, and I had to make sure I did everything in her best interest. She needed to get better and I needed to help her. She obviously wasn't going to be able to do it alone, and I felt like a horrible son for ever imagining she could.

Mom was quiet for the few minutes it took for a nurse to come check on her. The door opened and a new face appeared, smiling brightly.

"You're awake," she said as she approached my mother, looking at the monitor she was hooked up to. "How are you feeling?"

"I'm tired. And I feel like I can hardly hold my head up. My throat hurts a little. Other than that, I'm all right." She looked at me for just a moment, but then glanced back to the nurse, who was wrapping a blood pressure cuff around her arm. "Why am I bound to the bed?"

"You've had a rough night," the nurse answered as she studied the monitor, the cuff inflating with air. "The doctor will be in soon and he'll explain everything."

My mother was either satisfied with her answer, or didn't have the energy to ask more forcibly. Her head fell to the side, seeming to relax into the bed, accepting whatever was happening and that she was not in control of it.

"Everything looks good here, Mrs. Wallace. The doctor should be here very soon to talk to you."

"Thank you," I said as the nurse moved toward the door. She gave me a sad smile and then left us alone again.

"I'm so tired, Hayes," Mom said, her eyes closing.

"I know, Mom. I know."

It was ten minutes later when the door opened again. A man walked in who looked exactly how I would picture a doctor. Tall, glasses, white lab coat, stethoscope around his neck, pens in his front pocket. With him was a woman who looked professional, but didn't have the automatic designation of a medical professional. She smiled warmly at my mother while the man walked straight for the machines she was hooked up to.

"Mrs. Wallace, we're glad to see you awake and alert. My name is Dr. Stevens, I'm the attending on the floor today. This is Dr. Andrews," he said, motioning to the woman standing next to him.

"She's the resident psychiatrist." They both nodded at my mother, obviously not able to shake her hand, but they did reach out to me.

"I'm Hayes, her son."

"It's good that you have some support here," Dr. Stephens said. "Let's talk a little bit about why you're here, shall we?" My mother nodded and he continued, using the mouse and keyboard to bring up my mother's information on the screen. "You were brought in last night by ambulance, unresponsive, with low vitals. Someone at the scene said they'd found you with an open pill bottle and called for help. Upon arrival you were intubated, your stomach was pumped, and we administered intravenous drugs to counteract the pills you'd ingested. The pill bottle was provided by whomever was with you at the time."

"Luce," my mother whimpered, tears forming in her eyes. One slid down her cheek and I reached up wiping it away for her.

"How are you feeling now, Mrs. Wallace?" This was from Dr. Andrews.

"Please, call me Chelsea." She took in a deep breath and then let it out. "Honestly, I'm really embarrassed. And tired. And sad." Her voice cracked on the last word, and the next sentence was taken over by sobs. "I'm really, really sad."

Dr. Andrews reached her hand out and ran it slowly along my mother's shin, saying, "In order for us to figure out what's best for you, both physically

306 | Anie Michaels

and mentally, we're going to have to have a tough conversation, Chelsea. But I want to assure you, whatever you're feeling, however you got here, it's okay. You're going to have to be really honest, though. Both with Dr. Stevens, and with myself. Do you think you can do that?" Mom nodded. "That's great." Her eyes darted to me. "As a rule, I require this first conversation to be handled privately."

"I'm not going anywhere. That's how we got in this mess."

"Hayes," my mother's weak voice rasped. "This isn't your fault. Not even a little bit. And honestly, the last thing I want is for you to hear all this." Another tear slipped down her face, but before I could wipe it away she used her shoulder to awkwardly dry the stray tear. "I'll be okay."

I studied her, tried to make sure she meant what she said, that she wasn't just telling me what she thought I wanted to hear.

"I'm just going to go to the cafeteria to get some coffee. I'll be back in a few minutes." She nodded as I stood, and I watched her try to be outwardly strong, as if she was just holding on until I left the room, waiting to have some sort of breakdown as soon as I was out of earshot. I leaned down, pressing a kiss against her forehead. When I stood back up she turned her face away, and I took that as my cue to leave.

I walked down the hall, having no idea where exactly I was headed, and passed a waiting room.

Mrs. Harris was sitting on one end of an uncomfortable-looking couch, and McKenzie was lying down, her head resting on her mother's lap. Both of them looked to be asleep.

"Shit," I whispered, angry with myself for not even thinking about the fact that of course they'd be waiting all night for an update. I turned toward them and Mrs. Harris must not have been completely asleep because her eyes popped open at the sound of my footsteps and she immediately shook McKenzie's shoulder until she lifted her head.

When McKenzie's eyes met mine she jumped up from the couch and ran right into my arms. I didn't waste any time wrapping around her and burying my face in her hair. She smelled like home. Everything about her made me feel whole, especially the way she fit perfectly inside my arms.

She pulled away and linked both of her hands with mine, looking up at me expectantly.

"I'm really sorry I didn't come out here and update you guys. It was kind of a strange and overwhelming night."

"How is she?" Mrs. Harris asked, coming to stand behind Kenzie.

"She's in with the doctor and the psychiatrist. She woke up just a little while ago and seems upset, but okay." I let out a large sigh. "They strapped her wrists to the bed."

"Oh, Hayes," Mrs. Harris said, her words dripping with sympathy. "I'm so sorry."

I shook her words off, stepped back, pulling my hands from McKenzie's and running them through my hair.

"It's okay. I'm okay. I was just going to get some coffee."

"I'll come with you," Kenzie said, stepping closer to me again.

"No." I shook my head, looking down at the floor. "No, you and your mom should go home. My mom is fine medically. But I don't think she's up for visitors, and she's talking to the shrink right now. You guys should go home and get some sleep." I steeled myself for her touch when her hands gripped my t-shirt, effectively pulling me into her.

"Hayes," she said softly, "I don't want to go home. I want to be here, with you, to help."

Without touching her I raised my eyes to meet her gaze. "There's nothing for anyone to do. It's probably going to be a long day. You guys should go home."

Mrs. Harris stepped up behind McKenzie and put her hands on her daughter's shoulders. "Come on, let's give them some time, sweetie."

McKenzie looked hurt and confused, and it took everything in me not to reach out, pull her close, and tell her all the manic thoughts running through my mind. I wanted to explain to her why I was pushing her away, but I knew it would just make her cling to me tighter. This was better. For everyone.

"Tell your mom I love her, and that I'll be waiting to hear from her when she's ready."

I nodded at Mrs. Harris, and watched as she steered McKenzie out the door. They left and I let out a sigh. It was going to be a long day.

Forty-five minutes later when I peeked my head into my mother's room, I saw her lying on her side, hands tucked up underneath her head. Relief coursed through me knowing they'd let her out of her bindings.

"Hey," I whispered as I stepped into the room. Her eyes opened and she gave me a sad and weak smile.

"Hey, honey."

"How'd it go?"

"They decided I wasn't a threat to myself or anyone else. I'm being moved out of ICU soon. But I have to stay one more night for observation."

I walked around her bed and sat in the chair just next to her. I leaned forward, exhausted, and rested my elbows on my knees, bringing my chin to rest on my clasped hands.

"Mom?" I finally said.

"Yeah, baby?"

"Will you tell me what happened?"

She held my gaze for a few moments before she eventually looked away. I didn't know what was going to come next, if she was going to tell me or push it away. It felt as though we were in limbo, unable to go anywhere from there, unable to move forward unless something changed.

"Before I explain everything, I want you to know that I never wanted to die." Her words were strong and clear. In fact, they were the strongest words I'd heard her speak since we lost Cory and Dad. The strength in her voice surprised me, made me sit up straight, made every sleepy part of me wake up and listen. "It's been difficult, Hayes. I hope you never feel the kind of loss I've been wading through. Every day I feel guilty for checking out on you, but I couldn't find a way past the grief." She took in a deep breath, and then continued. "I was feeling a little better, trying to move through my days without getting lost in the sadness, but then Cory's acceptance letter came and it was another setback. Another part of his life he'll never get to live because of the actions of one person. It's not fair." Her voice, although still strong and loud, cracked at that point, and I fought the urge to go to her, to hold her close and tell her I didn't need to hear anything else, if only to spare her the pain of explaining it to me.

"With the wave of grief came more nightmares, and Hayes, I promise you, I just wanted to sleep. I wanted to sleep without images of Cory bleeding on the floor of a convenience store, or picturing the fear in his eyes before he was shot, or imaging what he'd look like on his wedding day, what his children would look like. I wanted one night where I could sleep in peace."

A tear slid down her cheek and she wiped it away, seemingly determined to continue. I didn't dare interrupt her.

"I took a sleeping pill, but the thoughts wouldn't stop. They wouldn't let me be. So I took another. That one managed to put me to sleep, but I just remember waking up from a nightmare, crying, and wanting to just *sleep*. I'm so tired, Hayes. So tired. So, I took two more. I think. I think it was two more. But, honestly, it could have been more. I'm not sure." Her eyes darted up to meet mine then, red rimmed and wet, but so completely clear and focused. "I *never* wanted to die, Hayes. I just wanted one night of not feeling. One night of numbness. I just wanted to sleep. I promise."

She finally broke down and cried. I stood from my chair and wrapped my arms around her, holding her as her body shook from the sobs. I'd seen my mother cry a lot over the last few months. But she'd always been crying from the loss of her husband and son. This was the first time she'd cried because she was acknowledging her grief and recognizing the fact that it was unhealthy.

For that reason, I cried along with her.

Chapter Twenty-Six

McKenzie

Three days had passed since I'd seen Hayes. The last time was in the waiting room at the hospital. I'd been so confused by that person. The one who wouldn't let me stay and help, wouldn't let me try and comfort him. But my mom dragged me out of the waiting room and then fretted over me the rest of the day.

Those hours we'd sat in the waiting room had been painful at first, not knowing what was happening or if Mrs. Wallace was going to be all right. My mom was frazzled, coming down hard on herself for not checking on her sooner. So, in an effort to distract ourselves, we started talking about anything but Mrs. Wallace.

That meant we talked about Hayes.

I told my mom everything. *Everything.* From the beginning. Starting at fourteen when Hayes was my best friend's cute older brother, to our first kiss at Cory's party, to where we stood that day, and everything in between. The best part was my mom listened, understood, and didn't pass judgment. I didn't get a lecture on getting involved with someone so soon after Cory's death, and I didn't even get a lecture about it being his brother. She just listened and then comforted me in her mom way.

"I was worried you wouldn't accept a relationship between Hayes and me," I'd said, sitting in an uncomfortable chair in the waiting room.

"Why, sweetie?"

"Ever since I could remember, you and Mrs. Wallace had been pretty clear you wanted Cory and me together. Being with Hayes seemed like it would be off-limits."

"McKenzie, Chelsea and I had the same dream every woman has with her best friend—that their kids will grow up and fall in love. But if you hadn't been with Cory, it wouldn't have mattered. What matters most, to Chelsea and to me, is that our kids are happy. If Hayes makes you happy, then I'll love him like I would have loved anyone who treated you right."

I let out a sigh, my head falling back to rest against the chair. "I hope Mrs. Wallace feels the same way."

"McKenzie, Chelsea loves you. She loved you with Cory, and she'll love you with Hayes. It might shock her, she might be surprised, but I really think she'll be grateful you'll still be a part of her life."

Later, when we'd gone home, she'd baked me cookies, fed me ice cream, and watched a *Twilight* marathon with me.

Saturday and Sunday passed with only one-word texts from Hayes, and I tried desperately to understand his situation, to think about how he must have been feeling and what he was dealing with. But every text I got from him that said, "Good," or "Fine," made me more nervous. He wasn't good or fine. I knew he wasn't. It wasn't possible.

Mrs. Wallace had texted my mom Saturday afternoon saying she'd been released from the hospital, but that she and Hayes needed a bit to settle in before they got visitors.

I was a mess. Hayes pushing me away had me feeling insecure and useless. But my mom was handling the situation like a pro, constantly telling me that they needed their space to heal—especially Mrs. Wallace—and that's what got me through until Monday.

I'd been on pins and needles all day, knowing that when last period came around, I'd get to see him. I wouldn't get to talk to him, to hold him, or kiss him, but I'd be able to look him over and gauge how broken he was. I'd get to use my eyes on him for a whole period, and at that point, I'd take whatever I could get.

The day dragged on and every class felt as though it took twice as long as normal. When it finally came time for the last period, I was practically sprinting.

I walked into the room and didn't see him, but that wasn't unusual so I took my seat and waited. And waited. When the bell finally rang and Hayes was nowhere in sight, I panicked as Mr. White walked to the front of the class.

"Due to unfortunate circumstances, Mr. Wallace will no longer be able to finish out the term here with us. We wish him the best and I know he'll succeed with whatever endeavors he pursues in the future. Now," he said, turning back to his desk, "Please open your text books to page 411, and we'll pick up where Mr. Wallace left off."

Never had words turned me cold like those. Never had I suddenly felt as though stones lined my stomach, as if I were tied to my desk and unable to move. My lungs were heavy, making it hard to breathe, and my heart was pounding as though I'd just run a marathon.

Hayes wasn't here.

Hayes wasn't coming back.

Then, suddenly, the weight lifted and I ran. If Hayes wasn't there, then I wasn't supposed to be there either. At least, that was the logic that had me sprinting out of my last period class, leaving everything behind.

I ran all the way home, stopping for nothing. The adrenaline pumping through my system was enough stamina to keep me going, even when the rain set in halfway there. I came up on my house, but I still didn't stop. I kept running until I saw Hayes's house, and when I turned that final corner, my eyes landed on Hayes himself.

Loading boxes.

Into a moving van.

That image alone stopped me in my tracks.

He didn't see me right away and continued to load a few more boxes. I was standing just down the street in front of his neighbor's house, watching. Finally, he came out of the truck, down the ramp, turned to walk into his garage, and spotted me. We stood there for a few heavy seconds, staring at each other through the rain, before he started toward me.

"Kenz," he said as he neared me. "I'm glad you're here. I've been meaning to call you."

I wanted to tell him I'd had my phone in my hands for three days waiting to hear from him, to tell him that he should have called, that I'd been worried sick about him, but I didn't. "How's your mom?"

"They released her Saturday, and we're just trying to move forward. She'll be fine, eventually."

We were both quiet for a moment, neither one of us seeming to notice the rain falling heavily down on us. Finally, I had to speak. "What's with the moving van?"

Hayes turned to look back at his driveway, as if he'd forgotten there was a U-Haul there, forgotten he'd just been inside of it. When he turned back to me his face was pained and he looked as though the words bubbling up in his throat were hurting him.

"My mom wants to sell the house. We're going to hire movers to come and pack up most of the

317 | Instead of You

stuff. I'm just loading the things she wants to take with us."

"Take with you?"

"Yeah, McKenzie. Shit," he said roughly, dragging his hand through his now soaking wet hair. "My mom needs to really focus on getting better. She needs to see a psychiatrist regularly, and she needs more care than I can give her here. So we talked it over and decided it would be best for her to be near her parents in Montana."

"Your mom is selling her house and moving to Montana?" There were so many things about that sentence that seemed impossible to me. The idea that the Wallaces wouldn't be just down the street, that some other family would be living in their house, it made the world feel a little colder and unfamiliar, like I'd jumped dimensions or something.

"Kenz," he said, the tone of his voice now apologetic, "we're both moving to Montana."

The earth might as well have opened up and swallowed me whole. Everything that kept me alive stopped working. I couldn't breathe, I couldn't think, my heart felt like a broken engine, refusing to do its job, churning and breaking and crumbling all at once.

"Kenz," he said again, this time stepping toward me. I stepped back and he stopped, his head dropping, his gaze falling to the ground.

"Mr. White said you weren't teaching anymore. I ran here to see if you were all right. If your mom was all right." I stopped, the words stacking up in my throat, jammed behind the huge lump forming there, with rain now soaking through my clothes. "You're leaving?" I tried not to cry, but it was the only way the words could come out, strapped to sobs. "For how long? You'll come back when your mom's better?"

It took a moment before he raised his gaze to meet mine, but he said no words.

"You're not coming back?" What world was I living in? This couldn't be reality. Not my reality. "Hayes, if you need to go with your mom to make sure she's okay, go. I want your mom to be all right too. But that doesn't mean we have to be over. You're acting like this is the end for us."

"It has to be."

My mouth fell open. Tears escaped both my eyes, mixing with the rain already streaming down my face, and my feet took me backward, away from the dagger-like words he'd thrown at me.

"Kenz, listen—"

"Listen to what? Listen to you tell me that you're leaving and we're over? Just days ago we were planning the next year of our life together, and now you're just ending it?"

"My mom—"

"Is sick, I know. I love your mom, and I want her to be happy and well. And I love that you want to be there for her. I'd never hold that against you. But I don't understand how this all means we can't be together." My words were frantic and tripping out of my mouth almost on top of each other. The words couldn't keep up with my thoughts and all I was thinking was why why why.

Hayes took a fast step toward me, grasping my shoulders before I could get away. I wanted him to stay with me, to choose to be with me, but I didn't want him touching me just then. It felt too raw, as though his hands were carving into me.

"I love you, McKenzie. More than I could ever love anyone. But this, us, it isn't right. Healthy relationships aren't born from death, they don't blossom in the dark, and they don't flourish while being hidden."

"We weren't born from death," I practically spit at him.

He shook his head ever so slightly, his grasp on me still firm. "If Cory were alive, I never would have been with you. And I'm not saying I was only with you because he died, but dammit, McKenzie, that's how it feels right now."

"This isn't fair. You can't just make me fall in love with you and then let me go like this. It feels like you set a trap and I've fallen in, and you're just walking away, leaving me behind." The rain was still pummeling us, and if I hadn't had anger burning through me, I would have been cold. But I wasn't shaking from cold, I was shaking from rage and pain.

"I wish I could explain how untrue that is, how I'll never be able to leave you behind. I'll never be able to just let you go, McKenzie. But as stupid as it sounds, and clichéd as this is, I'm letting you go because I love you so much." His arms pulled me closer to him, and even though I didn't want to, I let him bring me in. "I'm going to Montana, and I have no idea how long I'll be there. This is not the time in your life when you're supposed to be worried about your boyfriend and his mother. You're supposed to be young, carefree, live life, and you're supposed to fall in love, a lot." He closed what space was left between us, my chest pressing up against his, rainwater running down both our faces. "I want you. I want you so badly, but it's the most selfish part of me that would keep you tethered to me in that way. The best part of me, the part that loves you and wants nothing but goodness for you, wants you to fall in love with someone else instead of me."

"There will never be anyone instead of you, Hayes. And up until ten minutes ago, that fact alone made me the luckiest person on the planet. But if you do this, if you push me away, it'll ruin me. There will never be anyone else, and that will eat away at me for the rest of my life."

He pressed his forehead against mine and my hands gripped the wet fabric of his t-shirt, trying to hold on to him for as long as I possibly could. When one of his hands cupped my cheek, I tried to keep my eyes down, knew that if I looked him in the eyes it would be my undoing.

"I love you," he whispered. His lips pressed against mine and it was the saddest kiss I'd ever experienced. It was love and good-bye and I'm sorry all wrapped together, and I wanted to pull away, to yell at him, to tell him he was an asshole for making me love him and then throw me away. But instead, I kissed him back. Because there was a tiny part of me that knew it would be our last, and I wouldn't have traded our last kiss for anything.

Ever since Hayes Wallace had been my first kiss, I'd believed, somewhere deep inside, he'd be my last. But I had no idea we'd burn out so quickly.

I cried against his mouth, unable to keep it at bay any longer. I pulled away, took one last look at the face I loved, turned, and ran away.

Chapter Twenty-Seven

McKenzie

There was something to be said for being more heartbroken over a breakup than the death of a boyfriend. It had been six days since Hayes told me he was leaving, four days since he actually left, and every time my heart beat, I was sure it would be its last. The first day was probably the worst. I ran home, barged into the house dripping wet and shivering, and spent an hour in a hot shower trying to bring myself back to life. My mom came home, heard me sobbing in the bathroom, and eventually managed to get me out, dressed in my pajamas, and eating ice cream. Again.

This time, though, she joined me in more than just solidarity because I'd broken the news to her that Mrs. Wallace was moving to Montana, which she hadn't known. So, she was losing her best friend to distance, and I was losing my boyfriend to... what? To responsible heartbreak? Romantic martyrdom? I was swinging from a wild emotional pendulum. One moment I hated him. *Hated him.* And the next, I remembered every single thing about him that I loved and felt guilty for even entertaining the terrible thoughts of hate.

Of course I didn't hate him.

In the middle of the night, when I couldn't sleep and my mind was just a jumble of thoughts of Hayes, there was always one thing I knew for sure: Hayes loved me.

I couldn't understand why he didn't give us enough credit, or even the opportunity to make our relationship work, but I tried really hard to focus on the fact that he thought he was doing what was best. Best for me *and* best for his mom. In those moments when I would get really angry with him, I'd think of Mrs. Wallace and I'd try to remember what he'd sacrificed for her. And that made me love him even more.

Tuesday I'd stayed home from school. I could hardly walk down the hall without crying, so school wasn't a good place for me. But on Wednesday I'd decided to at least try. I'd never actually gone to high school at the same time as Hayes, but being in there, knowing he wasn't within the walls, made the school feel strangely empty. By the time I got to history, I'd told Mr. White I wasn't feeling well and went home early. I figured I'd tortured myself enough for one day. But the next day, and the day after that, I'd managed to endure the whole day. And by the end of day Friday, I'd made it all eight hours without crying.

I thought about him all the time, wondered where he was, what he was doing, but I never broke down and tried to contact him. I knew that would have just been painful for both of us.

Friday afternoon, though, I did find myself somewhere I hadn't been in weeks.

"I know you're the last person I should be talking to this about, but in a weird way, I kind of feel like you already know." I sighed and pulled at a few blades of grass. "The thing is, I'll always love you, and I'll always love him. And I'm really thankful I was lucky enough to love you both and feel loved by both of you." I ran my fingers across the letters of his name engraved on his headstone, and I wondered who would make sure it was taken care of since his mother and brother had moved so far away. I noticed a little bit of dirt in the *Y* of Cory, so I dug it out and wiped it on my jeans. "I will never have a best friend like you," I whispered, trying not to cry anymore.

"Hey, we resent that."

I turned to see Holly and Becca walking up the tiny hill toward Cory's gravesite. I smiled at them, feeling so thankful they'd come looking for me.

"How'd you guys know where I was?"

"We asked your mom," Becca said as the two of them sat down next to me. We were all quiet for a while, silent and thoughtful.

"I've never hung out at someone's grave before," Holly finally said.

I resisted the urge to roll my eyes, and said, "Me either. But I hadn't come to see him since he was buried, and I figured it was time." I gave a small laugh. "He's surprisingly a very good and nonjudgmental listener."

"What were you telling him that he would judge you about?" Becca's eyes were trained on me, and I knew she could tell something major had happened in the last week. Of all my friends, she'd

325 | Instead of You

been the most observant, the most skeptical about the excuses and stories I'd made up to cover my time with Hayes. But in that moment, it felt right that only Cory knew. I figured one day I'd tell them what had happened, how I'd fallen in love with my deceased boyfriend's brother, but today wasn't that day.

"Stuff," I said with a shrug.

"Have you heard from Hayes?" Holly asked innocently. I tried to make sure I didn't pull a face at the mention of his name. I needed to seem completely unaffected, even if just the sound of his name ringing in my ears made my heart beat faster.

"Mrs. Wallace called my mom last night. They made it to Montana. They're staying with her parents for the time being and she's starting her therapy next week." I said the words as fast as I could, not stopping to take a breath until the end, like ripping off a Band-Aid.

"I was really sorry to hear about his mom. I'm glad they decided to get her the help she needs," Becca said softly.

"Me too," I whispered. I looked over to Cory's headstone. "You hear that? Your mom's in good hands. She's going to be just fine. She just misses you." My voice cracked at the end of my sentence, my eyes stung, and my throat pinched. Both my friends reached out and rubbed my shoulder or my arm, letting me know they were there for me. I wiped away a tear and said, "We all miss you."

326 |Anie Michaels

After a few silent moments, Becca finally spoke. "The guys are at the mall. They want us all to go see the new scary movie that came out. Want to come with us?" She looked hopeful, as if she really wanted me to say yes, but was afraid I'd say no.

"Sure," I said, wiping my fingers underneath both my eyes, trying to make sure I'd dried both my cheeks thoroughly. "I love spending my Friday nights as the fifth wheel." I stood up, chuckling, then held out my hands to my two friends, pulling them both up as well.

"Hey, I was the fifth wheel for two whole years. You can spend an evening with your coupled-up friends." Becca said and then laughed.

"True. But someone has to buy me popcorn."

Three Years Later

Chapter Twenty-Eight

McKenzie

Somewhere, at some fancy university or research institute, college coffee houses across the country could be making big bucks by hiring laboratories to do research on prolonged caffeine intake and its effect on brain function and retention.

I was on my third mocha and the highlighter was practically singeing the page of my textbook as I swiped it across the important words. Or, at least, words I hoped would be important when it came time to take the test.

I was but a mere twenty-four hours from my last final of the term, which meant spring break was right around the corner. Not only spring break, but the first spring break where I was legally allowed to walk into a club and purchase and consume alcohol. It was on par to be the best spring break ever. All I had to do was make it through one more test.

My phone buzzed on the table so I flipped it over and read a text from Becca.

Officially on spring break, bitches.

It was a group text between Holly, Becca, and me. Holly and I went to the same school, but Becca had opted to go to a college out of state. It had been sad to drift away from each other physically, but honestly, we saw each other often. She always came home for breaks and summers, so I really only ever went about two months without her.

*When does your flight land?**

That was from Holly. She'd volunteered to pick Becca up from the airport as she was finished with finals already. The three of us would spend the first weekend in town, hit all the bars we'd been sneaking into for three years, and then drive home to spend the rest of the week with our families and other friends home for the break.

8:30 pm.

I hate that I can't hang out tonight. You guys have to have a terrible time since I'll be stuck at home studying still.

We'll make sure to party enough to make up for your absence.

Becca's good mood was evident in her text, and I smiled, knowing how good it would feel tomorrow to be completely done for a whole week.

Get back to studying. We'll pick you up tomorrow night and the first round is on me.

I knew I'd kept Holly as a friend for a reason. I turned my phone over, using the same logic that never proved to be true—that if I couldn't see the screen I wouldn't be tempted to pick it up—but I was determined to ace this test.

Tequila shots be damned.

I decided more coffee was necessary so I grabbed my wallet and walked toward the counter. I was sure the barista would turn me away, citing some sort of caffeinating limit I'd reached with my ninth shot in my last drink, but she simply took my order and then made my drink. I waited at the designated spot where everyone stood to receive their drinks, and when my drink was ready I steeled myself for another few hours of heavy cramming. Eventually, I'd move my study party to the library. But for now I would go back to my corner, put in my headphones, and try to focus.

I turned and only two steps into my journey back to my corner, my eyes fell upon him and my body simply stopped. As if I'd hit a brick wall. As if the connection from my brain to my legs had been severed. And it felt as though everyone else stood still too. The whole world came crashing to a halt.

Including Hayes.

Who was standing not ten feet away from me.

He looked just as uncomfortable as me, but he also looked something like sad.

Eventually the world started spinning again and my heart thumped back to life, but I was still stuck in my spot, completely unaware of how I was supposed to proceed. For months after he'd left, I'd looked for him everywhere. Every time I drove past his house I wondered if he was in it. At the movies, at the mall, I constantly was looking at every young, dark-haired guy, waiting to someday see him just appear. But once I moved away for college, I'd stopped. I knew he'd spent years on this campus, but I'd only been to two places with him, really. One bar and his apartment. Both places I avoided at all costs. We'd been in this coffee shop together, for a just a minute or two, but I'd convinced myself it was dumb to lose out on such a great study site just because once he and I breathed the same air there.

I was now regretting that decision.

He started walking to me and my brain shut down. It was just Hayes, slowly coming toward me, but he might as well have been wielding an axe for the fear it caused. He could do less damage with an axe in the long run.

"McKenzie," he said as he came to stop in front of me. His voice washed over me and I nearly shivered. It was strange the way his voice traveled along my spine and the unfamiliar feeling, the unfamiliar sound of him, simply could have knocked me over. He smiled a friendly but uncomfortable smile and said, "I figured I would run into you sooner or later."

My eyebrows drew in as confusion took over. My mouth gaped, but I wasn't able to form words yet.

"How've you been?" he asked, seeming to be genuinely curious.

How've I been? I had no response. I was still trying to figure out which dimension I'd transported into. He took another step toward me and I managed to close my mouth, my eyes still locked on his.

"I know this is out of the blue, and I'm really sorry about that, but can we sit? Have coffee? Catch up?"

He wanted to have coffee and chat? I could not have been more confused, but I mumbled, "Sure." I continued to my corner, convinced I was dreaming, but watched as Hayes ordered a drink and then brought it over, sitting in the chair across from me.

He eyed my textbook as he sat, then said nervously, "Statistics, huh? I avoided that class like the plague."

"What are you doing here?" Ah, finally, my mouth and brain were connected again.

He leaned forward, elbows to his knees, and clasped his hands together. "Well, I took a little time off but when I decided to go back to finish my certification and degree, I thought it would be a good idea to add an endorsement. So, instead of just being a history teacher, I can teach English too. Sometimes it gives you a better chance at finding a job when you are certified to teach more than one subject."

"So, you're a student again?"

"Classes start next week," he said with a nervous smile. He looked the same, but different. Older, maybe, but still just like Hayes. His hair was the shortest I'd ever seen it, and he looked as though he hadn't shaved in a week or two. I'd always loved his long, silky hair, the way it slid between my fingers, but the short hair only made his strong jaw stand out. He was the same Hayes—still stupidly hot.

"How's your mom?" I sort of already knew how his mother was. My mom was still best friends with Mrs. Wallace, but my mom was good about never talking about Hayes. I got important updates on his mom, which I was thankful for, but my mom understood that I needed him to be whitewashed from my life if I was going to survive.

"Good," he said, nodding. "Thanks for asking."

"I hear she really likes Montana."

"Turns out my mom's a cowgirl at heart," he said with a laugh that almost sounded painful, then he ran his hands over his face, pushing out a breath. Suddenly his eyes found mine and there was a sad urgency there, and a little bit of exhaustion if I read him correctly. "This conversation is bullshit." He scooted forward on his chair. There was still a table between us, but even the few inches that evaporated between us had my heart rate spiking. I could, in no way, deal with proximity in that moment. "Listen, I came back and I knew you went to school here. And I knew I'd run into you. I didn't think it'd be the very first day, but fuck if that isn't my luck."

"You didn't want to see me?" The question popped out of my mouth before I had time to even

334 | Anie Michaels

think the words. But the hurt was evident in my voice. For three years I'd been aching to see him. Even just a glimpse. A photo on Facebook, a look at him passing by as my mom Skyped with Mrs. Wallace, even just a photo on my cell phone when he called me. Not that he ever had. Even if I had pathetically refused to change my phone number just in case. I'd wanted to see him so badly, and it tore me open to think he hadn't wanted to see me.

"No, Kenzie, of course I wanted to see you." He moved even farther onto the edge of his chair and my lung capacity diminished. I pushed myself as far back in the previously comfy chair as I could, noticing it suddenly felt spiky. "I just hoped I'd have more than three hours to get used to the idea of being on the same campus as you before you appeared before me exactly as I imagined you would."

I had no response. The allusion that he'd thought about seeing me too did nothing but make my fingers tingle, so I clenched my fists.

"I just...," he started, but tapered off, looking at me with unrelenting eyes and a soft expression on his face. "It's really good to see you."

Nope. Couldn't do it. I unclenched my fists and started packing up my textbooks and highlighters.

"I have to meet my study group at the library. It's finals. I have one more test." *Which studying for is now a completely hopeless task.* "I have to go." *Before I crumble right here in front of you.*

"Right. Of course. I should have known...." He watched as I manically packed up my things and I felt his gaze on me, burning me through my clothes.

"I guess I'll see you around," I said, trying for casual and aloof, but I probably sounded rude.

"Hey," he said just as I'd taken my first step toward the door. I turned back to him slowly, trying hard to hold on to my last bit of composure. "I know this is weird and I probably should have warned you somehow that I was coming back, but I was really hoping we could be friends. Or, at the very least, not ignore each other if we passed on campus."

"I would never," I said immediately. Lies. I would totally.

"Kenz, I've known you your entire life."

"Not for the last three years." Again, the words sprung from my mouth like lightning. Quick and hot. And I almost regretted them. *Almost.*

His face dropped and I watched as he actually deflated a little. His shoulders slumped and his chest caved just slightly. That was okay though, because my chest had been caved in since he walked away from me that day in the rain. Now, I was walking away from him.

I turned, headed toward the library, and immediately found an empty stall in the bathroom and cried until all the tears stopped flowing.

I stayed up all night studying for my exam, but I didn't learn anything new. I read the same passages time and time again, trying to find some sort of logic in the words, but none came. The next day I passed my final—barely—and then went home and went to sleep. The look on Hayes's face right before I turned away from him was the last thing I saw before I drifted away.

Chapter Twenty-Nine

McKenzie

Loud banging on my door was what finally woke me. I looked at my phone and sighed. I'd slept through the morning. It was one in the afternoon already. I padded down the hallway toward the door, already knowing who was there before I even opened it.

Squeals greeted me as Holly and Becca burst through my door as soon as it opened even a crack, and two sets of arms wrapped around my neck. When the hugging and jumping was done they finally pulled away, all smiles. I tried to smile back, but I probably looked as though I was in pain.

"You said you were going to text us when you got up, but we got tired of waiting around for you," Holly said before taking a seat on my couch. She's spent a lot of time at my apartment and I knew she felt right at home there, which I loved. I felt the same way at her place.

"Sorry, I was really exhausted after yesterday's exam. I guess I needed more sleep than I anticipated. Did you guys have fun last night?"

"It was tons of fun, until Todd showed up," Becca said, feigning annoyance.

"Todd's here?" I ask Holly. Todd and Holly had managed to prove everybody wrong and survive three years of a long-distance relationship. He went to college an hour away. They saw each other often enough, but no one had thought they would last.

She shrugged. "He wanted to surprise me."

"It was cool. He brought a friend with him so I wasn't a total third wheel."

"Don't pretend like you didn't hook up with Scott," Holly teased. "Todd showing up with a friend was the best part of your night." Becca blushed but she didn't deny what Holly said. I smiled, glad my friends had enjoyed their night while I was trying to sleep off my run-in with Hayes.

"So, why'd you bail on us last night?" Becca finally asked, following me to sit on the couch Holly hadn't taken.

I had never told my best friends what happened between Hayes and me. My mother was the only person who knew, and if she told my dad, I had no idea. When he first left, almost three years ago, it was too hard to talk about and I didn't think anyone, especially Holly and Becca, would really understand. But now, looking at them, I figured enough time had passed, it was probably time to explain. Especially if Holly was going to be seeing him around campus; I'd have to explain the weirdness somehow.

"You guys remember Hayes, right?"

A confused expression crossed both their faces, and I understood; I was definitely coming out of left field.

"Cory's older brother?" Holly asked. I nodded. "What about him?"

"I saw him the day before yesterday. At the coffee shop where I always study."

"That's weird," Becca added. "What was he doing here?"

"He's going to school here," I replied, pulling my feet up under me, trying to get comfortable, a task I knew was impossible as long as I was talking about Hayes. "He starts next week. Something about getting certified to teach English as well as History."

"Wow, what a blast from the past," Holly supplied.

I took in a deep breath, knowing it was now or never. "Do you guys remember when he was our History teacher? For just a few weeks our senior year?"

"Yeah, it was right after Cory died, right? He stayed to take care of his mom. Isn't that why he left? Because his mom had some sort of breakdown and he had to take her away?"

"Right. He took her to Montana. But, something happened in those few weeks he was our teacher that I never told you guys about."

"Um, okay Miss Cryptic. What are you talking about?" Holly asked, sitting forward in her seat.

"I guess it started way before that, at Cory's sixteenth birthday party. Hayes kissed me. Out of nowhere. Just totally stole my first kiss and then he disappeared. I didn't see him again until Cory's eighteenth birthday, the night he died."

"Wait, what? You kissed Hayes? You cheated on Cory?" Becca sounded almost outraged.

"No, I mean, nothing had happened with Cory at that point. Hayes kissed me first, then Cory, and after that night Cory and I started dating. But there had always been something about Hayes that I was drawn to. It was silly and juvenile, or so I thought. But then after Cory's death, Hayes and I just kind of drifted together again." I paused for a reaction, but all I got were gaping mouths. "It was confusing and wonderful all at the same time. He was at our school and I was constantly over at his house trying to help him care for his mother, and we just, I don't know...." I let out a deep breath, a little overwhelmed by all the memories surfacing that I'd gotten so good at pushing down for the last three years. "Anyway, I fell in love with him and when he left, it hurt. And now he's back. It just kind of caught me off guard. I didn't think I'd ever see him again."

"You fell in love with him?" Becca asked, her voice soft and full of worry. The gentleness of it made my eyes well with tears and caused that familiar pinch in the back of my throat. I managed to nod, biting my bottom lip, but couldn't speak. "Why didn't you tell us, Kenzie?" Suddenly Becca was on my side of the couch and Holly was kneeling in front of me, her hands on my legs while Becca's arm went around my shoulders.

"I don't know," I cried as tears slipped down my cheeks. "He and I were so worried about upsetting his mother, the school finding out, people thinking we were insensitive to Cory. It was all so crazy, but we just couldn't stay away from each other. I loved him, so much, I still do. I was worried if I told you guys, you'd be angry with me. So, I didn't say anything. And then, before it ever really began, he left. So I never brought it up."

"You should have told us," Holly said quietly, her hand squeezing my leg. "We're your best friends."

"I know," I said, still crying through my words. "And trust me, I wanted to, I just didn't want to hurt anyone."

"Looks like you're the one who got hurt," Becca said.

I shook my head. "Hayes did what was best for his mom, I know that. It was just a crappy situation. But guys, now he's going to school here. I saw him two days ago and I literally lost the ability to form sentences." I let out a soft chuckle thinking about how just the sight of him had rendered me useless.

"What does he want from you?" Holly asked.

I shrugged. "Nothing. He just said he hopes we don't ignore each other if we walk past one another on campus."

Holly looked confused. "And you say you were in love with him? It seems weird that he would drop off the face of the planet and then just show up acting like everything was fine. Were things between you serious?"

"Like, I gave him my virginity serious," I said with a laugh, trying to act like the entire situation wasn't gutting me.

"Wait, what?" Becca asked, pulling away from me with her eyebrows drawn together. "I thought you went to college a virgin."

I shook my head. "No. I lost my virginity in Hayes's college apartment just a few blocks from here."

"Shut. Up." Holly gasped.

"I very nearly lost it in a tent at the Holstater compound that night we had that campout party, remember? Becca opened my tent and he was totally in there, sleeping in his underwear."

"Wow," Becca said quietly. "I can't believe all that happened and you never told us."

"At first I couldn't tell anyone, and then he left and it hurt so badly, I just tried to move on. Telling you guys any of it would have been too painful. But now, oh, my gosh...." The thought of seeing him walking through campus, holding some woman's hand, having to see him with someone else, it made my stomach roll. "Now I have to see him and pretend like I'm not falling apart all over again."

"So, you're still in love with him?" Holly asked.

I held up my hands and gave a defeated shrug. "I can't help it. There are times I wish I weren't, but it never went away and I'm not sure it ever will." I let out a large sigh. "This is not how I pictured my spring break starting."

"Tell you what," Becca said, standing from the couch with purpose. "We're going to go get lunch, come back here and watch a few chick flicks, and then we're going to go out and get you so drunk, you won't even remember his name."

"Girls' night!" Holly said as she clapped and smiled. I couldn't help but smile back. And the entire plan sounded excellent, so I agreed.

"I'll go put some clothes on."

I had the best friends. Seriously. My love for Becca and Holly only bloomed under their gentle care. They'd spent the entire day trying to make me feel better. They'd fed me, entertained me, and even given me a makeover, determined to take me out and find me some warm body to make me forget about Hayes. I wasn't opposed to their plan. I'd been with a few people since starting college, and all of them were just guys I'd used to fill a void. I never dated anyone and never started a relationship. In fact, one night was the most I'd spent with anyone in three years. I wasn't proud of my track record, but sometimes I was so tired of feeling numb, that any emotion would do. Lust was a perfect distraction, even if it was attached to a person who didn't care if they ever saw me again. At least with those men, I knew the score before the game ever started.

I was four drinks in and we were dancing in a trio in the middle of a club. The music was loud enough I could hardly hear my thoughts about Hayes pinging around my brain. That did not, however, stop my brain from imagining him everywhere. So I closed my eyes.

I wasn't drunk, but I was definitely buzzed. Dancing with my eyes closed made everything sway more, and I had to concentrate even harder on not tipping over, since Holly had convinced me to wear shoes with heels so high it was difficult to walk in them without alcohol in my system.

Suddenly there were hands on my hips and a hard body pressed into my back. My first thought was that perhaps it was Hayes. Maybe he'd found me. But I knew immediately it wasn't him because the hands felt foreign and my body didn't instantly come alive at his touch. My eyes opened to see Becca in front of me, giving me a thumbs-up, mouthing the words "He's cute" at me.

I reached down and placed my hands over his, trying to convince myself that his touch didn't make my brain scream, "He's not Hayes!"

I kept moving to the music and felt him lean forward a bit, his mouth coming to touch the shell of my ear.

"I've been watching you and your friends for a while. You're the hottest girl here and I couldn't understand why you were dancing alone." His fingers gave my waist a squeeze. "What's your name?"

"McKenzie," I said loudly.

His hands suddenly spun me around, which I didn't appreciate since the heels needed a little more thought and practice than he'd allowed. "Hi," he said with a smile. He was cute. But he was all wrong. His hair was too light, his face too round, he wasn't tall enough, and he just wasn't Hayes. "I'm Paul."

"Hi," I said, trying to smile.

"Wanna get out of here?"

I leaned a little closer to him so I didn't have to yell. "I'm here with my friends tonight. Girls' night." I smiled again, but this time it was an apologetic smile, and pointed over my shoulder to Becca and Holly.

"I'm sure they wouldn't mind. They want you to have a good time, right?"

He was cute and a little bit charming, and I imagined that lots of girls would take him up on his offer. Hell, last week I might have. But I knew I couldn't go home with anyone. Not while Hayes was saturating every thought I had.

"Thanks, but I'm going to have to pass." He shrugged with a smile, but then turned and wandered off, perhaps looking for a more willing participant.

Suddenly the noise of the music and the heat of the people all around were too much. I was wobbly and sweaty and I just needed one moment of peace and quiet.

"I'm gonna go on the patio for a minute," I yelled in Holly's ear. "I'll be back in a few."

"Want us to come with you?" she asked, still happily bobbing to the music.

"I'll be all right."

She gave me a thumbs-up and then I went to the bar, waited for a glass of water, then headed for the patio doors. Thankfully, there were only two other people outside and they were huddled together in the far corner, making out.

I took a long drink of my water, knowing I'd thank myself in the morning for it, and I pulled my phone from my pocket. I activated the screen and pulled up my contacts. I thumbed down until Hayes's name was highlighted, and then I paused.

I hadn't called him once since he'd left for Montana and I had no idea if his number was still the same, but I'd been thinking about calling him all day. Not once, in three years, had I called him.

But knowing he was in the same town as me made me itch to reach out. I was afraid it could only lead to more heartache, but at that point, everything hurt anyway.

I pressed the call button and held the phone up to my ear, fully expecting to hear an angry stranger yell at me for calling so late, or to be sent to an unfamiliar voice mail.

What I didn't expect was to hear Hayes's voice.

"McKenzie?"

Oh, God. His voice made all the hairs on my arm stand up. It was deep and raspy, like he'd been very close to sleeping when I called. Shit. He knew it was me. Damn cell phones.

"McKenzie, is that you? Are you all right?" He started to sound a little panicked and I hadn't meant that, so I answered.

"Yes, sorry. It's me. I shouldn't have called."

"No, wait, don't hang up. What are you doing?"

I looked around, thinking about making something up, but instead, the truth spilled out. "I'm standing on the patio at a bar. There's a couple dry humping in the corner."

"Are you alone?"

His tone was suddenly protective and the effect it had on me was terrifying. And also really wonderful.

"Holly and Becca are here. They're inside."

There was a silence between us and I wasn't sure what to say. I wasn't even sure why I called him. But I knew I didn't want to hang up.

"Do you guys need a ride home? Is there a designated driver?"

"We'll walk. I live just a few blocks away."

"It's just the three of you?"

"Yeah."

"Shit, Kenz. The three of you can't walk home alone."

"We do it all the time," I said, slightly defensive.

"Well, that makes me feel much better," he said, the sarcasm coming through loud and clear. He let out a breath and then said, "Just let me come walk you guys home. I won't be able to sleep now, knowing you'll be walking home alone. In the dark. Three beautiful college girls. In the middle of the night."

At that point I couldn't help but let out a tiny laugh. He sounded sort of like a grumpy father.

"I don't think they're ready to leave just yet," I said through my laughter.

"Are you ready?"

My breath stalled at his question. Was I ready to see him again? Was I ready to pass up an opportunity to see his face? To walk next to him?

To possibly take in his scent or feel the back of his hand brush up against mine?

No, I wasn't.

"I'm not ready to go home, but I'll take you up on a walk, if you're offering."

I heard muffled noises from his end of the line and imagined him sitting up from his bed, searching for his shoes. "Which bar are you at?"

"McFadden's. Right across the street from the bookstore."

"I'll be there in ten minutes. Wait on the patio for me."

"Okay," I answered softly, thinking to myself that I'd wait anywhere for any length of time for him. Still. And that made me both happy and sad.

"I'll be right there."

"All right."

It was silent for a moment, and I got the feeling he wanted to say more, but I just heard him let out a groan and then the line disconnected. I found a chair and sat down, waiting for Hayes and drinking my water.

Sure enough, ten minutes later, Hayes walked out onto the patio. I stood up when I saw him, a little shocked that he'd actually showed up, that he was actually standing in front of me. I didn't miss the way his eyes started at my face and moved all the way down to my feet, leaving a trail of warmth in the wake of his gaze. I swallowed hard and stepped toward him, stupidly wobbling on my heels. He was at my side in an instant.

"Need some help?" His question was sincere, his hand on my shoulder, keeping me steady.

"No, I'm okay. It's just these damned shoes." I look up at him, my hands at my sides but my fingers tingling with the need to reach out and just touch part of him. Even his shirt. Anything that would send a message from my fingers to my brain that Hayes Wallace was, in fact, standing right in front of me, looking just as handsome as ever, and that he was not a figment of my imagination.

"Come on," he said, nodding his head toward the door.

I followed him back into the club and he walked straight toward Holly and Becca on the dance floor. He tapped Holly on the shoulder and she turned around smiling, then did a double take, and finally shock registered on her face. Becca was staring at him with wide eyes as well.

"I'm going to take Kenzie on a walk. I don't want you two walking home. Call a cab." He shouted this at her over the loud music and then pressed a folded twenty into her hand. Holly looked down at the money, then back up at Hayes, and then to me, still confused. That was when Becca stepped forward, both her hands grasping the sides of my shoulders.

"Are you okay with this? You want to go with him?"

"Yeah, I'm good," I said, warming from the inside at my friend's concern for me, but also shaking from adrenaline at the thought of being alone with him. Her hands stayed on me as her eyes drifted to Hayes. She studied him for a moment, his expression never wavering, looking confident and possessive at the same time. Then her eyes came back to me. "You need to text me in an hour if you're not home. If you don't text me, I'll call you nonstop until I hear from you." I nodded and she turned back to Hayes. "If you fucking hurt her, I'll kill you."

"I get it," he responded, not unkindly. His reply was understanding and soft.

She nodded and then repeated, "Text me."

"I will," I promised. With that, Hayes led me out of the bar.

We'd been outside approximately ten seconds before he spoke. "So, I guess you told them what happened between us."

"I did. But only ten hours ago, so it's still pretty fresh in their minds. Which is probably why Becca went all mama bear on you."

He shoved his hands in his pockets and we slowly walked down the street. It seemed much of the student body was out celebrating being done with finals, so we passed many people on the street. Lots of girls who, like me, were wearing ridiculous shoes and short dresses, all walking in packs. Guys were out too, their heads turning with every girl that passed. The convenience store on the corner was full of people trying to buy beer. The pizza place was packed with people who preferred to sit and talk over the club scene. But after a few minutes, the farther away from the outskirts of campus we walked and the closer to the academic portion, the crowds dwindled and the night became quiet and calm.

It was strange, walking through campus with Hayes, both of us silent. But it was also surreal. Three days before I never thought I would see him again, and now he was right next to me.

"So, your mom is doing well?"

I had no idea what else we were supposed to talk about, so I went with something we'd sort of already covered.

"Yeah. It was rough at first. She started counseling and it was hard. After Cory and Dad died she'd tried really hard to just push everything away, tried to just go on, and that was probably her first mistake. So, when counseling started it was just her having to work through everything. It started with Cory, but once she started to work through it she realized that she'd never thoroughly mourned my dad, so then it was like she had to start over and trudge through the grief all over again. And then once she'd started to heal, I realized *I* hadn't dealt with their deaths either."

Something inside my chest tightened at his words. Not only did I ache thinking about him grieving his family, but I understood. I also went through a few weeks where Cory's death hit me hard after Hayes had left. I couldn't imagine what it felt like for him and I wished, more than anything, I'd been there for him through it.

"I'm sorry," I whispered. Sorry he'd gone through it at all, sorry I wasn't there for him, sorry about the entire situation because it sucked for everyone.

He looked over at me and met my eyes, saying, "It's okay. Mom is great now. She bought a ranch. She has horses and pigs and goats and chickens. I'm good, too. The only thing that's been missing for the last three years is beside me now, so I can't complain."

My heart stumbled. And so did I. Literally. My heel caught in a crack in the sidewalk and I would have gone down if Hayes hadn't reached out and grabbed my arm. He pulled me back up and I was pressed into his chest. His hand was still wrapped around my arm, and my hands were splayed across his front. He didn't move away and neither did I. I chose to focus, instead, on the way his chest was moving in and out rapidly with his breaths. Also, the way his other hand slid around my waist, pressing me closer to him. My breath caught and before I could stop myself, I let my head lean against him, let my hands run up him, let my fingers curl around his neck, and I held him. My heart started up again when both his hands wrapped around me. His head came low and he pressed his face into my neck, and everything in that moment was perfect.

He smelled the same and he felt the same, if only a little stronger. But he was still my Hayes and he still fit against me perfectly.

After a few long moments he pulled away, but not far. His hands came up to frame my face and he leaned forward, pressing a kiss to my forehead. It was a sweet kiss but I was torn between appreciating the gesture and wishing he'd pressed his lips against my own instead.

My hands rested on his forearms, my thumbs moving over the fabric of his t-shirt. I felt as though there were some invisible force field between us, holding me back. A very large part of me wanted to throw myself at him, to kiss him and be with him, but there was something there that kept me at bay. Fear? Fear that if I let myself be with him for even one night it would end up hurting more in the long run. Or it could have been anger that he'd left me to begin with? I didn't know exactly what held me back, only that it was a strong force because I was buzzing with need to touch him.

"I've missed you so much," he said, the words slightly mumbled as his mouth was still pressed lightly against me.

"I've missed you too," I said quietly. Then, "Ever since you left," with a little sting to my voice I couldn't contain. I pulled away a little, but not enough to break contact because I wasn't ready to let him go yet. His knees bent and his eyes were suddenly level with my own.

"Leaving you was the hardest thing I've ever had to do, Kenz. I've hated myself every day since, but I didn't have any other choice."

I did pull away at his words. "You didn't have a choice? *I* didn't have a choice, Hayes, because you left without giving me one. You made the decision for me. So, don't pretend like you were forced to leave me behind. You did that." I stepped away from him and turned, still wobbling in my heels. Not from the drinks or the height anymore, but from the adrenaline pumping through me. But I didn't get far before he was in front of me again, hands on the outsides of my shoulders.

"You were eighteen, McKenzie. Eighteen. No eighteen-year-old should be tied to a man who couldn't be there for her. You were going away to college. You were starting a new part of your life and I didn't want to be the person who held you back from that."

"You didn't even ask me what I wanted." My voice was a whisper.

"And if I had? What would you have said?" He moved in closer, his hands moving up; one stopping on my neck while the other moved to my cheek.

"I wanted you, Hayes. Any way I could have you. That's all I've ever wanted."

"That's exactly what I was afraid of—that you'd choose me and then eventually, when it didn't work out, we'd be over."

"But we're over anyway, Hayes."

"Not if I have anything to do with it." He said the words softly, his thumb running gently over my cheek.

I closed my eyes. My senses were so overwhelmed, adding sight into the mix was overload. His touch, his smell, the sound of his voice pleading with me, deep and raspy, was too much.

The fact of the matter was that I knew why Hayes left, and I never thought it was because he didn't love me. Quite the opposite, in fact. He loved me enough to let me go. It didn't really make it hurt any less, but over time, I'd realized that unless I knew he didn't love me anymore, I'd never fall out of love with him.

I didn't know what to say, but the silence felt too raw. Luckily, he spoke first.

"Come on, let's keep walking."

"Okay," I said on a breath just before he pressed another kiss to my forehead. Then he turned and his hand smoothed down my arm until it met mine, and he laced our fingers together. He took a step forward, but I pulled his hand back a bit. "Wait a minute." I reached behind me, bending a way that only girls who wore heels knew how, and pushed the shoes off my feet. I bent, never letting his hand go, and picked up the shoes. I held them up and said, "Not made for long walks."

He smiled, causing me to smile back, and he gave my hand a squeeze.

We walked for hours, until the sky turned an orangey-pink, slowly making our way through the small college town, passing my apartment three times. I never told him though, because I didn't want the walk to end. He never let go of my hand, keeping it in his the entire time. I wouldn't have had it any other way. Eventually, though, he caught me yawning.

"Shit, Kenz, it's six in the morning. I should probably get you home."

I shrugged. "Becca and Holly are probably still asleep." Holly had a key to my apartment, and after I'd called Becca as promised, she told me they'd wait for me at my place. I'd only had to send them one proof of life picture at 3:00 a.m. I hadn't heard from them since.

He looked at me and I watched as his eyes roamed over my entire face, like he was taking inventory or gauging my level of exhaustion. "My place is just up the road. I could show it to you. My coffeemaker is all set up."

I smiled. "Sounds great."

He led me to his place and I giggled. "We've walked past your apartment so many times!"

"I know," he said, laughing with me. "I just was afraid to say anything because I didn't want the night to be over."

"We passed mine three times." Our eyes were locked and it warmed me right down to my fingernails, knowing he was feeling the same exact things I was.

He opened his door and let me in, his hand releasing mine. I felt the absence immediately and hoped it wouldn't be the last time our palms were pressed together.

His apartment was bare, but that was understandable. He'd only moved in a few days prior and there were still boxes lined up on one wall in the living room. He walked to the kitchen and started prepping coffee and I took in the rest of his apartment.

I yawned again, feeling the exhaustion from being up all night taking over, but I wanted to fight it. I feared if I went home the magic of the evening would fade away.

"We don't have to do this now, Kenz. You look tired. I should take you home so you can get some sleep." I panicked. The last thing I wanted was to be away from him. He must have seen the panic in my face because he came to me, taking both my hands in his. "What's wrong?"

I looked down at my feet, feeling silly and stupid, but I managed to push the words out. "I guess I'm just afraid that if I leave and we go our separate

ways again, everything will go back to normal. Like
Cinderella and her dress. If I go to sleep, I'm
afraid I'll wake up, just like I have every other day
for the last three years, and you won't be there
anymore."

"Then stay with me." His words hit me like a car
slamming on its brakes. "We'll just sleep. I don't
have a couch yet, only a bed, but I'll sleep on the
floor. I'm not ready to let you go yet."

"Show me," I whispered, looking up at him. He
paused for a moment, his eyes searching mine, but
then he led me down the short hallway to his
bedroom. It looked more put together than the
rest of his house, with no boxes in sight.

His bed, however, made my heart stop. It was
the same bed from his old apartment. The very
same bed we'd shared three years ago. The bed in
which I gave him my virginity. I wasn't sure if that
fact had occurred to him or not, but it definitely
affected me. I blushed and my heart rate finally
sped forward. I tried desperately to seem as though
just the sight of his bed didn't leave me breathless.

"Do you have something I could sleep in?" I
asked, my voice shaky and soft. He let go of my
hand and moved to his dresser. He pulled out a
pair of basketball shorts and a t-shirt, then handed
them to me.

"You can change in the bathroom," he said with a
smile. He seemed nervous and I was thankful I
wasn't the only one. "There are towels in the
cabinet if you need one."

"Thanks," I said, then made my way into the bathroom. I shut the door behind me and then looked in the mirror. "Oh, good Lord," I said, leaning closer, as if proximity would change the monstrosity that was my reflection. I had raccoon eyes and my hair was all over the place. I quickly pulled it back into a loose ponytail and then washed my face. I changed into his clothes, taking a moment to bring the collar of his shirt to my nose and inhale. I was completely aware it took me into crazy stalker territory, but I didn't care.

I walked back into his bedroom, my clothes bundled up in my arms, but I didn't see him there. I put my clothes on the chair at his desk and wandered into the hallway, only to find him in the kitchen. He turned to me when he heard me coming, but he didn't say anything. His eyes did a sweep again from my face to my feet, but he said not one word.

The air in the room was electric, like it could catch fire at any moment. My heart beat fast, my breaths came even faster, but I didn't let the fear hold me back. I took a few steps toward him and held out my hand.

"Come and rest with me," I said gently. "There's no way I'll be able to sleep thinking about you on the floor." There also wasn't a great chance of me sleeping if Hayes was in the bed with me, but I kept that truth to myself.

He looked at my hand for a long moment, and then his gaze found mine again. I gave my hand a

361 | Instead of You

little shake, mustering up a tiny smile, and finally, he reached out and grasped my hand in his. Neither of us said a word as we made our way to his bedroom, but then again, there wasn't much to say. We'd rather sleep together than spend a moment apart, and that made me smile.

I climbed in first, feeling braver than I had in years, and when he lay down next to me I wasted no time moving into him. I rested my head on his chest, my arm draped around his middle, and my feet tangled with his. He seemed a little surprised at first, but it only took a second for him to relax and pull me closer.

"Is this okay?" I whispered, just before I yawned again.

"Yeah, Kenzie. Go to sleep," he said, and pressed a soft kiss to the top of my head.

I pressed in closer, unable to believe I was really cuddling with Hayes Wallace, but willing to live in the dream until I woke up.

"Uh, hey, Kenz?" His voice was a strange mixture of confusion and amusement.

"Yeah?"

"Why are your feet wet?"

I let out a laugh. "They turned black from the walk, so I washed them in your tub."

When I woke up, Hayes was still wrapped around me, but he was spooning me from behind. I was on my side, his arm acting as my pillow, his other arm draped over my waist, hand splayed across my belly. His front was pressed against my back and there was absolutely no space between us. I slowly woke, loving the feeling of his body encasing mine, and then I realized the hand near my face was entwined with my own.

We'd held hands while we slept.

I closed my eyes, willing myself not fall in love with him all over again.

The night before had been practically magical. After the initial weirdness, once we'd both decided to let our walls down, the rest of the evening had been incredible. We'd never lacked for something to talk about, there were never any awkward silences, and when he spoke about his life back in Montana I didn't find myself angry with him for it.

I was just so glad to have him back, in any capacity.

But lying there, his arms wrapped possessively around me, I found myself afraid long walks were all we had in store for us. I sighed, pressing my face into his forearm, trying to take in as much of the moment as I could. I must have woken him though, because his arm tightened around me and pulled me even closer, his face nuzzling into my neck. He took in a deep breath through his nose, and I stilled as his hand started to roam across my front, coming to rest just below my breasts.

"For three years," he said, his words a soft feather against the shell of my ear, "I spent my life thinking I'd never get to wake up to you again." His face pressed in close again.

"Hayes," I cried, half whispering.

"What, baby?"

Oh, God.

"What are we doing?"

At my question, his arm slid out from under me and I rolled toward him. He quickly pushed up onto his elbow and stared down at me. "I know what I want, McKenzie. I want us. I want you. But I know I'm the one who walked away before, the one who ended it. So, I don't feel like the ball's in my court." His hand moved from my chest and came to cup my face. "I've loved you through everything and I want you more than anything, but I understand if you get up, leave, and never give me more than a passing wave."

His hands were on me, he was over me, and his eyes were boring into mine. The same eyes I'd seen nearly every day of my life, and the thought of not seeing them every day for the rest of it seemed unimaginable.

So I did the only thing I felt right about doing.

I leaned up and I kissed him.

I must have caught him off guard because at first he didn't move. For just a split second I worried

I'd made the wrong decision. But then, *then*, he kissed me back. His hand moved to the back of my neck, holding me to him, and his tongue swept in, tasting me.

It was so much better than I remembered.

Suddenly, his arm was beneath me again and he was pulling me under him fully. My legs spread open to accommodate him, and he laid his weight on me. It was glorious. His hands were reacquainting themselves with me, running freely over my arms, my stomach, my thighs—as if they had no idea where to start and couldn't make up their minds.

When his teeth caught my bottom lip a moan escaped me. My breaths were coming faster, and my body felt as though it was about to ignite. His hips were resting between my thighs and my hands came to his waist, fingers seeking the hem of his shirt and smoothing up the warmth of his bare back. They were trembling, but I ached to feel him.

His mouth moved down my chin, pressing kisses down my throat, his hands bunching up the fabric of the shirt I wore.

"Do you want me to stop?" he asked against the skin of my neck.

"No," I rasped. I pulled up on his shirt, trying to get it off him, and watched with fascination as he reached behind him and tugged on the back of his shirt, removing it in that sexy way guys did. Then, without hesitation, I sat up and pulled my shirt off as well.

His eyes went straight to my breasts and something about the way he looked at me, with so much lust and love swirling together, had every part of me tensing. His lips came back to mine, and his hand smoothed over my breast, as he gently pressed me back into the mattress. This time, though, my legs wrapped around his waist as I tried desperately to bring every part of him closer.

He read me perfectly and ground into me, his erection pressing perfectly against my core, causing another moan to rip from me, disappearing into his mouth. My hands slid down his back and when I met the elastic of his basketball shorts, my fingers slid under, my hands palming his ass.

"These need to come off," I said. He grunted, his mouth moving down my throat only to have his lips latch onto my nipple, sucking me in, his hand palming my other breast. "Hayes, please," I rasped.

"Tell me what you want," he said between flicks of his tongue against my nipple and a long, hard suck that sent electric shocks straight to my core, making everything between my legs clench.

"I want all of you," I managed. He pulled back and my breast popped out of his mouth just as his gaze met mine. He moved lower, eyes never leaving mine. He gripped the edges of my basketball shorts and pulled them down, leaving me only in my underwear.

The night before I'd been wearing a tiny dress that called for even tinier underwear. Even though they bordered on uncomfortable, the look on his face at that moment, as his eyes perused the black scrap of lace covering me, was worth every moment of underwear misery.

"Holy fucking shit, Kenz. You're perfect," he said as his hands moved up my calves, slowly spreading me open. "Just like I remember."

I giggled at his response, loving the way simply the sight of me seemed to undo him. But my laughter stopped immediately when he ran his hands all the way up my thighs and up the crease of where my legs met my hips, framing my sex with his hands. His thumbs slipped under the soaked lace, causing a breath to shudder out of me. He rubbed me up and down, slowly dragging his thumbs against my already over sensitized core, his hands pressing my legs farther and farther apart until I thought I would burst from being so completely bared to him. The tiny panties I wore could hide hardly anything from him.

Finally, he grabbed the sides of my panties and pulled them down my legs, peeling them off me and tossing them to the floor.

"Now, you," I said, trying to sit up, wanting to get him just as naked as I was. But he had other plans. He wrapped his hands around my ankles, yanked me down the bed until my ass was on the edge of the mattress. I watched as he carefully placed each of my legs over his shoulders and brought his mouth down to me.

Just before his lips touched my skin, he said, "We'll get to me later." His breath ghosted over my hot center and then his tongue followed, taking one slow and leisurely lap up my middle. I made a high-pitched noise that wasn't really a word, but just the sound one makes when so much pleasure and sensation rocket through you. I couldn't speak, but I couldn't stay silent either.

I continued to make those nonsensical, whimpering noises as his mouth worked my sex. He licked, sucked, and kissed me like he'd been dying to do it ever since he'd left. Like it was his fucking job. I'd been with a few guys since Hayes, but not one had I allowed to go down on me. It was too personal, too intimate. Watching Hayes work his tongue over my clit, his eyes trained on mine, was a level of connection I'd never had before. He was playing me like a fucking instrument, determined to get that last note right, to make the song perfect, no matter how long he had to practice.

My fingers wound through his hair and my hips arched up to meet his mouth. He groaned against me, the vibrations sending a whole new wave of arousal over my body, and it was too much. My eyes closed, my mouth opened, and my head fell back. The rhythm of my hips was met by the lashing of Hayes's tongue. I held him to me, finding that perfect combination of his mouth and my hips, and moments later I came apart.

I was loud. I was practically feral. His hands came around to hold me down by the belly, and I cried out until my orgasm waned. As I came down, it was to the slow and measured laps of his tongue through my sex. With each pass over my clit I shivered, too sensitive not to. Finally, after the last spasm passed, he kissed me all the way from my core up to my mouth, taking the long route and making sure to cover as much ground as possible.

When his lips finally connected with mine, it was a slow and lovely kiss. I tasted fantastic on him.

"That was the most gorgeous and beautiful orgasm I think anyone's ever had," he said quietly as he pressed even more kisses down my throat.

I didn't have any words in that moment, but I knew what I wanted. I pressed on his shoulder, pushed him onto his back, and climbed over him. I moved down his body and grabbed the basketball shorts and his underwear, pulling both down his body, off his legs, and left them in a pile on the floor.

I climbed back toward him and at the same time he sat up, snaked an arm around my waist, and scooted backward until he was leaning against the headboard. I straddled him again, this time with nothing between us.

"Hey," he said softly, using his hand to push my probably crazy hair out of my face and tuck it behind my ear.

"Hey," I replied, smiling.

His hand moved back to cradle my neck and the arm around my waist tightened around me, bringing me closer. His cock was hard and hot between us, but he seemed focused on my eyes.

"This doesn't have to go any farther today, Kenz," he whispered. "I want you, all of you, but I can wait. I can wait as long as you need."

"Are you going to disappear again?" I watched him closely as I asked the question, not knowing what kind of reaction I'd get, but hoping it was going to be one I could live with.

His hands on me tightened and he brought my face even closer. "I'm not going anywhere again until you tell me to."

I took in a deep breath, trying to find the courage to leave everything out in the open, to find the strength to risk my heart one more time, hoping the payout would keep me safe.

"What if I'm looking for forever?"

His eyes darted back and forth between mine, but he never wavered as he said, "What if I told you you'd already found it?"

"Promise?" I asked, my voice more frantic than I'd hoped for. "Hayes, if you're not in this, not ready for a relationship, then please, walk away now before—"

"McKenzie, I love you. I always have. I always will. What kept us apart before, it's gone. Done. There is nothing in this world that is going to stop me from being with you. All you have to do is say yes."

I had no words. He'd said exactly what I'd been praying to hear for three years and nothing in that moment could have stopped my mouth from pressing against his.

The kiss started out reverent and grateful. I was worshiping his mouth, thankful he'd found a way back to me. But it slowly morphed back into the frantic kissing where hands roamed everywhere and I simply needed to have him inside of me.

I reached down between us and took him in my hand, my forehead resting on his shoulder. He was just as beautiful as I remembered. I circled my hand around him, moving up and down his shaft, loving the way his breath hissed out and shuddered back in.

"Babe," he rasped, his voice simply shattered. "Condom, top drawer," he said, nodding toward his nightstand.

I pulled it open and blindly rummaged through it until I felt the foil wrappers, then immediately brought one to my mouth, carefully ripping it open. I leaned back and then slowly rolled it down his shaft. With a loud breath he brought a hand between us, positioning himself as I leaned up on my knees. My hand met with his and together we guided him to me. I slowly lowered myself down, trying to concentrate on the way it felt to be full from him, to have him inside me after so long. His hands slipped around my waist, then ran up my back to my shoulders, curling around the tops, and pulling me down so very gently, until he was fully seated inside of me.

My head fell softly against his, our foreheads meeting, and we sat there, breathing each other in. I had never been so full, in every sense of the word.

"Jesus, Kenz," he whispered, his hands grasping at my shoulders, holding me down.

"Hayes, I need to move," I whimpered.

"Just give me a second. If you move right now, well, this will all be over before it really starts."

I wrapped my arms around his neck and pressed my mouth to his. As the kiss built, so did my need, and my hips moved to give me any kind of relief I could find. I rocked back and forth slowly on him, trying to give him the time he needed, but also trying to simply put out the fire that was quickly burning through me.

One of his hands moved from my shoulder down to my ass, holding me even closer, which only added more friction to my clit.

"Oh, my God," I cried, my mouth still pressed against his, but neither one of us were kissing anymore. I was clinging to him, grasping at his skin as my hips ground against him. The feeling of his cock inside me and the electricity of my clit rubbing against him in just the right way, were sending me into a stratosphere I'd never been to before. "Hayes," I whimpered, "I'm gonna come." I sounded afraid, and I partly was. Afraid of the enormity of what I was feeling. I was dangling on the precipice of the most powerful orgasm I'd ever had and the panic of feeling too much was definitely overwhelming, but not strong enough to stop me.

"I've got you," he said, still using his hand to make sure I was feeling everything I could.

"Hayes," I moaned. His hand tightened on my shoulder. Then, my entire body lit up. My core clenched around him as waves of pleasure rocketed through me. I grasped at him, trying to hold on as my entire body gave out on me. His hands wrapped around me and held me close to him, and I simply tried to breathe through my release.

After a few long moments of settling, of breathing and trembling, I finally came back around, and that's when Hayes picked me up and twisted, laying me on my back again.

"That was fucking amazing," he said, smiling down at me. I smiled back, lazily, but then gasped as he pulled out of me just slightly, then pushed back in. He smiled even wider, thrust just a little bit harder, and everything after that became one blurry and continuous form of sensual torture.

It was as if my body were so aware it was him, so thankful Hayes was the one inside me, it refused to come back down from the plateau. Everything felt magnificent. Every nuance was accentuated. A kiss on my neck wasn't just a kiss; it was a match on the wick of a firework. The caress of his hand against my skin damp with sweat was a boat crashing through the waves of a storm at sea. Every single thing about being with Hayes was magnified and exponentially better.

He took his time with me, almost as if he were trying to make up for all the time we'd lost, but I wasn't complaining. Nearly every fantasy I'd had about Hayes was fulfilled. He used me in a way that made me feel delicate, and he tossed me around, taking whatever he wanted in that moment. He made love to me, he fucked me, and everything in between.

In the end though, when he finally found his release, he was back on top of me, his lips to mine, and his hand cradling my face.

"This is us. Forever," he whispered as he shivered, the cold air in the room making our damp skin pebble. "It'll never be long enough, but I'll give you everything I can."

"I don't need anything but you."

Epilogue

Hayes

It'd been a little over one year since McKenzie had allowed me back into her life, even though I didn't deserve her. I'd gone back to Bellingham with every intention of trying to win her back, but also with the expectation that she'd turn me away—with good reason. So, when she took me back in the most gracious way, without one single instance of holding my past against me or using our time apart as a weapon, I never took it for granted.

Tomorrow she would graduate from college and I was so proud of her. School wasn't hard for her—she flew through every class she took—but she had this drive that amazed me. Her mom and dad were coming down to watch her ceremony and then to take us out for dinner. The surprise was that my mom was coming with them.

About a year after my mother and I had been in Montana, when she'd seemed stable and I'd had some counseling of my own, I told her about McKenzie. I told her everything. I'd done it in her therapist's office, hoping for the best but knowing it might have been a trigger for a setback, and I wanted to do it the best way for my mom. At first, after listening to my story, she cried. It took nearly ten minutes for her to calm down enough to explain that she wasn't crying because my and

McKenzie's relationship upset her, but more so because she felt responsible for the outcome.

From that day forward she'd been my biggest cheerleader and tried to convince me every day to go back for McKenzie.

I'd dated other women in Montana, each one a desperate attempt to cover a wound, to try and force myself to move on even though I knew, so very deep down, it was impossible. My mom had been polite and kind to each one, but never missed an opportunity to tell me I was being an idiot for trying to make myself forget about McKenzie.

They hadn't seen each other since four years prior, but I knew my mom was anxious to wrap her arms around her, to see her again, to feel that love she'd thought she'd lost. She'd always known McKenzie would be her daughter one day, and above everything else, she was so glad that hadn't been lost along with everything else. I wanted my mom there when I asked McKenzie to be with me for the rest of our lives.

McKenzie was asleep next to me, like she'd been every night since the first we spent together here. We both seemed to understand that there was no reason to be apart any longer. That first day, after our long walk through an entire night, we made love until neither one of us could move, and then the next morning she went to her house, loaded up her car, and moved in. Neither of us ever looked back.

I let my eyes wander over her, loving the way her wild hair was everywhere, the way her legs never stayed on her side of the bed, but also the way—even in sleep—she kept me close.

It was with the same surety I'd felt since my brother's party when I finally kissed her and confirmed what I'd thought was true—that she was the only one for me—the same certainty, that I knew she'd end the day wrapped around me, wearing my ring.

The End

Acknowledgements

First, always, thank you to my family. My husband, especially, for.... I don't know....keeping the kids out of our room when I'm trying to write. Even though you're not very good at that.

Thanks to ALL my beta readers. I think I had more beta readers for this book than any other. And that stemmed directly from my fear of writing something new. Joanne, Danielle, Michelle, Dana, Ali, Rachel, Stefanie, Lesley, Keena, Ashley, and Andrea T. – your input was invaluable and I am so grateful to have had such wonderful readers for this book.

To all the ladies in Anie's Awesome Teamsters – THANK YOU for being such a great sounding board for me and offering up advice and opinions when I need your input. You ladies are such a great resource for me and help me more than you probably realize.

Olivia, thank you for always being such an awesome editor. I appreciate not only your opinions, but your professionalism and your enormous bank of knowledge. Thank you, also, to everyone at Hot Tree Editing.

Becca, my girl, I love you. Thank you for not only beta reading this book, but for handling the teasers for me. And, for always being a genuine friend when those are so hard to come by in this business. I love how 85% of our conversations aren't even about books, but about our lives because our friendship goes deeper than just books. At least.... I hope it does. This is awkward....

Ena and Amanda at Enticing Journey, thank you for handling any and all events for this book. Whether it was the cover reveal or the release blitz, or any other event you've worked on for me, it was always handled professionally and effectively. You both do a truly awesome job.

To all the writers in my Sprinters group, thank you for being there to push me when I need more words. Most of this book was written knowing I'd have to check in with any number of you, so I kept the words coming. Who knows how long it would have taken otherwise.

Books by Anie Michaels

The Never Series

Never Close Enough

Never Far Away

Never Giving Up

The Never Duet

Never Standing Still

Never Tied Down

The Private Serials

Stand Alone Novels

The Space Between Us

The Absence of Olivia

Instead of You

The Presence of Grace – *coming in 2016*